EDUCATED BY THE EARL

ANNABELLE ANDERS

ANNABELLE
ANDERS

Educated by the Earl

Copyright 2021 by Annabelle Anders

Cover by Barbara Cantor, Forever After Romance Designs.

Edited by Tracy Mooring Liebchen

Proofed by Laura Dickey

❀ Created with Vellum

"The coach is outside, Primm," Victoria Shipley announced, staring across the schoolyard from inside. A gust of wind rattled the windows, and she could practically feel the chill even though a fire burned steadily in the hearth. "It's beginning to snow, so you mustn't delay setting out."

"I hate leaving you here without any help. If I had realized I'd have to go, I never would have given Jenny the holidays off." Augusta Primm wrinkled her brows. As the founder and director of her school, Miss Primm's Seminary for the Refinement of Ladies, she was Victoria's employer but also one of her dearest friends.

"I'll manage fine without a housekeeper." Victoria ignored a subtle twinge of unease. "It's not as though you could have predicted your mother would fall ill." She squeezed her friend's thin but strong hand. "It will be good for you to spend the holidays with your family. I'll use the time to get ahead on my lesson plans."

"I don't know..." Primm removed her spectacles and

squeezed the bridge of her nose. "I wouldn't think much of it if Liam hadn't been the one to write." Primm had mentioned a few times that her mother had a tendency to exaggerate her maladies, but Victoria couldn't remember ever seeing the headmistress looking so distraught.

At the age of three and thirty, Miss Primm had not accomplished all that she had by being sentimental. She was the strongest, most energetic, and most grounded woman Victoria had ever known.

"I feel dreadful abandoning you here alone for the holidays—without Jenny to manage the house! You, my friend, are not accustomed to fending for yourself. If I'd anticipated this, I would have insisted one of the other teachers remain here with you."

Which was precisely why Victoria was glad she hadn't. It wouldn't have been fair to the teachers, who—aside from Miss Fellowes who was spending the holidays chaperoning one of their students—had family gatherings to attend.

"I'll manage fine. I'm not helpless. One would think I was one of our students. And I won't be alone, really. I have Mr. and Mrs. Driver nearby if I need them." The elderly couple lived in a cottage on the school grounds and worked as janitor and cook while school was in session. "And I can always visit Lady Annesley in town."

"I know. I know. It's just that I promised you that we'd spend a quiet holiday together, what with your aunt's passing last summer. Come with me, Victoria. We can make other arrangements for the early return students."

Victoria had considered going along more than once, but she'd then imagined herself as an interloper. She refused to intrude on Primm's family at a time like this.

According to letters Primm had received from her

brothers, Miss Primm's mother hadn't been the same since the death of her oldest son two winters before. And this latest missive that had arrived from Primm's brother had been urgent.

"I'm eight and twenty, for goodness' sake. Please, Primm, you mustn't worry about me." Victoria squeezed her friend's hand again. "Your mother needs you." Tomorrow was never a certainty, and most people didn't comprehend the importance of family until they were gone.

Victoria had learned that lesson the hard way.

Primm nodded and then her expression turned fierce. "I sent word to Piers. I don't care how much he loathes our father. If he doesn't come home for Mother's sake, I'll strangle him."

Primm was the only sister to five younger brothers, twins and then three younger. Four, actually, following the death of the eldest twin.

The younger twin, Piers, had been bestowed with his courtesy title, Earl of Rosewood, and would one day be the Marquess of Starbridge. From what Primm had said, even before his brother's death, he'd been the worst sort of fellow—a reckless and inconsiderate rogue. Having been raised with no real responsibilities, he must have been horribly spoiled. And although he was the new heir, he hadn't so much as returned home once since the funeral.

Victoria could hardly imagine such a man coming from the same family as Primm.

And yet, her friend spoke of him with great fondness. Lord Rosewood, in fact, seemed to be her favorite.

Even so, if he didn't rush to his mother's bedside when the family needed him most, he'd deserve any punishment his sister chose to inflict. It wouldn't be the first time he'd disappointed his sister.

"It's not entirely his fault," Primm stared out the window. "My father doesn't make it easy…" But then she pressed her lips together.

Victoria kept her opinion to herself and instead offered reassurance. "He'll be there." Even the most self-centered rake couldn't deny a plea from his mother, who very well could be on her deathbed.

"I hope so."

Victoria glanced outside. "But you need to set out. I'm already going to worry about you traveling in this weather."

Primm gave a tight-sounding laugh. "That will make two of us. You should come with me. That would solve everything."

"Go." Victoria lifted Primm's coat and scarf off the nearby chair. "Button up. If the storm worsens, make the driver stop at the nearest inn. Arriving earlier isn't worth risking your safety." She assisted the taller woman into her jacket and then handed her a navy knit hat to pull over her dark brown hair.

A hot brick and a lap quilt would be waiting for Primm inside the carriage, but the temperature outside was already frigid, and the drive to Starbridge Abbey, although it could be made in a day's time, was a long one. Victoria nearly reconsidered her decision to stay behind but no family would appreciate guests at such a time as this.

"Write so I know you've arrived safely," Victoria ordered.

"I will." Primm blinked, her eyes bright behind her spectacles, and then stepped back, straightening her shoulders.

The two of them were good friends, but the other woman

was also *Miss Primm*. And Miss Primm, school headmistress and formidable teacher of all subjects imaginable, wasn't the sort to invite affection under any circumstances. She must be truly worried about her mother to even have allowed Victoria to clasp her hands. "Lock the doors. And don't go rambling around the school late at night. I know you, and you'll conjure up all sorts of terrifying scenarios if you do."

"I shall confine myself to the residence the moment the sun sets." She reached into her pocket to withdraw the small journal where she kept her daily lists. "And when you return, I'll be fully prepared for the next term."

Primm stared at her and then, possibly surprising them both, seized Victoria in an awkward hug. "Thank you. I'll make this up to you."

"There is nothing to make up. Now go." Victoria laughed, blinking back the stinging in her eyes before Primm noticed that she was anything less than confident about being left behind.

She followed the taller woman outside. And once Primm had climbed into the coach and settled inside, Victoria waved and then stood alone in the flurries, watching until the luxurious carriage turned out of sight.

With it gone, she sighed into the ensuing silence. Victoria appreciated the solitude for now but would no doubt tire of it within a few days.

She shivered.

Or possibly a few hours.

Although Victoria had, in fact, *felt* alone for most of her life, she'd always had other people around her.

Today was December nineteenth. The early return students would begin arriving back at the school on January fourth. She was going to be entirely on her own for sixteen days.

Rubbing her arms for warmth, she rushed back to the single door of the small residence she and Primm shared. The comfortable dwelling had been built onto the side of the building so that it was separate from the students' and other teachers' quarters but also connected. As the director's assistant, Victoria appreciated the privilege of returning to a private chamber each night. And although she hadn't found it necessary to learn to cook since most meals were provided by the school, she appreciated the small kitchen.

She could make herself tea and put together very simple fare if necessary. But it had been Primm who'd planned on doing the cooking over the holidays.

Victoria had been employed at the school for nearly a decade, but this was to have been the first holiday she and Primm would have spent together. The first few years, she'd spent holidays with her parents, and then later—after their passing—she'd spent them with Aunt Delia.

Bedelia Beasley had been considered insufferable by most who knew her, but she'd always put Victoria's well-being first. In the end, she and her aunt had grown quite close.

Victoria stepped inside the foyer and closed the door behind her.

Now what? Despite the reassurances she'd given Primm, now that she was alone the next few weeks stretched out in front of her like a dark and stormy sea.

The sound of howling winds spurred her into motion. She double checked the locks behind her and then made her way to the back of the residence where she then checked the door between their private chambers and the school hallway.

Her hand on the lock, however, she paused.

Had Primm or Mr. Driver secured all of the school's exits? She unfastened the locks she'd just set, entered the school, and rushed through the corridor leading to the front entrance. So long as she focused on the tapping of her shoes echoing on the hard floor she could almost imagine today was like any other day. She could ignore the fact that the school would sit empty for over a fortnight.

She increased her pace and then breathed a sigh of relief when she rounded the corner to the large double doors set in the center of a brick arch.

Which were both locked. *Of course* they were locked.

Nearly an hour later, after checking each classroom and the empty dorms, Victoria returned to the residence feeling somewhat more at ease.

What would she be doing if Primm hadn't left?

She stared at the comfortable settee in the small parlor and then the tidy desk in the corner. She had plenty of lesson plans to write up and endless books to read. Furthermore, in the rush of the end of term, she'd gotten behind on her correspondence. Her mother, who was spending the winter in France, was due a letter, as were Collette, and Olivia, as well as a few of the school's more generous financial donors.

If she was going to accustom herself to her present state of isolation, she was going to have to keep herself busy.

And so she set herself to work.

By four that afternoon, while mapping out the first week of new classes, the snow had thickened to the point that the large lawn outside was hardly visible. Trees were beginning to sag under the weight of it, the corners of the windows were frosted, and gusts of wind moaned to fill the silence. It was as though Victoria and the school had been plucked up and dropped into another world.

She might have kept right on working if not for the rumbling of her stomach.

Drifting into the kitchen, after rummaging in the larder, she found bread and cheese to make up a meal.

The recipes that Primm had promised to teach her to cook taunted Victoria from where they sat on the worktable, so while waiting for her tea to steep, she flipped through them.

Roast with squash, Brussels sprouts and carrots, mince and Twelfth Night pie… Most of the ingredients sat on a shelf in the larder but would likely go untouched. She'd walk them over to Mrs. Driver's tomorrow, assuming the snow let up.

Which it would. Because December storms never amounted to much in England. Mother Nature waited for February and March to dump those on her favorite country.

Although, Victoria mused while sipping at her tea and nibbling on a piece of cheese, this particular storm showed no signs of letting up. She'd been diligent about adding logs to the hearth but even so, the temperature in the room had dropped considerably. She wrapped up the remains of her meal and moved about the room lighting candles.

The last thing she needed was to have to go searching for tapers in the dark. Especially on her first night alone.

Thinking to add the a few mundane tasks to her daily list, Victoria changed out of her lavender gown and into the heavier of her two night rails, a luxurious velvet dressing gown, and a pair of woolen slippers. Soothed by lifelong habits, she then brushed out and braided her long, light-brown hair into a single rope that draped over her shoulder and down her front.

Without a fire burning, the temperature in her bedchamber had become nearly unbearable. She glanced at the empty hearth, contemplated what all might be involved in building and lighting a fire, and, as a practical matter, relegated tackling that to tomorrow. Having decided to postpone that particular chore, she gathered the quilt and one of the pillows off the bed and carried them back to the settee in the parlor.

She had known the two servants who handled such chores didn't work while school was in session. She simply hadn't truly mulled over all of what that meant.

And it wasn't that she didn't know how to build a fire in the hearth, just that she'd never needed to do so.

A pang of longing struck her from out of nowhere.

If Aunt Delia hadn't passed, Victoria would have traveled to London where they would spend the holiday together. The two of them would attend various parties and on their nights in, sit together in her drawing room where a fire would be blazing in the giant hearth that nearly took up an entire wall.

Lost in the emptiness of that moment, Victoria would have done almost anything to be reading to her aunt.

Her aunt's housekeeper, Mrs. Dinkers, would have served them tea or broth, and when Aunt Delia began to nod off, Victoria would return to her chamber where a golden light would be flickering in the small hearth and her bed would have been cozily inviting, having been prepared with a warming pan.

She had felt safe knowing her aunt was one chamber

away and other servants on the floor above and also below her. She'd felt comfortable in belonging there.

She sniffed and then pinched her lips together. That was the past. This was her future.

Her aunt's solicitors had approached her shortly after the funeral regarding selling the Mayfair townhouse, but she'd told them she wasn't ready. Beasley House was the most recent place she'd considered home and since funds weren't an issue, she'd instructed them to taper the staff to a minimum until the following summer. By then, she'd most likely not be feeling so sentimental.

Primm had offered her time off in deference to the family death, but Victoria had declined, insisting that she'd already spent too much of her life in mourning.

She'd accepted the condolences of her aunt's friends and then returned north for the autumn term. People depended on her here at the school, and the last thing she'd wanted was to be alone.

Which she found ironic, considering her present circumstances.

Victoria shuffled around the parlor, drawing the drapes closed and then arranging a bed on the sofa. After selecting a book, she doused all the candles but a few and settled into her makeshift bed.

Once the few tapers beside her had burned down to the nubs, Victoria set the book aside. The hour wasn't all that late, and she anticipated she'd lay awake for some time, but as luck would have it, keeping oneself busy while alone was more tiring than she had imagined.

She ventured out from beneath the heavy quilt one last time, added fuel to the fire, and then carefully replaced the screen before returning to snuggle into the sofa.

Not allowing herself to dwell on the wind howling outside, she closed her eyes and fell asleep.

VICTORIA HAD no idea what time it was when her eyes popped open, but whatever had awakened her sent unease racing through her limbs.

The fire had burned down to nothing more than an amber glow, and aside from the pale slant of moonlight breaking through the curtains, the room was cast in darkness.

Thump, thump, thump. It was coming from the foyer—from outside. That must be what had woken her up.

Her unease inflating to a cold, twisty fear, she remained huddled beneath the quilt like a statue.

Thump, thump, thump. The pounding sounded louder —violent.

Desperate.

What sounded like a man's voice filtered inside. She had no choice but to inhale when her chest nearly exploded.

Who on earth would come visiting in the middle of the night? The wailing sounds outside provided a reason. The storm hadn't abated, and whoever was outside must be frozen.

Normally, the thought of someone in trouble or danger would have her springing into action, but caution tempered her concern.

She was alone.

Thump, thump, thump. She thought she heard the words, *"Damnit, Auggie!"*

Auggie? Augusta? That was Miss Primm's name.

Victoria slid her feet onto the floor and... waited.

A sharp explosion reverberated from the kitchen, nearly shooting her out of her skin.

Whoever was outside had broken a window. They were breaking into the residence!

But rather than get up and off that settee to grab the fire poker, or fetch any sort of weapon she might use against the intruder, or even run and hide, Victoria remained glued to the spot where she sat.

More sounds fluttered into the parlor—of glass falling, hitting the floor and breaking into pieces.

"Who…?" Her voice sounded more like a croak. She swallowed hard. "Who is there?"

"Damnit, Auggie, will you come around and open the damn door?"

Who on earth dared call Miss Primm by such a name? An old friend? One of the students' parents?

A lover?

"Miss Primm is not here!" Victoria shouted. "Go away!" Having a strange man break in while she was alone here went beyond her worst nightmares.

"It's bloody freezing out here! I don't give a possum's ass if my sister isn't here. Open the fucking door before I break it down."

Did he just use that… word? And he expected her to open the door for him? But as affront rolled through her, something else he'd said penetrated the fog of her indecision.

Sister?

"Tell me who you are first!" Finally, she pushed herself off the settee to hastily retrieve the iron poker in case she needed a weapon.

"Rosewood!"

As in… Piers? "Miss Primm's brother?"

"Unfortunately. Can we dispense with these introductions until I'm inside?"

"Please?" Really, the man lacked even the most basic of manners.

"Are you…? God in Heaven," he responded. "I'm going back around to the front door, and if you don't open it, I'm breaking it down."

Air blew in from the kitchen—cold, blustery air—robbing the parlor of whatever warmth remained from the fire, and Victoria shrugged back into her dressing gown. She touched her hand to her hair, of which half had escaped her braid, and then slipped her feet into her slippers.

Thump!

Anxious he'd carry out his threat, Victoria scurried through the foyer to the door. "I'm here. Stop being an idiot!" she shouted, throwing open the locks.

The door flew open and, along with a blustery wall of snow, a tall presence pushed his way inside and slammed the door behind him.

Whether it was the timing of his arrival, his violent entrance, or the fact that he was at least a foot taller than her and looked to be half frozen, Victoria let out a scream.

The second after that, the frozen intruder crumpled to the floor.

*I*f Miss Primm's oldest brother died because Victoria allowed him to lay freezing where he'd collapsed, it was quite possible she'd be fired. Not only would she be fired, but she'd also lose her best friend.

The thought spurred her into action.

Since teachers at Miss Primm's were at least partially responsible for the well-being of nearly seventy-five young ladies ranging from the ages of eight to eight and ten, upon accepting employment, they were all required to learn the most basic of lifesaving techniques.

Unfortunately for Victoria, and perhaps for this intruder as well, nearly a decade had passed since Victoria had sat through such instructions.

Thinking she needed a plan, and to gather her composure, Victoria backed away. Ignoring Lord Rosewood's inert form, she returned to the parlor, where the first thing she noticed was the fire dying in the hearth.

Warmth. He was going to require warmth. She hurried to the kitchen and returned with wood to build the fire up again. At first, she thought she'd smothered it, and her breath caught in her throat. Seconds later, an orange flame peeked out from beneath to lick one of the new logs she'd added, and she exhaled a sigh of relief.

But before satisfaction could truly set in, her mind jumped to her next hurdle.

The Earl of Rosewood's hulking form lay crumpled on the cold floor of the foyer, whereas the warmth from the fire was in here, several feet from where he needed it.

When that weak orange flame flickered in the bitter breeze coming from the kitchen, Victoria frowned. What on earth had he been thinking? Breaking a window like that?

Palms together, she held her hands in front of her mouth and forced herself to rationalize her situation.

He was not a murderer or intruder; he was merely Primm's brother.

Who must outweigh her two-fold—if not more.

Giving the fire a stir, she propped the poker in its rack then returned to the foyer and lowered herself beside him. "Lord Rosewood?" She shook his shoulders. There was no way she could get him into the parlor without his help. "Piers?"

"I need a minute," he answered without opening his eyes. She hadn't paid attention to his voice when he'd been shouting at her, but the husky tones summoned a whisky-like burning in her chest.

When was the last time she'd been alone with a man? Years? A decade?

His eyes remained closed, and she shook him again, dismayed that his thick wool jacket was icy and damp. "Get up," she ordered. "You need to get out of these wet clothes."

"That's what all the ladies say. Where's my sister?" His

words slurred, but a dark smile stretched across his mouth nonetheless.

"I don't mean…" Victoria pinched her mouth together. She was the *assistant director* of one of England's most prestigious ladies' seminaries; she ought to be able to manage a single half-frozen earl. "Miss Primm left for Starbridge Abbey this morning. Which is where you ought to be."

She fisted her hands around his collar and jerked… and yet he didn't budge.

"Damn Auggie. My sister takes endless pleasure in showing me up."

She felt his eyes burning into her even though she could barely see them.

"That's been easy enough for her, as far as I can tell." Victoria jerked on his collar again and this time was able to get him into a sitting position.

With his help, of course.

"Is it your wish to lie here on the floor all night, or would you like to come into the parlor and dry off by the fire?"

"With or without my clothes?" His voice floated through the darkness like smoke from an expensive cigar. It settled low in her belly before she shook off the effects and nudged him.

"With, of course," she answered tersely. Primm had warned her that the eldest of her younger brothers was a rake. Obviously, she hadn't exaggerated.

Victoria pushed herself to stand and then pulled at his arm. He brushed her away, but she ignored him and tugged on his elbow anyway.

Once she had him standing, Victoria used all her strength to urge him into the parlor before his legs gave out on him again. "It *was* warm in here," she explained. "Until some buffoon broke one of the kitchen windows."

He answered with a grunt.

"Are you injured? What on earth were you doing out there in the middle of this storm? In the middle of the night?"

"I'm fine. A few scratches, maybe." They'd made it into the parlor by now, and she was pleased to see that the fire was almost roaring. But, before he could sit down, Victoria began unbuttoning his coat.

Cad or not, he was Primm's brother. He was a human being.

And even if he was an arrogant beast, he was as susceptible to illness as the next person. Neither of them spoke while she tugged at his jacket and then unwound the knit scarf from his neck.

"Only a fool would travel in this weather without a hat." Chunks of ice clung to his inky hair.

"I was wearing one when I set out." He swayed, watching her from half-closed lids. "At least I think I was." He frowned.

Victoria dragged his sleeves down his arms and then pulled Primm's favorite wing-backed chair closer to the hearth. "Sit here. Close to the fire."

"I'd rather you warm me up. Where did you come from, Angel?" He didn't resist when she pushed him into the seat. In slightly better light, she was startled to note that his lips were almost blue.

"Tea. I'm going to make tea."

"No tea. Auggie must have a bottle or two of whisky around here somewhere."

Victoria ignored that and, after lighting a taper, padded

away to the kitchen. Once there, however, she caught herself.

Even with the fire she'd left burning in the stove, the room was freezing, and what had been a pristine countertop and floor was now littered with shards of glass and a thin layer of snow.

"Go back into the parlor. Those slippers won't protect you." His breath skimmed the side of her face, leaving a tingling, fluttery sensation.

Victoria hadn't even realized he'd followed her. She stiffened, leaning away from him. She wasn't at all happy that this man had disturbed her night—even if he was Primm's brother. She was even less happy about him ordering her around.

"I need to make tea." She moved to approach the stove, but he caught her arm.

"I'll get it."

"You can't. You can barely stand up."

But he only shrugged. "I'll tend to this mess. Go back to the parlor."

Every fiber of her being hated that he would be so heavy-handed after showing up uninvited in the middle of the night. She hated even more that he was right about her slippers.

The curtains on the broken window billowed from another gust, sending an almost violent shiver rolling through her. The room, which was most uninviting, needed sweeping and Victoria wasn't even sure where Jenny kept the broom.

Rather than argue, she lifted her chin. "Fine."

Never had she heard such a mocking chuckle. It was as though he'd read her mind.

She spun around and brushed past him, flinching when her arm brushed his. He ought to be cold. He had ice in his hair, for Heaven's sake.

And yet, heat flooded her limbs from a simple touch.

If anger could physically emanate off a person, hers ought to be hot enough to warm the entire residence.

She marched back into the parlor, confused and tired but also disheartened at the realization that she wasn't quite the calm and independent woman she'd considered herself to be.

Victoria lowered herself onto Primm's chair, feeling helpless, and stared into the fire. She'd been protected all her life—coddled. She knew this, but experiencing the unexpected consequences was like having icy water thrown in her face.

She'd been born the daughter of a viscount who'd taken care to ensure she never experienced lack or insecurity. In addition to that, as Primm's assistant, Victoria was confident, refined, and capable of handling some of the school's most troublesome students. But what mattered most, she knew, was her ability to handle parents.

Parents and benefactors.

The more basic skills she lacked, however, might not be so insignificant. Was this why Primm had been reluctant to leave her alone?

She placed another log to balance on the fire she'd built and jumped back when it collapsed on itself.

True, a few gaps in her education needed to be filled, but she wasn't unintelligent. And now was as good a time as any to learn. Perhaps a few days fending for herself was a blessing in disguise.

"The kitchen is now safe for those delicate little feet of

yours." Lord Rosewood had returned but rather than enter, was leaning against the doorframe.

Without even entering, his presence managed to fill the room. Which, oddly enough, despite his cavalier demeanor, exuded protection and warmth. Minutes ago, he'd set her nerves on edge, so why was it that now he could quiet her mind?

But then she realized the quiet had nothing to do with him—not with his person, that was. But the wind no longer howled from the direction of the kitchen.

He must have affected a temporary repair to the window.

"Thank you," she said.

Simply because he was an intruder didn't mean Victoria should abandon her manners. She wasn't all that sleepy, and more than anything, she wanted hot tea. She craved the warmth of cradling the cup, the aroma steaming into her nostrils, and the liquid to warm her belly.

She rose, but he hadn't moved.

Was he… asleep standing up?

"My lord?"

Nothing.

"Lord Rosewood?" She took a step toward him. "Are you all right?"

He opened his eyes. They were glassy and unfocused. But then he shook his head. "Fine, I'm fine." But he didn't seem fine at all.

For the second time since his arrival, Victoria assisted him into her cozy parlor. This time, however, he didn't reach the chair but instead buckled onto the settee.

Only after ascertaining that he wasn't going to topple off

did she step back to contemplate her next move. "I'll... make that tea then."

What else was a respectable lady to do with a frozen earl who'd broken into her residence in the middle of the night?

"Tea," he parroted, slumping backward.

Back in the kitchen, she was pleased to confirm that he had, in fact, cleaned up all the glass. A large piece of wood had been wedged into the window.

Removing the kettle of water from the stove, she then prepared two cups of tea. She added sugar to both of them, arranged them on a tray, and returned to the parlor.

Where she found him slumped asleep on the settee. His arms tucked across his chest and he had one booted foot draped over the armrest but left the other planted solidly on the floor.

Mentally apologizing to Primm, Victoria tiptoed through the dark to her friend's chamber, tore the coverlet off Primm's bed, and then returned to throw it over Lord Rosewood.

And since Victoria's own chamber was even colder than the kitchen had been, she fashioned a second bed of sorts on the carpet in front of the hearth.

This way, at least, if the buffoon on the couch stopped breathing or anything else so inconvenient, she could... do something to revive him. Indeed, he was obnoxious and far too arrogant for her liking, but he was *Primm's brother*, after all.

First thing in the morning, she'd send him on his merry way.

*E*very bone in her body ached but at least she was warm.

Victoria burrowed deeper under her cover, vaguely wondering when her mattress had become so uncomfortable. And that reminded her she'd fallen asleep on the floor.

She opened her eyes and poked her face out just enough to see that the fire hadn't gone out. And as she had not added more fuel, then that meant that—she rolled over to stare at the settee—Lord Rosewood had.

The harrowing events of the night before had not been a nightmare. No, Lord Rosewood was indeed quite real.

Sitting up but careful to keep the quilt around her, she hugged her knees and sighed. In the pale morning light filtering through the curtains, she could make out his features even better.

He certainly didn't look like an earl—not one she'd ever met, anyhow. In fact, with his unshaven face, unruly black hair, and stern chin, he looked more like a highwayman than the heir to a marquess.

In complaining about her brother, Primm had failed to disclose how ridiculously handsome he was.

He was more handsome, even, than Lord Kingsley—the man Victoria inevitably compared all other gentlemen to.

She closed her eyes and remembered the face of the man who'd begged her to end their betrothal because he'd fallen in love with another woman.

Victoria had forgiven him, and despite all her aunt's efforts to steer her back into society, her experience with the ever-so-charming Earl of Kingsley had been enough to induce her to not only swear off men but marriage in general.

Having postponed her wedding four times—yes, four!—so that she could mourn the loss of close family members, only to have it ultimately canceled by the groom, she'd decided fate must have other ideas for her life.

And now, she was exceedingly content in her position at the school.

She and Primm were in strong agreement as far as the patriarchal institution was concerned. A woman who took a husband didn't only relinquish her assets but her right to make independent decisions regarding her very existence.

Which wasn't a problem if one's husband was a fair man, such as Kingsley was to Olivia Redfield, the woman he had eventually married. Victoria had wanted to hate the young woman but had quickly learned that hating Olivia was impossible. Not when the young Countess of Kingsley was kind and generous and had overcome so much in life already.

And ironically enough, Lord and Lady Kingsley were now some of her most cherished friends—apart from the school that was.

A glance around the untidy room reminded her of the decision she'd made the night before—to be more self-efficient. A woman ought not to fall apart merely because she's without a cook and housekeeper.

Or because her night's rest had been interrupted by the untimely arrival of an arrogant rake.

She would make a list of all household chores she needed to learn. Then, if she had questions, which she likely would, she could seek out Mrs. Driver. Perhaps Mrs. Driver could instruct her in one of the Christmas recipes Primm had left on the worktable.

Victoria would also lay out a fire to light in her own chamber that night. She glanced at the flames keeping the parlor warm. Thick ash and a tired blackened log covered most of the surface. After it burned out, it would need cleaning.

She could do that. She could clean out a hearth. How hard could it be?

She'd do all this before darkness set in again.

The lump of masculinity on the settee shifted and mumbled incoherently, spurring her into action.

Victoria wriggled out from the warmth of the blanket, folded it, and draped it over the chair. Then, with that done, she hurried into her chamber—not because she had any great reason to rush, but because moving kept her warm.

The snow still blustered outside, and without a fire in her chamber, frost had built up on all the windows. She could even see her breath when she exhaled.

Shivers raised the hair on her arms as she shimmied out of her dressing gown, and her near frozen fingers fumbled to lace up one of her woolen gowns—lavender, of course, because that particular color made up most of her wardrobe. She unwound her braid, dragged a brush through her hair one hundred times, and then pinned a neat chignon behind her head.

Staring into the looking glass, she almost felt like her usual self again. She would need every last ounce of her confidence if she was going to cope with the thawed-out brawny earl sleeping in her parlor.

He could not remain here with her—alone. Already the situation was most improper.

The very first rule a lady learned was never to be caught without proper chaperonage. As an expert in this field, Victoria could hardly afford to break it.

If so much as a single whisper of gossip got out regarding the earl's presence here... Victoria shuddered. It was unthinkable.

He must have ridden here, so he must have a horse. But even if Lord Rosewood had to walk, she had no doubt he could manage the few miles between the school and the inn.

Bolstered by her resolve, she returned to the parlor. But as she approached the settee where she'd left him, her heart skipped a beat.

Because he lay still. Very still...

Too still.

And her nostrils picked up a coppery scent in the air.

Please don't let him be dead!

She touched her hand to his forehead. Hot. He was burning up!

A combination of relief and horror swept through her. The first because he was alive, and the second because, as she leaned closer, the coppery smell grew stronger.

One of the kitchen linens was wrapped around his hand,

and that linen, which was normally white, had been stained with a combination of black, scarlet, and red.

It was soaked with blood.

The air seemed to swoosh out of the room, and Victoria fell back onto her heels.

"What's the matter, Angel?" Deep green eyes met hers.

For an instant, she forgot he was ill, injured, and a cad. Because those eyes, fringed by glorious black lashes, seemed to see right through her.

And the gravelly tone when he called her Angel made her aware of her heartbeat... which she inexplicably felt everywhere—her ears, her throat—not to mention her chest.

"You cut yourself. You should have said something," she answered.

"It's nothing." He managed a listless shrug.

"You're bleeding," Victoria insisted. "You could die!"

He closed his eyes and inhaled before opening them again—vague, unfocused, but also a little mesmerizing.

"And you're burning up." Panic gripped her insides, all but paralyzing her.

Before she could stop him, he'd swung his feet to the floor and was sitting up. He swayed, though, and she had no doubt she could unbalance him with her little finger.

"I'm fine," he growled.

"You are not fine, you... you... buffoon!" Victoria all but exploded—her noble intentions went up in flames right along with her temper.

She inhaled through her nostrils and, getting another strong whiff of his blood, immediately regretted doing so.

Her lack of control over this situation was ridiculous.

Victoria Shipley, *Miss Shipley* to her students, was not the sort of person who lost her temper or panicked easily. On the contrary, she was the person to turn to in all social circumstances. She was the person who kept the waters calm.

It was part of why Primm trusted her so implicitly.

And already, this... *buffoon* had caused her to lose far too much of her composure.

"Settle down, Angel. No one is going to die." Even fevered, he cocked a brow at her as though she amused him.

"You cannot die." She sat back, thoroughly exasperated. "Primm cannot lose another member of her family."

His gaze shot to hers. "What do you mean, *Another member of her family?*" Finally, he was taking her seriously. "Has something happened—?"

"No!" Victoria realized her exact words. "Well, yes. But I assumed you knew. Your mother had an attack, at least your brother was concerned enough to send word of one. It's why Primm—why Miss Primm isn't here. She left early yesterday for Starbridge Abbey." And not for the first time, Victoria sent up a prayer that her friend had made it safely through the storm.

Lord Rosewood swallowed and then turned to stare toward the window. She expected some sort of expression of concern, but all she could see was cool indifference.

He truly was the most genuine of cads imaginable.

"Isn't that why you're here? So that you could escort your sister to Starbridge Abbey?" she pressed, annoyed and disappointed. Such a good-looking gentleman ought to be at least partially good on the inside.

No answer. Of course.

She just needed a plan.

A plan. Oh, yes. He needed to... Go!

She normally had no difficulties giving orders—managing. But with this man, she felt somewhat out of her depths. "Look," she began. "Perhaps you could—"

"Who are you?" He dragged his gaze away from the window and met her eyes, his stare pricking her like hundreds of tiny thorns.

It was odd to not be formally introduced, but under the circumstances, Victoria had no choice but to set aside her reservations. "Miss Victoria Shipley. I'm the assistant director of the school."

"You're Augusta's assistant?"

"I'm the *assistant director*," she said. Because there was a difference.

He smirked at that and then pushed himself to his feet. "I need to find my horse." He rubbed his chin with the hand that wasn't wrapped in a bloody cloth. "She ought to have made it here on her own."

It was the last thing she expected him to say. But he did not look arrogant and uncaring at that moment. He was *concerned*.

For his horse.

Even though his mother was quite possibly dying that very minute. Although, according to Primm, their mother had exaggerated the nature of ailments in the past. So… perhaps his lack of urgency in regard to Lady Starbridge could be forgiven.

But… *"Made it here on her own?*—You rode her here?"

"She threw me, but she knows the area." He frowned. "A branch weighed down by snow spooked her." He leaned forward to stand but only made it halfway before flinching and dropping back onto the settee. Beneath the flush of his fever, his skin turned white—most notably, around his mouth.

Wincing, Victoria pressed a pillow behind him, steadying him as she did so. If any of her students were thusly injured, she could have sent for the local physician. Doctor McBride could bring his little black bag and fix them up good as new. Victoria could then write a report and send for their parents if necessary. Procedures… that was what she was used to.

Lists. Objectives. Administrative goals.

But there was no one available to send for the doctor. Even if she could make it across the field to Mr. and Mrs. Driver's cabin, she wasn't sure that would be a good idea. Mrs. Driver wasn't the sort of person one entrusted with secrets.

Could Doctor McBride even get here through the snow?

Victoria needed to do something, however, because if that wound wasn't cared for soon, it was going to putrefy. Even then, dash it all, a lesion could kill a person if allowed to fester.

She glanced down at the bloodied bandage and her heart sank. Sending him away today was no longer an option.

"Let me look at your hand," she demanded, annoyed that she was going to have to risk her and the school's reputations.

"Why don't you find that whisky for me first?" His lack of propriety ought to be more off-putting than it was.

"Really?" She raised her brows. "It's not even noon."

"Or gin. Doesn't really matter. Just bring me whatever Auggie's hidden away in that brown cupboard she keeps by her bed." The earl met her skeptical gaze and winked. "For medicinal purposes."

Alcohol. Right. And he was right in that Primm kept a brown cupboard in her chamber. When they'd gotten news of a former teacher's engagement to a duke, Primm had surprised Victoria and the other teachers by bringing out a decanter of brandy for them to make a toast.

"I didn't realize you were injured last night." She pushed herself up. "We should have done something about it then."

Besides the brandy, she needed a few other supplies—soap, water, and a new bandage.

"Bring a needle and thread too."

"Did you lose a button?" she asked but then realized why he would need them. "I am not going to sew you up."

"I wouldn't expect a princess like you would."

"You're infuriating, do you know that?" Every time she felt a smidgeon of sympathy for him, he opened his mouth and made her want to throw something at him instead. She shot her gaze around the room in search of something to launch.

Not really. She wouldn't really throw something at an injured person.

"By all means, take your time, Miss Shipley. It's not as though I'm sitting here in pain."

Victoria refused to be goaded into exchanging insults with this man. Sending him a scowl, she instead marched out of the room in search of supplies she could use to fix him up.

The sooner he was well, the sooner he could be gone.

Standing at the door to Primm's chamber, however, it struck her that she was not without resources.

Miss Addie, who taught biology and anatomy, also kept a primer for any students interested in taking the apothecary exam one day. Such a manual would have remedies, mostly, but perhaps instructions on suturing.

Lord Rosewood had accused her of being a princess and he didn't even know her! And it was not any sort of compliment.

No, he'd called her that implying that she was spoiled and needy.

She hadn't viewed herself like that for a very long time. Since teaching and then being promoted to her current position, she'd become efficient, hard-working, and capable —*dash it all!*

Except for a few of the most basic aspects of survival, apparently.

She left Primm's chamber in favor of the door leading into the school. She unlocked it, pushed the door open and turned into the stairwell to climb to the second floor. She didn't feel at all guilty for rifling through Miss Addie's books. Her most useful find, however, was the medicine chest the anatomy teacher kept.

It held tinctures, poultices, and small cards explaining how to use them. Victoria settled onto the floor with the suturing kit that included various needles, catgut, and... was that human hair? But also a chart showing various stitches.

It was...

Surprisingly, very similar to crocheting. After a quick inspection, she replaced the chest's contents to bring it back to the residence with her.

Contemplating the task of actually sewing up his injury, she once again revisited the option of hiking through the snow so she could ask Mr. Driver to fetch the doctor. If asked, she could always tell the couple that Lord Rosewood had arrived early that morning.

And once she'd held up her responsibility to ensure his well-being, she could send him away so she could once again focus on teaching herself some of these more basic skills she lacked.

Clutching the chest under her arm, Victoria drifted toward the window to assess the conditions she'd have to hike through.

Inside, the classroom was much colder than usual, but standing by the glass, it was downright frigid. She hugged the chest, amazed but a little in awe of how the world had changed from browns, greens, and blues to nothing but white.

Piles and piles of white.

Except for a lone individual walking in the direction of the stable.

A tall, disturbingly familiar individual wearing a black greatcoat and holding one arm awkwardly despite his masculine swagger.

"You have got to be joking!"

Infuriated more than she was concerned, Victoria took one last look around the classroom before rushing back down the stairs. What if she hadn't seen him?

It would be just her luck for the buffoon to lose consciousness in the snow. How was she expected to drag him back inside?

And he couldn't die. Good lord, he couldn't die.

He might be arrogant and annoying, but he was her employer's brother. And Primm would be devastated if Victoria didn't prevent him from freezing to death.

Even if it would have been no one's fault but his own.

*U*pon seeing the black sheen of Artemisia's hindquarters, a wave of relief flooded Piers. The mare turned her head, flicked him a glance, and then turned away, as though irked that he'd questioned her ability to find shelter in the storm.

"Don't look at me like that. You're the one who threw me." He moved slowly as he entered—slowly because every joint in his body was screaming. With each step he took, his pulse pounded painfully behind his eyes.

Having survived Waterloo at the tender age of ten and six, he was embarrassed that he'd nearly succumbed to the elements on the short journey between London and his sister's school.

He wasn't particularly fearful of dying, per se, but he didn't fancy the idea of being done in by something as innocent as a low-hanging branch on a quiet country road.

Despite the storm, he and Artemisia had been making good time enroute to the school. Piers was familiar with the road, and the moonlight reflecting on the snow had aided his visibility, giving him the confidence to allow the mare to trot along at an efficient pace.

He wouldn't be in this sorry condition if not for the weight of the snow. As bad luck would have it, a single branch gave way over the road at the precise moment Piers rode beneath it.

Two seconds later, he'd been flat on his back, staring up at the ghostly limb while it swayed back and forth.

Unfortunately, the shadowy movement had not gone unnoticed by his mount. Before Piers could so much as catch his breath, the sound of Artemisia's galloping hooves had disappeared in the distance.

Piers had taken inventory of his condition, his arms, hands, legs, and feet. They'd been freezing but uninjured—for the most part. However, the occasional stinging pain on his left side had been an unexpected annoyance and caused the walk the last few miles to Augusta's school to take twice as long as it ought to have.

Miss Shipley's disheveled but ethereal appearance when she'd finally opened the door had almost made the walk worth his effort.

Her hair was the color of good scotch, brown with burnished golden strands hanging around her face and down her back. Her bare feet had peeked out from beneath a maroon velvet gown, and for an instant, he'd been certain she was a figment of his imagination.

Although, if that had been the case, the dressing gown wouldn't have concealed her figure so effectively.

And the woman would have been mute. Because females such as her, *proper ladies* to be more specific, were inevitably more trouble than they were worth.

Her scream had likely shaved ten years off his life.

And the woman who'd pestered him this morning was a far cry from the angel who'd opened the door. No doubt one of his sister's colleagues.

Confounded bluestockings.

The world would make more sense when bluestockings actually looked the part.

Artemisia's ears perked up, he heard approaching footsteps outside the barn, and then the object of his thoughts burst through the whistling winds outside.

"What are you doing out here?"

Speak of the devil.

Eyes the color of chocolate stared at him accusingly as she peered around the door. Her cheeks were flushed, her mouth pinched in a disapproving line and her arms crossed over her bosom.

Even the storm couldn't protect him from her. Smoothing a hand along his mare's coat, Piers did his best to ignore her.

"Do you want to catch your death?"

Piers continued stroking Artemisia's back, hoping Miss Shipley would give up and return to the residence. But she would not be so accommodating.

"She's beautiful!" She'd entered instead. "Is she yours?" Her mouth relaxed ever so slightly as she stared in wonder at his horse. How long would it take for those pretty pink lips to soften beneath his?

Ignoring the thought, he met her gaze and rolled his eyes.

She took a moment to scowl and then focused on Artemisia.

"She's beautiful." Miss Shipley repeated as she approached.

35

Auggie's assistant wore a knitted cap on her head, and a thick gray wool coat hung to the top of half-boots. The only visible part of her was that face.

Which, ironically enough, was one of the most classically perfect faces he'd ever seen.

"You're supposed to be a silver-haired spinster with a giant mole on your nose," he muttered. Not silver-haired, exactly, but whenever his sister had mentioned her assistant in one of her letters, Piers had imagined such a woman to resemble his old governess—right down to the beady eyes and visible nose hairs.

"What? Why would you say that?" Her posture, even now, would likely make any general proud.

"Auggie's letters." This version of Miss Shipley was too young and too damned pretty to be the person his sister had described. More than once, Auggie had written of her appreciation for Miss Shipley's brutally efficient and no-nonsense focus on the school's success. She'd written that Miss "S" possessed more starch than anyone she'd ever met and that she was indispensable to the running of the school.

"Primm said I had a mole on my nose?" Miss Shipley's brows furrowed.

What would this woman look like if she could ever unwind enough to smile?

"She mentioned you were a dragon with the students." His words—not Auggie's. But any woman so dedicated to propriety as this one supposedly would have to be one.

Even if she didn't exactly look the part.

Except for the not-smiling thing.

Auggie had bragged that she needn't worry about losing Miss Shipley's expertise to marriage, as she had her previous assistant. Piers had assumed that had been

Auggie's round-about way of saying that the woman was an antidote.

Obviously, he'd been wrong.

More likely, Miss Shipley was one of those women who opposed the institution itself. A feminist, like his sister, who preferred the "living death" to tying oneself to a man.

His sister, of course, used the term sarcastically. According to Auggie, marriage, rather than spinsterhood, was the true living death.

Piers, ironically, couldn't argue. An intelligent woman such as his sister would be miserable if forced to endure the constraints of marriage.

"I don't feel like much of a dragon." The corner of Miss Shipley's mouth twitched, more of a wince than anything else. "May I pet her?" She held back.

"You know horses?"

"I used to ride quite a lot." She rubbed her hands together. Bare hands. In chasing him outside, she'd not bothered to don any gloves. "A very long time ago."

Piers nodded. "Don't approach her from behind."

"Of course not," she retorted as she approached. To avoid spooking the mare, she had no choice but to stand beside him.

The sight of this woman's pale, bare hand stroking Artemisia's shoulder mesmerized him.

It was the most graceful he'd seen this woman yet. The night before, and earlier that morning, she'd been anything but rushing about awkwardly—stumbling and then marching, to be more accurate.

And this close, her perfume brushed his senses. The scent was barely noticeable amidst the dirt and cold inside the stable, yet it was strong enough to stir an overactive libido.

The wind gusted outside, and a swirl of snow curled inside through the door. This storm wasn't letting up today.

"What else do you know?" he asked. "About my mother?"

He dropped his gaze to the ground. Ever since his brother Elijah's death, he'd avoided going home. His blood ran cold at the thought of facing his father—this time as his father's heir.

Starbridge Abbey loomed like a trap—or a prison. Eli wasn't there.

And although Piers did occasionally long for the company of his younger brothers, they were going to have to come to him. He stretched his shoulders.

Was it possibly his mother's illness was actually serious?

Miss Shipley's hand stilled, but she didn't look at him. "Your brother Levi sent the missive. They believe she suffered minor apoplexy. Primm hadn't planned on going home but was concerned enough to change her plans." The sound of her voice provided more information than her words themselves.

His sister had never been the sort to panic.

A drop of sweat slid down the center of his back despite the bitter cold. Was he wrong not to panic as well?

He couldn't travel in this weather. Even if he was in better physical condition himself, he couldn't put his horse in danger.

"You shouldn't have come out here," he said.

"I wouldn't have, but..." She cocked an accusing brow. "You weren't thinking of traveling today, I hope? Because like I said—"

"You couldn't have Primm losing any more of us." Piers answered for her.

"Would you please come back inside? Your horse is fine."

He glanced around until he found what he needed. "Let me drape this over her." But when he reached up for the rug-like covering hanging over the stall, pain in his side nearly had him doubling over.

"Give it to me." She grasped the edge of the blanket.

"I've got it." He didn't let go. "She'll spook. I need to—"

"Then let me help you."

Piers hated feeling weak but allowed her to follow behind him and assist in draping it over Artemisia's back. The covering wasn't much, but it would help the mare retain heat. Today, he wished he were as resilient in harsh weather as his horse. Piers stared at the magnificent animal, imagining himself dropping right here—bedding down on some straw. That way, he wouldn't have to think.

"Come inside." Miss Shipley's hand on his back jolted him. "Please. You're burning up."

A sudden all-over weakness prevented him from arguing with her.

The snow whipped at his face before they'd even stepped outside and for the first few moments, the cold was almost inviting.

She relinquished his arm just long enough to close the stable door behind them while Piers tilted his head back and allowed the frozen crystals to land on his face.

"What is the matter with you?"

"You," he mumbled. And the snow. And Auggie for traveling to Starbridge Abbey before he could catch her. And Elijah.

And now, apparently, his mother.

Piers blinked to dismiss the fog enshrouding him while Miss Shipley dragged him through the drifts, head down, cursing intermittently at his slowness. Why wouldn't his limbs obey normally? What the devil was the matter with him?

He shook away the pounding in his head and focused on taking one step at a time. Miss Shipley wasn't at all happy with him, but it wasn't as though he could rest anymore without knowing Artemisia had made it to the stable safely. What kind of man could forget about his horse?

Not until the door slammed closed behind him, shutting out the howling of the wind, did he realize they were back in Augusta's residence.

"I found a medicine chest in our natural science teacher's classroom—it's normally for students, but under the circumstances, I hardly think she'll mind that we've borrowed it. And if I'm right, it has everything we need to fix your arm." She was behind him, mercilessly tugging his coat off his shoulders. He hissed when she dragged him back into the parlor. He'd forgotten about his arm.

Once planted on the settee again, he watched as she opened an old brown leather chest and rummaged inside. And since she was taking forever, he closed his eyes.

Sleep. Sleep would be wonderful. But he needed to check on his horse. "Artemisia."

"Is fine."

His would-be nursemaid had ceased her buzzing and lowered herself beside him. "Why does there have to be so much blood?" she muttered under her breath as she unwound the linen. "Of course, you'd have to put your hand through the window."

"You didn't answer the door," Piers pointed out reasonably.

"I would have!" She peeled away the last of the muslin strip and then set it aside. "Eventually. If you'd bothered sending word of your pending arrival, accommodations could have been made for you. At least then I would have had some idea who it was pounding on the door in the middle of the night. How would you feel? A woman alone? You could have been anyone! And me, here without protection!"

Piers closed his eyes, oddly enough soothed by the sound of her voice now—soothed that she didn't expect him to answer her—that he didn't have to make conversation. She expected nothing of him.

But all thoughts of being soothed exploded when...

She stabbed him!

Wide awake again, he stared down at the oozing red gash on his arm and seized her hand. "What are you doing? For God's sake, woman!"

"I'm sewing this closed."

He withdrew the needle with a hiss, swiping it out of her fingers. "I'm not a blasted pin cushion. Did you find Auggie's whisky?"

"I have turpentine and vinegar." With such a contrary response, she killed any softening he'd had toward her.

"To drink?"

"To bathe your wound." She pointed to the cut. "Isn't that what you want the whisky for?"

"I want whisky to dull the pain of your company." He groused. But it also came in handy while sewing oneself back together. "Give that to me." He examined the needle, which she'd threaded with catgut, and grudgingly acknowledged was precisely what he needed.

Before he had to ask again, she was once again in his favor when she placed the mouth of a bottle at his lips.

Whisky.

Needle in one hand, his other oozing blood, he had no choice but to tip his head back and trust her to pour it in.

He swallowed twice, but she kept right on pouring until he was choking and coughing with a most regrettable amount dribbling down his chin.

"Enough," he managed.

This woman was a mess.

But the few drams he had managed to swallow provided a familiar warmth. And numbing... enough so that he could focus his attention on the cut—a surprisingly straight line on his inner forearm that was about six inches long. Partially dried, but oozing blood and pus, he frowned to note a few red streaks forming along the edges.

"Pour a splash of whiskey on it." Piers scowled as he met her eager gaze. "Not the whole bottle this time."

Her eyes narrowed back at him, but she nodded.

"Careful now."

Piers watched closely as drops and then a slow, steady stream drizzled onto the wound. He kept careful watch despite the burning because she required supervision. Also, because he didn't want to see more whisky wasted than was necessary,

Before she could wash away the extra liquid, Piers had already drawn the needle through his skin. Feeling vaguely nauseated, he allowed the catgut to pull the flesh together, looped it and then tied it off.

"Doesn't that hurt?"

"Not even a pinch," he lied even as red clouded the edges of his vision.

Judging by the glare she sent him, she didn't believe him for an instant.

"Tie them off separately. Pierce the skin near the edge, but not too close, or it will tear," he explained even as that weakness returned. If he passed out and she needed to finish this up, he preferred she didn't sew him to one of the pillows. "Pull it taut, but not tight."

Her eyes were wide, and she herself was pale, but she nodded.

"Afterward, use the turpentine and vinegar." Piers blinked, forcing himself to focus. He'd closed half the wound, but when he went to make another stitch, the needle would have fallen from his fingers if she hadn't taken it from him.

She made a perfect stitch and then met his gaze.

"Like this?"

He nodded. "Pack it with a poultice... after... honey or lavender...."

And that was the last he remembered before the world turned black.

*V*ictoria stared at her handiwork on the unconscious man who'd collapsed onto the settee after she'd finally dragged him back inside. She'd always had an aversion to blood, but the greenish-white liquid oozing out of the wound had been far worse. No wonder he'd wanted whisky.

Nonetheless, she was remarkably satisfied with the stitches she'd made, which were small and perfectly symmetrical. And as long as she could ignore the fact that this was human flesh and not muslin or cotton, it was not all that different than mending or sewing a hem.

She tied off the ends, snipped the last thread, and doused the gash with the vinegar and turpentine. Then, pleased that it wasn't oozing now, she applied a honey-soaked dressing and bound the covering loosely with linen before arranging him as comfortably as she could onto the settee.

Wobbly, but also proud, she rose on shaking legs and let out a long sigh of relief. Perhaps she wasn't as useless at this sort of thing as she'd initially thought.

With her unexpected guest subdued, she could finally tackle the first item on the list she'd made for herself earlier.

Cleaning out the hearth and laying a new fire.

Victoria moved the screen aside, eyeing the black sooty mess with determination. A warm fire was something she'd taken for granted her entire life.

Now where did Jenny keep that small shovel and pail? Following a bit of searching, Victoria experienced another small victory when she located them in the back of a small storage closet by the larder. So when she returned to the parlor, she was emboldened to tackle the hearth.

Mastering this task made her feel almost… virtuous.

She needed to learn how to perform such basic chores. Not having done so before now had indeed put her at an unexpected disadvantage.

And what better way to learn than to do them? Already today, she'd learned how to stitch flesh.

Half an hour later, hands blackened and her back sore from leaning over, she relit the fire and deemed it not perfect but good enough.

And for the remainder of the morning, she persisted in working through her list quietly… But was the small residence perhaps a little too quiet?

When she stopped to check on her patient, she'd expected him to snore or awaken with some requests, but he lay more still than he had before. So still, in fact, that she crouched on the floor beside the settee and hovered over him to see that he was, in fact, breathing.

Uncertain as to what to do, she returned to the kitchen to make herself some tea. On her way back to the parlor, however, guttural sounds from the settee nearly caused her to spill the hot liquid. Relieved but also ready to chastise him for making such a commotion, Victoria hurried inside and set the tea aside.

But he wasn't awake.

He'd tossed off the quilt she'd placed over him. Sweat poured off his face as he turned his head back and forth on the pillow.

"Lord Rosewood?" She knelt beside him.

"Can't breathe." His eyes shone an even brighter green but were unfocused and glassy. She doubted that he even saw her.

"You can't breathe?" She leaned over him, perplexed. He was breathing, gasping, actually.

"Eli. I'm here." His stare landed on her, his hazel eyes pleading for…?

Elijah? Primm's brother who'd died almost two years before.

"Do you want water?" All it took was a few words from this man to have her feeling helpless once again. "Whisky?"

He tugged at his collar, looking frantic.

He was burning up—and not from the fire she'd lit in the room earlier. Instead, he was burning up from the inside.

"Let's get you out of these." Instinctively, she struggled to undress him. First his boots and stockings, and then his waistcoat.

"Air," he mumbled. He'd quieted somewhat, but that was equally as terrifying. Did that mean he was better, or did that mean he was worse?

She tried cooling him with lavender water and soaked his shirt in the process. It was tucked into his breeches, making it… impossible.

He was a single gentleman. But he was also possibly

dying. Dare she? And yet, she didn't have much choice. He could die!

Ignoring her qualms, she unfastened the buttons of his falls, the backs of her fingertips pressing into his belly— which was rigid and tight.

Six buttons in all, and then all that remained was to slide them off of him. She pinched her eyes closed and rubbed the back of her neck.

"You are lucky, my lord, that I am a confirmed spinster," she spoke out loud to herself, staring at his feet instead of her hands where she fumbled with the fabric around his hips and... "Otherwise, I'd likely have a fit of vapors."

This wasn't at all like when Lord Kingsley—her betrothed at the time—had been injured. Having been shot, he'd hovered between life and death for nearly a week. But there had been doctors present to save him, nurses to tend to his needs, and there had been Olivia—the woman he'd eventually married.

While he'd fought for his life, Victoria had barely summoned the fortitude to visit him once a day.

It was no wonder he'd married someone else.

But this was different.

She was different.

And there were no nurses nor physicians to call upon.

She untangled the breeches from around his feet and trailed her gaze back up.

The length of his linen shirt, which ended just below his nether region, allowed her a vivid glance of his lower half— or third, rather. His calves were elegant and shapely and perfectly complemented the thick muscles of his thighs. Curling black hairs dusted his pale olive skin, not too much, but just enough. Her heartbeat pulsed in her ears that she would sit alone with him like this—that she would undress him!

Victoria forced her gaze back to his face.

The shirt. She needed to get him out of that wet shirt.

But first…

She located the quilt and covered his lower half.

"Can you sit up, my lord?" She leaned over him.

He opened his eyes, but she had no idea if he saw or heard her.

"Lord Rosewood?" she asked. "*Piers?*"

He blinked. "Do you ever smile?"

"Not when I have an earl burning up on my settee," she answered, relieved more than affronted. Even half-delirious, the man was incorrigible. "I need you to sit up. Help me get this shirt off you."

He surprised her by nodding and lifting himself enough for her to pull it over his head.

The pulsing grew stronger, and she swallowed hard to quiet it. It was silly, really, that she should find herself so affected by a shirtless man.

Sinewy shoulders tapered to smooth forearms and elegant wrists. His hands were slim but strong-looking, the nails cut blunt along the tips of his fingers…. Which she couldn't help but imagine to be dexterous and efficient.

A tremor rolled through him, and she pulled the coverlet up, effectively ending her study of the rippling muscles that made up most of his belly.

"You finished the stitches?" he murmured.

"I did."

"Good." His head fell back onto the pillow again, and he closed his eyes. Thick black lashes swept along the tops of his cheeks, and even relaxed, his jaw looked determined.

When he wasn't making snide comments or insulting her, this man was almost beautiful. "And you used the turpentine—"

"And vinegar. Yes. Are you thirsty?"

"Um-hm." He dipped his chin. "Willow bark?"

"Oh. I think I have some of that in the medicine chest." She rummaged and brought out a packet.

"Put it in the water."

As she opened the packet and prepared the tonic, the muscles in the back of her neck eased. He was *alive*.

She hadn't realized she'd been holding herself so rigidly.

"Here." She slid one hand behind his neck, helping him to drink. "You scared me. Please do not go outside again. I'm not very experienced at any of this and…." She was the one to shiver this time. "Please. Just don't put yourself in harm's way again."

Mindful of his arm, she leaned close and assisted his head back to the pillow. Although she braced herself for him to make another inappropriate comment, one didn't come.

"Can I get you anything else?" she asked.

"More whisky?" His ghost of a grin had her shaking her head.

It had been foolhardy of her not to have bothered learning such skills long before this. As a teacher, as a person responsible for the well-being of dozens of young girls, she ought to have made it a priority.

"Miss Shipley?"

She lifted her gaze back to his face. He wasn't smirking or frowning.

"Yes?"

"You're doing fine." His tone was reassuring.

"You don't have to say that."

"But I do." Another ghost of a grin danced on his mouth. "Can't have you getting discouraged and giving up on me."

"It's not as though I have a choice." She choked on a laugh. "Sprawled out in my parlor like this, you're impossible to ignore."

"No smile," he mumbled.

"What?"

"You laughed without smiling." He closed his eyes. "I'm going to sleep again."

"Don't die." She was only half-joking. "Primm would never forgive me."

But he'd drifted off already, leaving her once again to the quiet of the otherwise empty residence.

"My lord?" Her voice came from far away.

A cloth cooled his forehead and then his lips.

"Can you drink some more? I have another dose of the willow bark mixed for you."

It was Miss Shipley's voice. The aging spinster who wasn't aging at all. His eyelids were heavy, and his tongue felt like cotton.

"I will. But you…"

"Yes?"

"You need to check my arm." Fire burned in his head and he could barely think. Even so, he knew that his wound might be the cause of it. "Clean it again."

Although too weak to open his eyes, he felt her presence as she leaned over him. Nervous energy vibrated around her and knowing he needed her help, it was not unwelcome.

Blessedly cool air met his chest where she drew back the quilt, and then the wrap on his arm loosened as she unwound it.

"I used a honey poultice, but… oh."

"What?"

"It's… redder than before."

"Are there lines?"

"Little ones. And more of that green substance."

Damn.

All he could hear were her breaths. "It's putrefying, isn't it?" Her voice caught.

"Clean it again." His attempt to sound commanding failed and desperation sounded in his voice instead.

"I'm going to apply more whisky this time."

As much as Piers hated wasting good liquor, it was probably for the best.

"Use it liberally." He could tolerate pain, but it was possible he'd pass out again. "Willow bark first."

"Of course."

He didn't know this woman from Eve. In fact, he'd deemed her something of a pestilence before meeting her. And yet, as her hand slid into his hair, holding him up so he could swallow the medicine, he found her… comforting.

He drank, then cracked his eyes open enough to watch her fold a linen square and place it beneath his arm. And getting a glimpse of the wound, he was inclined to agree with her.

He'd been stupid to let it get this far.

"Willow bark is in the tea, along with a splash of whisky," she said.

"I think I love you."

"You won't love me for long. I'm going to address this

greenish substance first," she sounded overly cheerful—no doubt an attempt to keep calm. "I'll use the turpentine and vinegar mixture. Foul-smelling stuff."

"Good girl."

He hissed as she dabbed around the stitches.

When she finished with that torture, she held up the bottle of whisky. But before tackling the wound again, she tipped her head back and took a long swig.

Piers would have laughed out loud if he wasn't so weak.

Composed now, she held his arm again. "Are you ready?"

"Just do it," he said, preparing himself for the stinging. "Try to pour so it goes inside." That would allow it the greatest chance to get at the source of the problem. If this didn't work, poor Miss Shipley might very well face Auggie's wrath after all.

Damnit.

"If you say so."

The uncomfortable burning from the fever gave way to the fire on his arm. Red-hot, stinging... but not unbearable.

"I'm sorry. I'm so sorry." Miss Shipley sounded more distraught than he was.

"Don't wipe or cover it," Piers managed through clenched teeth. "Let it sit like that."

"Very well." She poured a little more. "It's drenched. I'm so sorry."

"No, no. That's good." She was holding his hand now. Or was he holding hers? "Thank you," he breathed. *Don't leave me.*

"You're going to be fine, Piers. Do you hear me?"

When she went to pull away, he squeezed her hand. Just a few seconds more.

"I'm not leaving. I promise," she soothed. "I'm right here."

He should release her hand but couldn't bring himself to do so. Just a few minutes more.

WHEN NEXT PIERS opened his eyes, it was dark but for the flickers of fire across the room along with those of a few candles. Curled up in a large chair adjacent to the settee, Miss Shipley sat watching him.

Escaped whisky-colored strands of her hair reflected the flames burning from the hearth. She wore an apron over her dull-colored dress but managed to look angelic again. When she realized he was awake, her eyes flew open wide, and she leaned forward to rise.

"Don't get up." His voice came out hoarse.

She swiped at her hair, tucking it behind one ear, and rose nonetheless. When she reached his side, she lowered herself to the floor beside him and touched a hand to his forehead. The vague scent of her perfume teased him. It was clean with only a hint of something floral.

Her breasts, which filled his line of sight, heaved when she gulped in a breath.

"I think it's broken. The fever." Her voice wobbled. She dropped back onto her heels, and when she brushed away a strand of hair, it was shaking.

Shadows etched beneath her eyes, and that pinched mouth of hers was almost white.

"How long?" He cleared his throat. "How long have I been asleep?"

He vaguely remembered burning up and then uncontrollable shaking. And the burning in his arm.

"Two days," she answered.

Two days!

He raised his arm to examine it. Red but not angry, and it was absent most indications of infection.

"I used all the whisky, I'm afraid." She took hold of his wrist, turning it carefully.

He liked the feel of her touching him, and it was... unexpected.

"You got drunk while I lay here dying?" he teased, satisfied to see some color return to her cheeks.

"On the wound, you buffoon." She shook her head. "That and half a bottle of gin. You're lucky Primm keeps such a well-stocked liquor cabinet."

"That's my Auggie. Prepared for any emergency." He flicked his gaze to his arm again, this time noticing the tiny, even stitches she'd sewn ridiculously close to one another as though embroidering an insignia. But they were holding, and the cut no longer appeared to be festering.

"I believe I'm going to live after all," he announced, sitting up and trying not to groan. He should be grateful to her—he *was* grateful to her, but he also hated that he'd gotten himself into such a state in the first place. "You should get some sleep."

"Not yet. What if the fever comes back?" She raised a cup to his lips. How many times had she done that?

Tea but with white powder—the willow bark—and the bitter citrus of gin.

Not his favorite, but an acceptable substitute.

"Drink." The command summoned fleeting images that felt more like a dream.

Weak, but bored with himself already, he slid his feet to the floor. When he wavered, she wrapped an arm around him.

"This cannot be a good idea."

"Artemisia—"

"I checked on her this morning," she answered. "She has everything she needs. She's fine."

He wouldn't have expected her to consider his horse. This spinster had more fortitude than he'd given her credit for.

"Thank you," he offered. He had intended to spend the holiday with Auggie here at the school, but his sister wasn't here. She wasn't here because his mother had apparently experienced another of her episodes.

Although, there was also the possibility that it was more than that. The desire to be with his mother warred with the aversion he had for his father.

He couldn't stay away forever, damnit.

"The storm?" he asked.

"It seems to be letting up."

"I should go." And yet, in his present state, he doubted he'd make it to the end of the drive.

She laughed at that. But still no smile. "You aren't going anywhere in your condition."

"What a mess."

Miss Shipley, who was seated beside him now, neither agreed nor disagreed.

"I didn't go home last year either." Piers stared into the fire.

"I know."

At this, he exhaled a harsh laugh. "My sister does not approve."

"She does not." And then, after nearly a full minute passed... "She said you don't get on well with your father."

"That's putting it mildly."

"I am sorry about your brother."

"I mourn the hell out of him." Eli had been his twin. They'd been inseparable for most of their childhoods. But Piers was seven minutes younger than Elijah had been, and as they'd gotten older, those seven minutes had come to matter greatly.

He'd been mourning the loss of his brother for years.

Their father had kept his oldest son separate from the rest of them so he could teach him the running of an earldom. As a result, he hadn't much interest in his second son —or any of the others, for that matter.

So Piers had traveled the world, seen new lands, fought in a war, and eventually dabbled in trade. He'd done all the things Eli never could.

Miss Shipley's gaze, although sympathetic, was also accusing. "I'm sure your other brothers miss you."

"You wouldn't understand," he exhaled. "Eli was my twin. He was… a part of me."

"You're right. I can only imagine."

Piers swallowed. Even his throat hurt. "When Eli died, part of me died with him." It didn't matter that they'd not gotten on well in the end. He had still been Eli.

And now he was gone.

"You are not your brother," their father had told Piers as they stepped away from the grave. *"But you'll have to do."*

All he'd wanted was to grieve the loss of his brother, but anger with his father had eroded even that. So Piers had left early the morning after the funeral. It was the last time he'd been home.

"But you did not die." Her answer wasn't at all sympathetic.

Piers couldn't quite read her expression. "I came here so

Auggie wouldn't have to spend the holidays alone. I thought she'd want my company."

"But you have me instead."

Piers hadn't yet decided if that was a good or a bad thing.

RECOVERY

"You're lucky you have family to go home to. Your brother is dead, but you have, what, three other brothers and both of your parents? And more, from what Primm has told me. Aunts, uncles, a grandmother."

"Is that why you aren't away for the holidays, then? Are you an orphan or something like that?"

"Something like that."

He simply nodded. It hadn't been fair of him to speak to her like that. She'd helped him. She'd ladled medicine into his mouth, washed the sweat off his body, and then built up the fire and covered him in quilts when he'd been chilled.

Every muscle in Victoria's body ached. Not from pain or injury, but from work. From making fires, boiling water, but mostly from tension brought on by the fear that her patient would expire any moment.

Even now, she wasn't wholly confident in his recovery.

"I'm sorry." His voice was so low that she barely heard his apology. "It's just… complicated."

Victoria burst off the settee. He was weak, and likely not thinking straight, but she couldn't hold back her criticism. "You are not the only person in the world to lose someone you loved. *People die.*" She'd spent a good part of her life coping with death. Victoria crossed to the fire and smoothed her skirts. Now that her guest was conscious, what was she supposed to do with him?

"Right." But he didn't sound as though he agreed with her.

He was improved but certainly not well enough to travel. Which meant she couldn't send him away.

The thought niggled that she ought to tell Mr. Driver about him... But he would tell his wife, who would tell Miss Jefferies, who would no doubt tell her employer, Lady Annesley...

Which would have been equally effective as posting it in the *Gazette.*

It was the middle of the night, and she'd barely slept in the last few days. Now that his fever had broken, she could finally return to her chamber. She'd laid out the fire. All she'd need to do was strike a flint, and it would be cozy.

Comfortable.

Familiar.

"How is going home for the holidays complicated?" She asked instead. "I understand you're at odds with your father. But your mother needs you. As, I'm sure, do your brothers and Primm. Are you angry with your brother for dying? Is that it?" She'd been angry at her sister for dying. And then her parents.

She wasn't angry with Aunt Delia. She just missed her.

"I'm not angry with Elijah." But he *was* angry; she heard it in his voice.

Victoria turned her back to the fire, and upon taking note of his ruffled hair and the stitches on his arm, felt more than a little guilty for goading him.

It wouldn't do either of them any good for him to wear himself out again.

"Lay back down." She crossed to him. "I'm sorry for your brother. It's none of my business."

She fluffed the pillow and pushed him onto it.

"I'm not angry with him," Piers said.

She'd stopped thinking of her patient as Lord Rosewood the second time he'd passed out. Mostly because when she'd addressed him as "my lord," he never answered her.

So, for now anyhow, he was Piers.

"Then who are you angry with?" She didn't really expect an answer.

"I don't know," he mumbled, practically asleep again already.

Having listened to Primm complain about her brother's lack of concern for their family over the past year and a half, Victoria had not expected to feel sympathetic toward this man.

And yet, she did.

"It's all right." She brushed her fingertips through the hair that fell across his brow. "It's all right."

She sat watching him sleep, and only when she felt certain his fever wasn't returning did she return to her chamber. And although her mind was filled with dozens of unanswered questions about the gentleman recovering on the settee in the parlor, the moment she climbed under the counterpane, she drifted into a dreamless sleep.

· · ·

THE SCENT of coffee teased her into wakefulness. Victoria burrowed deeper into her mattress and imagined Primm bustling in the kitchen and brewing her bitter beverage. It would have to be Primm since Victoria only drank tea.

Coffee was an abomination.

Contemplating climbing out of bed and making herself a strong cup of tea, Victoria rolled onto her side and sighed, relaxed and comfortable.

Until the recollection of the past few days slammed into her.

Primm's departure—Piers's late-night arrival—and then the two terrifying days when the threat of death had lurked over the parlor.

Someone was working in the kitchen. Had Mr. Driver taken pity on her and brought his wife over to assist her? Had Primm returned?

Either scenario was enough to induce Victoria to throw back the covers and hastily shrug into her dressing gown. She barely took the time to locate and slide her feet into her slippers.

But when she turned the corner to the kitchen, she froze. Because standing upright, shirt untucked and sleeves rolled up, was the last person she expected to find.

Using his uninjured arm, Piers was attempting to roll out... pastry dough?

His hair was in disarray and his shirt wrinkled, but he didn't look as though he was about to topple over as one might have expected. Not twenty-four hours before, he had been knocking on death's door, and now he was...

Baking?

He acknowledged her with a quick glance and shrugged his shoulder toward the makeshift repair in the window he'd broken. Returning his attention to the dough spread out on the worktable, he asked, "Do you always sleep well into the afternoon?"

She ignored the question.

Because although she'd managed to stop for the occasional few bites of bread and cheese in between caring for him, she hadn't eaten a hot meal since before Primm left.

"What are you making?"

"Egg and cheese bread. One of my grandmother's favorites."

That was...surprising.

"You?" She stared at him. "*You* are going to cook it for us?"

"Unless you would prefer to take over," he answered.

She'd planned on sustaining herself with yet another meal of unperishables, but her belly chose that moment to growl, and of course, he heard it.

Rolling the dowel back and forth with his palm, he slanted her a smirk.

"I'll take that as a no." Using one hand, he flipped the dough over and rolled again. "Your larder is full. Auggie was prepared to make a full Christmas dinner for the two of you, I imagine. Were you going to let all of it go to waste?"

But she was still distracted by this side of him. She was... impressed.

"I've never known an earl who could cook." In all her life, she'd never imagined that her inability to cook would be something she'd feel embarrassed about. But here she was, standing in the kitchen feeling sheepish.

Something about this man... She pinched her mouth together.

"You forget. I've mostly been the spare." He awkwardly

EDUCATED BY THE EARL

turned the rolling pin with his one good arm. "While my dear brother was kept locked away learning my father's ways, Auggie and I learned other skills—like cooking. Lucky thing, as I haven't always lived places where I had the luxury of someone to cook for me."

Victoria couldn't help but imagine where those places might be—the deserts of the far east? Craggy highlands? Or perhaps even the savage lands of America.

Wherever she imagined him, she had no doubt that he... fit. Even while terribly ill, this man was more comfortable in his own skin than any person she'd ever met. Perhaps that was what made him so maddening.

"Primm mentioned you've done some traveling," she said, making an attempt at civility.

"Some." He tossed the pin in the air and caught it with the same hand.

When he turned to her and flashed a decidedly wicked grin, Victoria took a step backward. Dear heavens, he'd managed to release butterflies in her chest with a single glance.

This was the rogue Primm had told her about.

She clasped her hands together to keep them from fluttering uselessly. She needed a distraction, and the task he was attempting seemed to require two hands.

"May I help?"

"I've got it." He moved to use his injured arm.

"No. You mustn't!" She crossed over and went to take the pin from his hand. "I'd rather not sew you up a second time. I've seen enough blood to last a lifetime."

But he didn't relinquish the pin.

"Do you know how to use it?" He cocked a questioning brow.

Victoria stared down at the flattened dough. It couldn't be that difficult, could it?

"You don't, do you?" He made a disapproving sound.

"Did you *cluck your tongue* at me?" She squinted over her shoulder at him. She had to tip her head back since he was so much taller than she. This close, he made her feel smaller than usual.

He made her feel delicate.

With her stare caught by the whiskers around his mouth, Victoria temporarily lost her string of thought. And she didn't comprehend his words right away.

"What?"

"Dust flour on your hands and then brush them over the pin."

But that sounded terribly messy and unnecessary. "I managed to stitch you up. I think I can do this."

"My apologies." Making a half bow, he stepped away from the worktable. "By all means, do your best."

Victoria lowered the pin across the dough and then began rolling, transferring a good deal of her weight to the dowel.

Dismay struck right away, however, because the dough tore in two, more than half of it sticking to the wooden pin.

He was beside her again. "Brush some flour on those fragile little hands of yours. Looks like I'm the teacher today."

My hands are not fragile.

He reached around her, and even one-handed, he easily scooped the dough off the pin.

"Primm always brags that her students learn from the best. What, my *dear Miss Shipley*, do you teach?'

My dear Miss Shipley. The words hung in the air.

Wondering how he'd managed to make her name sound improper, Victoria frowned. She had never been ashamed of the skills she taught, yet she felt the need to apologize for the second time that morning. This man was more than insufferable. He was... impossible!

She stared down at her hands, still uncertain about covering them with flour.

"Oh, Lord, you're the token manners teacher, aren't you? Give me your hands." She held them up, and he unclenched her fists. Without any warning, he then tossed flour onto her palms. "Rub them together."

"*Decorum and Comportment*—in addition to music." She lifted her chin even as she noticed how dry her hands felt. "Harp, the pianoforte, and violin. And voice." Despite her own less-than-melodious ability to sing, she knew the principles.

"The truly important skills." He laughed out loud at her this time. "Spread the flour over the wood."

Holding the dowel with both hands, she cautiously slid them up and down the rod. She paused, however, when he made an odd choking sound.

"Am I doing it wrong?"

"Not at all." He shifted.

"It is fundamental for a lady to carry herself properly before entering society," Victoria continued dusting the pin as she defended her area of expertise. "Before graduating, every student is required to master my subjects. What kind of a world would we live in without them?"

"Without manners?"

"And music."

He shook his head. "Dust the dough. And pinch these

pieces together, like this." His voice rumbled right behind her. He was helping her again.

Enduring his random criticism, she reshaped the dough. And when she placed the dowel on her handiwork, he leaned forward, covering her hand.

"Don't push too hard, or it will tear again."

What had happened to all the air in the room?

She struggled to focus on the task at hand with him standing so close to her—his hand guiding hers as she rolled the pin, his chest pressed into her back.

Much more of this and the flour on her hands would turn to paste.

"Easy now. You aren't pounding out a song on the pianoforte." He loosely guided her wrist with his uninjured hand. Even as tingling awareness spread from her belly to her fingertips and toes, she couldn't help bristling at his know-it-all-ness.

Victoria needed to make herself perfectly clear.

"When a lady steps into a Mayfair drawing room, her demeanor sets the stage for the rest of her life. If she is timid, she will be overlooked. If she is loud, she will be dismissed as uncouth. The conversation she makes reflects her inner strength. She requires confidence but must carry herself with grace in all circumstances."

"Right," he said.

"Yes. Right," she said through clenched teeth.

Her students would be lost without the skills they learned from her. They were valuable and important and… beautiful!

Victoria's classes mattered! She side-eyed His Lordship. *Drat him.*

~

Miss Shipley, Piers realized, was a passionate woman. While teaching her the basics of shaping the pastry boat and then grating the cheese, he couldn't help goading her as she described damn near every last detail of what surely must be Manners 101.

"But you no longer mingle with the *ton* yourself, do you?" he accused. "You are a teacher."

"*Assistant director*," she corrected him. She brushed her hair out of her face, and Piers didn't bother to tell her that she'd left flour on her cheek. "I have friends, well-heeled friends, who I associate with when I'm able. In fact, if Lord and Lady Kingsley hadn't traveled for the holidays, Miss Fellowes and I could have spent Christmas at Sky Manor."

Sky Manor. "Miss Fellowes is..." Piers searched his memory. "The Earl of Kingsley's sister, is she not?"

"She is."

"So, another teacher is one of those so-called well-heeled friends?"

She sent him a very dark, admonishing look, which didn't scare him a bit.

"Believe what you wish. But I also attend local functions. Sometimes I even convince your sister to join me. I organize the school's parent meetings, special gatherings, and fundraisers." And then she met his gaze with a scowl that was the equivalent of a child adding, "*So there.*"

Despite Miss Shipley's uptight nature, or perhaps because of it, he was finding her to be surprisingly delightful.

Charismatic.

And he immediately comprehended why his sister

deemed Miss Shipley vital to the running of the school. It wasn't that she was notably capable on any academic level. Or that she possessed one of those scientific skills Miss Primm's students inevitably learned.

Dear Miss Shipley, he deduced, was the school's figurehead.

As Miss Primm, Auggie ought to have filled that role, but she was too efficient, too impatient—*too damn smart*—to waste her time charming donors or attracting students from aristocratic families.

Not that she couldn't. As the daughter of a marquess, Auggie could rightfully lay claim to the title of a lady. But upon failing to land a husband by the age of five and twenty, she'd legally claimed her dowry and spent it establishing the school. And for years now, she'd rejected the title in favor of being Miss Primm—in favor of dedicating herself to her vocation.

And as he learned more about Miss Shipley, he silently commended his sister for knowing precisely what she was doing.

Even if her assistant director was practically clueless when it came to being proficient at anything practical.

Miss Shipley all but destroyed a second egg by slamming it onto the edge of the bowl.

"It's not a mallet," he chided.

Ignoring the stitches tugging along his right arm, Piers positioned himself behind her again.

"Tap the egg on a flat surface, not the bowl. Horizontally, like this."

"Why not the bowl?" Her voice sounded a little throaty and breathless.

"The edges push the cracked shells up into the

membrane of the egg and break it. Start with a gentle tap, eventually adding more force. Now, pry it open with your thumbs and..." He forced her to use a little finesse, his fingers directing hers.

Ironically, he didn't mind teaching her. He didn't mind that it provided him with an excuse to touch her hand or lean in and inhale her perfume. This particular spinster was more damsel than dragon. Nothing wrong with that. Nothing at all.

"Gently." The back of her wrist was delicate, almost fragile.

And yet, she exhibited the finesse of an elephant.

"This one didn't break!"

"See that broken piece there? Use the shell to scoop it out."

"I've got it."

"Perfect." He couldn't help but praise her success—she sounded so damn proud.

The pulse in her wrist fluttered beneath his thumb.

Piers had not expected to be attracted to this woman. She was the sort of lady Eli would have pursued—the sort his parents would have chosen for him.

And yet, his debauched imagination had taken him to a very wicked place when she'd dusted flour over the rolling pin. Ah, the things those pretty little hands could do...

An unexpected wave of fatigue crashed over him, and he stepped backward.

"Now what do I—?" She turned around to ask but something in his expression gave him away. "You need to lie down again. This was too much for you."

"We haven't cooked it yet."

"I'll manage." And yet he allowed her to bully him out of the kitchen.

"Don't burn them," he said, mounting a weak protest. Piers truly had been looking forward to a decent hot meal.

"Then tell me what to do." She wasn't leading him into the parlor but toward the back of the residence—the bedchambers.

"Bake the pastry and cheese until it starts to brown. Then add one egg to each and bake another five minutes. Do not walk away. Don't get distracted. It only takes a second to burn them. Where the devil are we going?"

"You can sleep in Primm's bed. The settee is too small for you."

"Good God, she'll kill me." Piers recalled his sister's large bed made up with luxurious bed linens. It was the one thing he knew his sister liked to splurge on. He raised an arm and sniffed. "I haven't bathed in days." What the hell—? Was that—

"I bathed you in lavender water."

No wonder he smelled like a meadow in springtime.

But wait. She had *what—?* He stumbled but caught himself on the wall.

True, he'd wakened to find himself naked beneath the quilt but hadn't considered how he'd gotten that way.

He glanced back at her. And then his twisted mind shot back to the image of her hands sliding up and down the rolling pin.

She, however, was apparently more preoccupied with the possibility of a hot meal.

"How long did you say I needed to bake the cheese?"

If she'd been impressed by what she'd seen while bathing him, she obviously wasn't letting on.

"Piers?"

"What?" His gaze landed on the bed.

"How long does it usually take?"

"How long does what take?" Half his blood had left his brain, which for some reason was imagining her hands squeezing water out of a cloth, and then rubbing—

"The bread—to brown. How long does it usually take?"

"Ah…" Pastries. Egg. Cooking. "About a quarter of an hour."

"I didn't realize how hungry I was until just now." She drew back the counterpane for him. Patting the mattress, her eyes glowed with anticipation. "Now come and get into bed."

Piers blinked. Did she mean—?

"Do you need help with your arm?" Her frown returned.

Of course she didn't. He rubbed the back of his neck, frustrated that he'd allowed his mind to jump to sex—with his sister's manners teacher, no less—when he could barely keep himself upright, let alone…

"I'm fine."

He must be running a fever again.

"I could—"

"Thank you." He pointed away from the bed and toward the exit. "Don't burn the pastries."

"Are you sure—?"

"Go."

He could hear her grumbling even after he'd closed the door.

A HOYDEN?

*V*ictoria inhaled the buttery scent wafting from the pastries and set them on the worktable. It would serve Piers right if she didn't wake him and instead sat down alone to eat her first hot meal in what felt like weeks.

Although, it hadn't been weeks, just a few days, really. But with all the upheaval of his arrival and the days blurring into the nights, it might as well have been.

Fearful she'd burn them, as Pier seemed to expect, Victoria had forgone dressing properly while waiting for the bread boats to bake.

She glanced down at her night clothes—her gorgeous dressing gown now covered with flour—and sighed.

This person she'd become since Primm left wasn't like her at all. In fact, it was the very opposite of her nature to be so discombobulated. And though part of this was due to her failing at keeping the house livable, she blamed at least half of her frustrations on the man sleeping in Primm's chamber.

Piers Primm, the Earl of Rosewood, was too handsome for his own good—too handsome for her equilibrium. A single glance from his piercing hazel eyes turned her into a graceless ninny.

She stared at the bread as it cooled and fanned her cheeks with one hand. Of course, she was going to wake him. He was Primm's brother—a guest—for heaven's sake.

Almost tea-time already, Victoria bustled between the small dining room and the kitchen, setting out two sets of silverware, napkins, glasses, and as an afterthought, a bottle of wine. Careful not to wake her patient yet, she tiptoed back to her own chamber so she could tidy herself and don something more appropriate—something that would make her feel more herself.

Which she needed—desperately.

One glance in her vanity, and she almost felt like crying. With flour on her face and the weave of her braid half undone, she looked more like a hoyden than any respectable teacher she could recall.

I look like a hoyden.

She turned to the side, glancing at her reflection over one shoulder, and then faced herself again.

I, Victoria Shipley, resemble a hoyden!

For the first time since coming to work at the school full-time, she missed having her ladies' maid.

How did the farmworkers' and merchants' wives perform all these chores day in and day out and still make themselves presentable for society? *But, oh!*

Not society. Victoria halted her thoughts.

She'd always felt sympathy for the poor and even the middle class—because they could never experience the same privileges she'd been born into. Victoria closed her eyes.

There had been times she'd looked down on them for failing to act with any manners—for being undignified.

It wasn't that she hadn't been sympathetic. She had *known.*

She had known they lived very different lives than her, but she'd been…

Ignorant.

Those who lived outside of society's inner circle were likely mostly only concerned with… survival.

Caring for themselves, their family, and their homes wasn't an option. And there was no end to it. There were no summer holidays for them—no house parties. Only days stacked into weeks stacked into years of…

She stared at herself and touched the ends of her braid as a fraction of their hardship crowded her perspective.

It had only taken three days for Victoria to resemble a harridan.

She was exhausted.

Rattled, Victoria scrubbed the flour off her face, hands, and a few other unlikely places. Then, in selecting a gown to wear, she chose an older, serviceable woolen frock and covered it with an apron. It didn't matter that it wasn't as pretty. Nor did it matter that the knot she pinned at the back of her head was tight and unflattering.

The only person who'd see her was Piers.

She was not about to dress up for him. They weren't in Mayfair, and she wasn't attending any balls.

No. Her prettier gowns would have to remain in her wardrobe. At least until Jenny returned. When the new term began, Victoria could go back to normal—albeit, with a new appreciation for others.

Fortified by her ablutions but still caught in a tailspin, she marched across the corridor and knocked on Primm's bedchamber door. "It's ready," she announced.

She heard footsteps, and then he peered out.

"Did you sleep?" she asked.

"On and off." He lifted his gaze to stare over her shoulder. "I kept waiting for you to wake me so I could put out the fire."

"What fire?"

"The one consisting of charred bread boats." He sniffed and then rubbed his thumb along his bottom lip. "But perhaps I worried for nothing. Have you proven me wrong?"

"Really?" She jammed her hands on her hips. "Why am I even surprised? And why should I even care?"

Victoria spun around, too irritated to look at him.

But before she could escape, he'd snagged one of her arms from behind. "Wait, Miss Shipley... Victoria."

She tugged, and his grip loosened, but his tone halted her hasty retreat.

"That was unkind of me." His voice, oddly enough, sounded sincere. "I'm sorry to imply that you couldn't handle it. Forgive me?"

There was no practical reason for her eyes to be stinging with tears. It was a simple apology from a man who was practically a stranger to her. She dipped her chin.

What should his opinion of her matter? She was happy enough to eat alone. She didn't require his company. She didn't need him or anyone!

"Allow me a few minutes to wash up, I'll join you shortly," he added.

"Do as you wish." She exhaled loudly and then, without looking back, marched down the short hall to the kitchen. Not completely trusting this side of him, she collected the tray she'd put together earlier and carried it into the dining room. The sight of the table she'd laid out earlier stilled her.

What good were the decorative candelabra and vase of silk flowers if a person couldn't cook a meal?

Bringing them out earlier, she'd thought they looked pretty. But now... they just seemed... ridiculous. Pointless.

Along with the embroidered napkins and delicate silverware. She lowered the tray onto the table and sighed.

She would return them to the linen closet rather than be taunted by her misplaced priorities throughout the meal. She realized it was too late, however, when she looked up to see him standing just inside the door.

"I didn't burn them." Her voice was stilted. "I watched them just like you said—"

"They're perfect."

Victoria swallowed, her throat unusually thick, and then stepped back from the table. The eggs had long since cooled, but the bread was still warm.

Piers surprised her by assisting her onto one of the chairs. "All of this is beautiful." He moved around the table to sit across from her.

"Thank you."

It *was* beautiful. She *liked* beautiful things. But did they even matter?

"I didn't—"

"It's just that—"

They both went to speak at once and then stopped at the same time.

"I shouldn't tease you." He cleared his throat, laying his napkin on his lap.

Trouble was, she didn't mind most of his teasing. In fact, she rather welcomed some of it.

Or she had until she saw herself through his eyes.

"It's just that…." She inhaled, picking at the egg with her fork.

"I hope I haven't ruined the meal for you? A while ago you said you were starving."

She scooped a portion onto her fork and took a bite. It was…

"I am. Oh, this is delicious." She blinked. "You'll need to show me how you made the dough." Since he'd finally found his manners, she would let bygones be bygones.

And, at this point, there was no reason to pretend she knew anything at all about cooking.

He dipped his chin. "You can make them with pork sausage, or vegetables, or chicken. I'm sure Auggie has the recipe written somewhere. In case I don't get a chance to show you before I leave." He stuffed a large bite into his mouth.

He'd been here three days now, and it was the first time he'd mentioned leaving.

"The snow stopped." Victoria dutifully commented on the weather.

Outside, it was already getting darker. How could he leave when he'd barely had enough energy to finish cooking their pastries?

And why, she wondered, wasn't she shoving him out the door?

"I feel chastened—weak," she admitted. "To realize that I'm so incapable of performing tasks that I...." She cleared her throat. "That I before might have dismissed as below me." She forced herself to take another bite, her eyes burning at her confession. She waited for him to tease her again. When he stayed quiet, she glanced up to read his expression.

But there wasn't any condescension in his eyes. And he wasn't laughing at her.

"Not many ladies would admit to that—or even care."

Victoria's very existence centered on being a lady. Likely, she'd dutifully thanked the midwife for catching her out of her mother's womb. As the daughter of a viscount, she'd never held a title, but the rules of propriety and gentility were the cornerstones of her foundation.

And yet here she was, sharing a private residence, no servants in sight, working as assistant director at a school for girls and...

Cleaning out hearths...

And she had nobody.

No parents. No siblings. No aunts.

No children of her own, and most notably, no husband.

Which was fine. That was just as it should be.

But if Piers remained here much longer, she'd soon also be without her good reputation.

Her dinner companion touched a petal of one of the silk daisies in the bouquet she'd set out.

"People who open their minds," he said. "People who allow themselves to view the world differently than they've always known—are not weak. Rather the opposite."

Victoria finished chewing and then swallowed the delicious bite. His words almost sounded like a compliment. And yet… She didn't deserve compliments.

"I am a teacher, Piers." She was teaching young girls how to make their way in the world. "I'm supposed to know what I'm doing."

"So, then, you learn. Become a student again."

A student? The idea ought to make her feel like she was going backward, but instead, it was refreshing.

The light from the candles reflected in his eyes, and the small dining room closed in around her. Not in a stifling way but in a cozy one. And she didn't feel alone.

Uncomfortable at having drawn so much attention to herself—to her troubled thoughts—she lifted her fork. "Are you a student?"

"Always," Piers answered without hesitation. "It comes with traveling. New places, new experiences."

"Tell me your favorite destination."

She was making proper conversation. How long had it been since he'd sat down to a proper dinner? How long since he'd made conversation with a proper *lady*?

Since rejecting his family, he'd rejected other aspects of his heritage as well—notably, the constraints of behaving in society.

Miss Shipley had, however, likely saved his blasted life. He could put forth some effort for a meal or two.

"I don't have a favorite." He poured wine into her glass and then filled his.

He'd gotten used to keeping to himself, but Miss Shipley, however, asked all the right questions to keep him talking beyond what he normally would. By the time they finished the last of the wine, she had him convinced that he did, in fact, have two favorite destinations: Paris and New York.

"What of you?" he asked. "Have you had a chance to travel?" What did teachers do when they sent their students off for the holiday?

"My father took us to Belgium… before the war. I wasn't yet ten, and I mostly just remember the crossing—which was not at all pleasant."

"You have no wish to see more of the world?" he asked, pushing his empty plate away.

Her brow furrowed. "I… No. If I wish to know something about foreign lands, I can read about them in a book, or…" She smiled. "I suppose I can ask you. But I prefer the steadiness of home."

The steadiness of home… "What a stifling notion."

"Is that why you avoid yours?" she asked. "Is that why you were traveling to the school and not to Starbridge Abbey?" Of course, she would revisit this matter again.

"Perhaps." Piers leaned his elbows on the table. "Or perhaps I didn't want my sister to spend Christmas alone. You aren't normally here for holidays, are you? Surely my sister could have hired a caretaker?"

Miss Shipley dropped her gaze to her almost-empty dish.

"She could have. But some of the girls return before the new term begins. They require a teacher to be here when they begin arriving."

She'd not answered why she hadn't gone away herself. Piers wouldn't press, but he didn't move on to a different subject either. Instead, he sat watching as the candlelight danced over her features. She shifted and then sighed.

"My aunt passed in August." She stabbed her fork into the bread. "She was the only family I had left." And then she met his gaze, trying to look brave. "Your sister could have hired a caretaker as she's done in the past. But instead, she took pity on me. We were going to cook the Christmas meal together. She was going to teach me. And after, we planned on delivering the baked goods to three particular families in need."

The stiffening of her spine made it plain that the last thing this woman wanted from him was sympathy.

"That sounds like Auggie." But with his sister's change in plans, Miss Shipley had been left alone to fend for herself.

Fend for herself in a large, cold school, alone except for... him.

"I'll show you. If you like." Even if he could make it safely home through the snow piled up outside, a few days oughtn't make much difference.

If he had a penny for every time his mother claimed one illness or another, he'd... be richer than he already was.

"That's kind of you, but you really need to leave as soon as you're well enough to travel. If word gets out that you are here..." She shook her head. "Some might find it excusable, given the storm and your injury. But many will not. Most will not." She levelled him a very teacher-like stare. "I believe you are quite aware of this."

He was. "Let me worry about that." Piers pinned his gaze on hers. The two of them had been together for three days now. "Unless you're expecting guests, we ought to be able to go unnoticed a few more days."

"Mr. Driver might show up any day."

Fair warning that Piers really ought to get the hell away from the school and this woman while he could.

But some devil had him throwing caution to the wind. He winked. "If anyone questions your virtue, I could always marry you."

Her response wasn't what he expected. "It's not only my virtue I'm worried about." She scowled. "There is the school's reputation to look out for."

Piers's brows shot up. Most unmarried ladies would be contriving strategies to keep him there. And yet, she wasn't.

She put the school first. Just as his sister would.

"You don't want to marry me?" He knew the question was arrogant, but he also knew that it… wasn't. "You don't want to hang up your ruler and chalk in favor of being a countess?"

"My training is more valuable if I can help shape the next generation." Miss Shipley frowned as she rose and reached for his empty dish. "You should go back to bed, my lord. I'm happy to see you've an appetite, but if you're going to be healthy enough to travel, you need to rest."

"I've already spent too much time lazing around."

"Just sit, then. You'll find plenty of interesting books in the parlor." She was shaking her head. "But for tonight, anyhow, you are not allowed in the kitchen."

"You are going to wash the dishes?" Piers teased, pretending disbelief.

"Yes. I believe I can manage that." She smirked without looking up at him. "Now, go find a book. Or write a letter. I'll look in on you once I've finished."

"Promise?"

She snapped her head up to meet his gaze and he couldn't help but get a little lost in it.

Because Victoria didn't look at him like a proper spinster would. They'd just finished eating a hearty meal and yet the sparkle in her coffee-colored depths hadn't gone away.

No, Miss Shipley was still hungry.

Dropping her gaze and fussing with the dishes, she pinched those lips together again.

"Find something to read," she finally answered. "You might learn something new."

AN INSTRUCTOR

*V*ictoria tried ignoring the tingles in her chest, knowing he watched her as she exited the small dining room. And as she scraped the leftover food into a bucket near the door, she reaffirmed to herself that he really must make his departure soon.

Surely he wasn't sincere in his offer to help her cook a Christmas meal. It must have been brought on by the wine, good food, or the romantic glow from the candles.

She shook her head, placed the plates on a shelf, and wondered.

What if it had been a genuine offer? What would that be like, to celebrate Christmas with him? With a man?

But then he'd joked about marrying her. Of course, the offer wasn't a serious one.

Victoria removed her apron and hung it on the hook near the door. It was an unconscious act she'd seen others do numerous times—Jenny, the cook who normally prepared meals for them, or Primm. But she'd never considered the significance. It left her feeling… satisfied.

But what if he was willing to help her with the baking? If she didn't take him up on his offer of assistance, when would it be done?

Would those families even care who helped her pack the contents of their baskets?

To assuage her conscience, Victoria could almost make the claim that, as Primm's brother, Piers was a sort of brotherly figure.

But then long-held beliefs of rigid rules brought such thinking to a screeching halt.

It was true that he'd needed shelter from the storm. If she were in London, in Mayfair, and they were discovered, she'd have no choice but to marry him or retreat to some distant country estate in shame.

For showing compassion to a stranded traveler.

And this was the system she'd been raised in. It was the system she... believed in. She perpetuated it in every class she taught.

She glanced around the kitchen. Having actually cooked something now—having created a meal, simple though it was—the worktables and stove and pots and pans seemed more meaningful now. A kitchen was vital to any house— for survival and nurturing and comfort, but it was also a place of possibility.

How many times had she had the same impression upon stepping into a ballroom, or later, into a classroom filled with green girls who had looked to her to learn the secrets to having a successful come-out?

Of course, Victoria had realized the irony that she taught ladies how to find husbands despite the failure of her own dismal betrothal.

Even years later, on her rare visits to Mayfair, she occasionally heard whispers that her engagement to the Earl of Kingsley was still the longest betrothal never to result in a wedding.

It was a joke that no one would ever make to her face. Because she was the esteemed Miss Shipley. She was not a fraud. Primm kept her for not only her skills, but her connections.

These things mattered. Of course, they mattered.

But even as she marched along the corridor toward the parlor, niggling doubts plagued her.

And by the time she arrived at the open door, she paused. "I'll take you up on your offer if you meant it." Victoria threw her words into the quiet room.

He stood with his back to her, staring outside the window where moonlight scattered flecks of silver onto the pristine drifts of snow. When he finally turned, it was with raised brows.

"My offer?"

The fact that he didn't remember truly was proof that he hadn't really meant it.

"To take your sister's place. To-to help me with the baking and the cooking. Seeing as the families will be disappointed otherwise. Primm's made it into something of a tradition. It's nothing fancy—ginger snaps, a few biscuits, and some preserves. The baskets are stacked in the back of the larder." She was babbling, and she never babbled. "As long as you're feeling up to it. And until the roads are clear for you to travel, that is."

He wasn't laughing. And he didn't look put out.

"But what of all those wagging tongues?" he asked.

Victoria inhaled.

What about them?

"No one needs to know you are here. And if someone finds out," she shrugged. "You are Primm's brother. Why wouldn't you visit the school?" The thought struck her that he could just as easily assist her if he took a room at the nearby inn, but she didn't voice that.

Because she didn't like being here alone.

He might be obnoxious, but it was comforting going to sleep knowing another person was just feet away.

"You want me to stay?" He had his back to the window now. "To teach you how to bake?"

"And cook a few more meals, if you don't mind." She nonchalantly moved farther into the parlor and, still waiting for him to answer, lowered herself onto one end of the settee.

There was risk involved, but... he was already here, and truth be told, she didn't want to spend Christmas alone.

"I'll do what I can," he said, glancing at his arm. "I suppose I owe you."

"For saving your life?" She scoffed.

"I suppose that's worth something." He sounded serious as he crossed the room to join her.

"I wasn't sure I could do that—sew your arm up." She grimaced. "But I think it might be the most useful thing I've done in years."

"Why?" It was a simple question. "Why is it the most useful thing you've done in years?"

"Because I've dedicated my life to propriety and etiquette," she answered without thinking. "Not that those things aren't useful as well," she added.

"Really?"

Victoria exhaled. "In their own way, they are useful. They are important."

"I'm not arguing with you."

So why did she feel the need to explain?

"My father was Viscount Whitley." That was part of it. "He was a good and decent gentleman who valued tradition and honor above all. But he was also capable. My mother," Victoria searched for words to adequately describe the woman who made her who she was today. "My mother was an earl's daughter, and as such, a very proper and refined lady. It was perfectly natural for her to raise her daughters thusly." Victoria made a dry-sounding laugh. "She liked to remind us that since father was only a viscount, we weren't actual ladies. If we wished to be respected as such, we needed to work harder than most."

"Work harder?"

"Yes, harder," she confirmed. "My earliest memories are of my sister and I—together in our posture devices—sitting on these tall wooden chairs in the nursery with steel rods along our backs, leather straps around our waists, shoulders, and foreheads. The tighter, the better. We wore them for our reading lessons." Rationally, looking back, Victoria knew those practices had been harsh. But... "My mother would tell us how proud she was to raise such elegant daughters."

Margaret had complained, but Victoria had been more concerned with pleasing their mama.

Her mother had always been strict with them. Because it had mattered. Hadn't it?

Vague memories of her mother rushed in—sensations more than images.

"I remember Mother hating the loose-fitting gowns that had become fashionable just before my come-out. They were highly improper, she said." And while other girls walked around looking free—breathing—Victoria and Margaret had been forced to wear corsets so tight their shoulder blades nearly touched.

The discomfort of it meant that they were... better. It had meant she and Margaret were all that was good and proper. They might not be titled ladies, but they deserved their place in society.

And if Victoria hadn't been required to sit out her most valuable years waiting to marry Lord Kingsley, her life would have unfolded exactly as her mother had planned it.

She had been betrothed to the earl before she'd been born. But every time she and Lord Kingsley had set a date for the wedding, someone in her family had died, and they'd had to postpone the ceremony so she could observe the proper period of mourning.

"My sister doesn't allow such devices here, does she?" Piers's tone startled her.

"No," she answered.

"It sounds like torture."

"I know that. I realize that now..." In her first few years teaching, she had tried using backboards on a few students. But upon discovering scrapes on one of the girls' shoulders, she'd been horrified.

She would have discontinued the practice even if Primm hadn't stepped in.

Her chest tightened at the thought. It had taken actual harm for her to see that the practice was cruel—that kinder, gentler methods also improved posture.

What other lessons had she gotten wrong?

Victoria hugged her arms in front of her, not sure why she was telling him any of this. "My mother didn't mean to be cruel. She thought learning proper bearing and manners was the best for us."

"And you think it best for your students?"

"I did." She stumbled over her use of the past tense. "It's vital if they're to enter society." And then she turned to him. "It's different for ladies. Take you for instance, despite rejecting both society and your family's expectations, you are, and always will be, accepted in society. But with ladies…" She frowned. "A single misstep ruins them forever.

It wasn't fair. It wasn't fair because men were forgiven.

Whereas women were not.

Women were ruined—they *decreased* in value.

"I don't suppose it's fair. And yet ladies line up to participate," he pointed out.

"We—they—don't have a choice."

He watched her, running his thumb along his jaw. She wished she could read his mind. What might she learn? Was there some secret to going through life and not caring what people thought about you?

"Why?" she asked. "Why do you reject it?" Primm had told Victoria once that she believed he'd reject the title if he could.

"Because none of it is real." He didn't take long to answer.

The hierarchy, traditions, mannerisms, and rituals. Was he right?

The world was made up of dirt, water, air, food, and fire, and then there was her world.

A world that was…

Not real.

Victoria began moving around the room, tidying her

books on the small desk in the corner and then unfolding and refolding a quilt.

Piers had answered her question, and yet she wanted to know more. Because for her, decorum and society were very real. They mattered. They made up the fabric of life.

She unfolded and then refolded the quilt again.

She'd lost everyone who had ever loved her. This was all she had left.

Despite the differences he had with his family, when he spoke of his mother or brothers, it was obvious he cared for them. And yet he and Primm—to some extent—had rejected their heritage.

How bad of a person could their father possibly be?

And it wasn't as though Piers could ignore them indefinitely.

Could he? He had brothers. If he didn't marry, the line would go on.

Piers could travel south after the snow melted, continue shirking all the responsibilities he'd inherited in the wake of his brother's passing, and live exactly as he pleased.

But no. He *cared for them.*

She half laughed. "You truly think none of it is real?"

"SOME IS." Piers tempered his opinion for her. "The money is real. The privileges are real."

She turned back to stare at him, and for a moment, he forgot what they were discussing. Vulnerability softened her features and confusion clouded her dark eyes.

"You never smile, do you?" He now had some sort of

understanding why she looked so grim. Her mother had trained it out of her.

She tilted her head. "Pardon?"

He reached out to touch her mouth, and she jerked back. "What are you doing?"

"Come here," he said.

"Why?"

Piers's mouth stretched wide as he imagined some of life's greatest pleasures.

"Just trust me and try it. Smiling is an outward sign of happiness—joy—or even anticipation. But you, Angel, seem to be out of practice. No doubt those muscles are weak from disuse."

He remembered one event he'd attended in Mayfair years ago. The ladies had not laughed. They had… tittered. Most of the smiles had been coquettish.

"Anticipation?"

"You aren't all starch, or I wouldn't be here, Miss Shipley."

"Victoria."

"Victoria," he held her gaze.

And then, by God, the temperature might very well be freezing outside, but the sun shone in that parlor.

Because she *smiled* at him.

She only held it for a second before dropping it, but the glimpse had Piers wanting nothing more than to make her smile again.

"You don't always have to follow the rules." He edged closer to her. "The world won't end if you break a few."

His suggestion, unfortunately, summoned a frown of worry to her brow. "I can't do anything that will harm the school."

"I'll stay. I'll help you with your charity baskets, and after, I'll make myself scarce so you can deliver them on your own."

"Once the roads are clear?"

Even though Piers was fairly certain the nature of his mother's ailment had been exaggerated, he was going to have to travel to Starbridge Abbey after all.

But he could wait a few more days.

She was nodding, slowly. And an aura of risk hovered around her. And something else—sexual tension.

It hovered in the whole damn room.

What other rules might she be willing to break?

LAUNDRY DAY

*P*iers's presence pressed into Victoria. It touched her, not in a physical sense, but low in her belly, adding weight to an unsettling desire to be near him.

Up until now, the attraction had been subtle and sporadic.

Piers was handsome—more handsome than Lord Kingsley. And he was more daring than any person she'd ever known. Or was that recklessness? Regardless, his lack of inhibitions presented some tantalizing possibilities.

Gabriel Fellowes, the Earl of Kingsley, had not been the only man to ever show interest in Victoria while she'd mingled with the *ton*. But when other gentlemen had danced with her or strolled with her through moonlit gardens, she'd kept barriers erected around her.

Because she'd been engaged.

Her father and Lord Kingsley's father had never signed contracts, but they might as well have. All her life, she'd expected to eventually become the Countess of Kingsley.

She had been engaged for her entire life—right up until

she hadn't been.

And for some reason, after it all fell apart, she'd left those barriers in place.

The bulk of her wardrobe was gray or lavender, and yet Victoria had lived her life thinking in terms of black and white.

Rules were straightforward and the consequences for breaking them unavoidable.

And yet, after just a few days on her own—and with this man—ambiguity had crept in.

She hugged a quilt in front of her. "We will cook tomorrow, then?"

"Yes. We will cook tomorrow." He leaned forward. "Unless…"

"Unless?"

"Unless you want me to teach you something else."

Her eyes flew wide. Because she knew exactly what he was offering.

Shaking her head, she backed toward the door. "Cooking is fine."

As she exited the parlor, the sound of his soft laughter wrapped around her like mystical smoke.

And she couldn't help wondering what it would be like to extend her education even further.

Sleep didn't come to her as easily as it had the night before. Not that she wasn't physically tired, but because she couldn't keep her mind from imagining Piers's eyes, or the way he sometimes touched his bottom lip, or the way he moved, exhibiting a natural power but also grace.

And she played his words over and over in her mind. *Unless you want me to teach you something else.*

Did he offer only because she was female and presently

convenient? It cannot be because he was falling in love with her.

She was not without looks, and she knew this, but that had never made a difference for her before. On a few occasions, in London, she'd been considered a diamond of the first water.

But since everyone knew she was spoken for, it hadn't meant anything.

Piers was attracted to her. She didn't doubt that. But was that all?

When she was finally able to push him out of her mind, other issues that had her questioning the foundation of her existence kept her awake.

She taught comportment and music. But decorum was not just about a lady's outer life. It affected her soul. That way, she would feel equal to those around her. This was what parents of her students expected their daughters to learn.

To have ironed into them.

But how could she teach these concepts properly if she no longer believed they mattered?

By the time the sunlight filtered through the window, she hadn't any answers, nor had she gotten much sleep.

And she would have remained in the warmth of the bed if not for her guest.

She was excited to see Piers. No, she was excited *to begin her lessons* with Piers. She knew how to manage a manor—perhaps learning the details of maintaining a household would bring about a better perspective.

Braving the cold, she slipped out of bed, tore off her gown, and then examined her wardrobe. Her fingers itched to bring out one of her older, but prettier gowns.

Because she was attracted to him? Or was there some part of her that was rebelling against her doubts?

She grimaced, acknowledging that the only reason she wanted to wear one of her prettier gowns was because she *wanted* to look pretty, *dash it all.*

She could wear the conservative gray-blue frock made of heavy muslin, or…

She could wear her newer rose linen that gathered intricately around her waist and made a swishing sound when the skirt swirled around her legs.

What mattered?

What was real?

She exhaled and removed the gray-blue, pulling it over her head and lacing up the front before she could change her mind.

The rules she intended to break did not require that she be pretty. They required her to be strong and self-disciplined. She was only breaking rules that were keeping her from being truly independent.

Which had nothing to do with Lord Rosewood.

Those resolutions, however, flew right out of the window when she stepped outside of her bedchamber and collided with a solid wall of…

Male.

Bare male chest, to be more precise.

"What are you doing?" she gasped.

Except for his unfastened breeches and unlaced boots, her guest was walking around the residence naked.

To make matters worse, she found it nearly impossible to drag her gaze away from all that skin. She had touched it.

She had rubbed a damp linen cloth over those sinewy slopes and lines. She'd appreciated the silky texture of his skin along with the smattering of curling hairs spread out from his chest that trailed down his abdomen in the shape of a T.

She'd had no choice but to rub him down in order to alleviate his fever.

"Nothing you haven't seen, right?" He stared down at her, making no effort to cover himself. "You did say that you bathed me," he reminded her.

And once again he was the incorrigible rake his sister had told her about. Why did he have to do that?

Heat rushed from her chest to her neck and into her cheeks. "I did."

"I thought so." He casually touched her arm. "We're washing the blood out of my clothing today. I'm sure you have something that needs washing as well. This is the sort of thing you need to learn, isn't it?"

Was this what he'd meant by offering to teach her something other than cooking?

Laundry? And although she was still distracted by the expanse of skin he was showing, she had to admit that such a skill would come in handy after he left.

But before they went any further, she desperately needed to explain something.

"It is true that I bathed you while you were incapacitated," she said. "But I did nothing that was inappropriate. I... preserved your modesty to the best of my ability—most of it, anyhow."

She had been tempted to look beneath the tails of his shirt—as any woman might be. But instead, she'd acted the lady and kept his nether region covered. She'd used the damp linen on his torso, legs, and feet, but not...

Her face grew hotter as she recalled the swirls his leg

hairs curled into when she'd squeezed the lavender water over them.

At the time, she had been almost out of her mind with fear and fatigue, but commitment to propriety had outweighed the temptation to succumb to her curiosity.

And now, with his gaze piercing every secret thought she'd ever had, Victoria lifted her chin to meet his stare squarely.

"You're an interesting woman, Miss Shipley—Victoria."

"Not too interesting, I hope."

"Why? Why wouldn't you want to be interesting?"

She shrugged, wondering why she couldn't seem to keep her thoughts to herself while conversing with him. "Because... that would mean I—"

"Yes?"

"That would mean I don't fit." As members of her family had died off, one by one, she'd fought the unsettling notion.

Was that all it was? A breakdown of sorts brought on by the isolation of the storm and then Lord Rosewood's startling appearance in the middle of the night?

She frowned and stared down at her hands. She'd thought she'd rid herself of such doubts. With any luck, before the new term began, she could work through this... episode.

"Victoria." He stepped closer. He wasn't touching her, but it felt like he was. She tilted her head up so she could meet his stare.

"It's okay." His breath fanned her face. "Trying new things... it's okay."

All her life, she'd believed the opposite. New was second best. It was common and tawdry. Traditions and propriety —being *good* at maintaining both—were all she had.

She studied his eyes—green with flecks of brown—and didn't even flinch when his fingertips brushed along her cheek. It took all her resolve not to sway into him. She inhaled, needing air… needing…

This wasn't part of her great epiphany. Was it?

"Laundry," she breathed. "Let's try laundry." And while she still had the strength to do so, she stepped back.

He rubbed his fist in a circle above his left breast, scrutinizing her.

Thinking.

"As good a place to start as any," he said. "Laundry."

PIERS LEANED AGAINST THE WORKTABLE, watching Miss Shipley. She was so damn serious at everything she did. And yet, he found himself more and more intrigued.

"Did your grandmother teach you this as well?" she asked, glancing over her shoulder at him. Her arms and back must be straining already. Bending over the tall wooden bucket, raising and lowering the wooden plunger, and then turning it was not easy work.

"Now rotate it," he answered. "I learned in the army." His stint had been a short one. As soon as his father had discovered he'd lied in order to enlist, his commanding officer had sent him packing with all manner of threats. "It's a skill that has come in handy more than once."

"I've seen Jenny do the wash before, but I had no idea it was so exhausting." Victoria stopped to catch her breath, wiping one sleeve across her brow. Her face was flushed from when they'd heated the water, and half her hair had escaped the tight knot at the back of her head.

But her chocolatey eyes were shining now.

With each step of the process, that scared deer expression she'd had earlier had faded away. He'd quickly surmised that whereas success built this woman's confidence, she was terrified of making mistakes.

She didn't trust herself.

She crossed her arms to stretch her shoulders but then went right back to work, plunging and turning. "I'd never used turpentine before. But now I've used it on both your wound and bloodstains." She went to reach her hands into the mixture—

"No!" Piers grabbed her from behind. "You'll burn the skin right off your hands." She could cook, clean out the hearth, and sew up wounds all she wanted, but he'd be damned if he'd allow her to hurt herself in the process.

"Move." He took control of the plunger and used it to lift the soaked fabric out of the water. Not perfect, but good enough. He had dozens of others folded away in the Mayfair townhouse, likely as many at Starbridge Abbey. She'd only been mixing them for about five minutes, but he'd filled a second tub for rinsing and wasn't inclined to draw out the process.

It may be a novelty to her now, but it was work—hard work. This gave her just enough of a taste to appreciate it.

Piers hefted the soaked shirt into the basin of cooler water using the plunger. A few days before, he hadn't even known this woman. Now he was wondering if he was ruining her—not in the social sense but in a sense that he was washing the gentility out of her.

She peered into the water from behind him, crowding his space now in addition to his thoughts.

"No wonder," she said.

"No wonder what?"

"No wonder they look at my hands."

"Who?"

"The village women I meet sometimes at the mercantile —and their children. I noticed theirs were often dry and cracked, but I never fully comprehended why."

Piers didn't turn to look at her but churned the shirt in the cold water.

"I assumed it was because they didn't use creams…" The catch in her voice warned him that she was upsetting herself again.

He stepped back and handed her the plunger. "Rinsing is the same. Up and down, just like you did in the lye."

Words couldn't have calmed her half as effectively as good manual labor did.

By the time they'd finished rinsing his shirt, twisted it out, and hung it near the stove to dry, along with a few other items, Victoria was nearly as soaked as the garments they'd been cleaning.

Piers caught her gaze and cocked a brow. "Well?"

She brushed her hands down her skirt and nodded. "That was eye-opening." But then she grasped his arm and, only because he allowed her, turned him toward the door. "And it was quite enough for you today. What will it be, my lord, the settee or bed?"

If he felt completely himself again, he would have argued. But as it was, his bruised rib and some weariness from the fever had caught up with him again.

"Settee." He didn't like laying alone in the bedchamber.

"I'll roll out the leftover dough from the bread bowls. They'll be good to use?"

"It's usually better the second day." And yet, Piers wasn't thinking about food. He was restless.

She walked behind him; her hand pressed into the center of his back.

The warmth of her hand reminded him of the conversation they'd had the day before.

He spun around and, before she had a chance to move, dropped his hands onto her waist.

He didn't care that her gown was damp against his chest.

"What are—?" She tilted her head back to meet his stare. "What are you doing?"

"Does this mean you're finished for the day?"

"Finished with what?"

"Learning. Breaking rules." He wanted to kiss her, but he paused.

Victoria Shipley might be relatively inexperienced, but she was not immune to the sparks flying between the two of them. She'd given herself away every time he'd caught her staring at him. And those damned delicate blushes of hers only served to warm him in other areas.

She'd have to be an idiot not to know what was happening.

Miss Shipley was no idiot.

"Maybe," she answered. "I don't know."

Piers backed her against the door and dipped his chin so she would hear nothing but his whisper.

"Put your arms around my neck," he instructed.

And just as she'd followed his instructions all morning, she did exactly as he said. Her hands trailed up his bare chest. She had the softest hands, but she'd also proven them to be strong.

Piers nudged his hips against her. She'd endured his

sarcasm and irreverence without complaint. It didn't make sense.

"Why are you here?" Why wasn't this woman attending some Christmas house party in London? Or residing over some grand country estate as lady of the manor?

She was the perfect product of gentle upbringing. She was beautiful, and the sound of her voice alone could stop an entire army. But what he really wanted to know was, "Why aren't you married?"

She vibrated in his arms and then buried her face against his chest. "I don't know."

VICTORIA COULD HAVE TOLD him the obvious. She wasn't married because her fiancé had wanted to marry another woman. After being engaged for over two decades, Lord Kingsley had decided he didn't want her.

She closed her eyes, remembering the afternoon her betrothed had come to her, begging her to cry off their engagement. She had not argued. She'd agreed, going so far even as to put him at ease—to wish him happiness.

But she had not wanted to marry a man who didn't want her, even if it broke her heart to set him free.

With Piers's presence wrapped around her, a startling question taunted her. Had Lord Kingsley, in fact, broken her heart, or had she already been broken?

"You don't know why you aren't married, or you don't know why you are here?" Piers was so close that Victoria's ability to reason vanished along with the steam rolling off her wet gown.

He was close—he'd trapped her in a way that she wasn't

interested in freedom. And as her breath mingled with his, her blood flowed like lava.

"I was betrothed to the Earl of Kingsley for years." Her chest tightened. "But I ended it to teach."

That had always been her story. Her reputation would have suffered worse if the truth had come to light—that it was Lord Kingsley who'd wanted to end it.

Shortly after, he'd publicly engaged himself to Miss Olivia Redford. Victoria hadn't remained in London to face the aftermath.

Piers's steady stare burned into her now, as though he was trying to read her mind.

"You," he scoffed in disbelief. "Ended your betrothal so that you could teach and raise funds for an all-girls school?"

"Y-yes." She dropped her gaze to the base of his neck, where the tell-tale pulse evidenced that his heart raced as quickly as hers.

"Really?"

She snapped her head back up at that. "What do you mean?"

"Did it make you feel guilty? Or did you feel magnanimous for making such a sacrifice? And what of Kingsley? Did you break his heart?"

The suggestion was laughable. "I didn't break anyone's heart."

Piers dipped his chin. "Did he break yours?"

Lord Kingsley hadn't broken her heart. He had broken something less tangible.

He'd shattered her faith in... life. The faith that had begun crumbling the day Margaret passed away after her horrible illness. Victoria had loved her older sister more than anyone else in the world. She'd been the first person

Victoria ran to when she was happy, when she was sad, when she'd succeeded, and when she'd failed.

Her sister had been her touchstone.

Since Margaret's passing, Victoria had endured too many deaths—too many disappointments for that faith to be revived.

Teaching, however, being a part of the school, had rekindled it just enough.

"My heart was not broken." She studied the flecks of blue in his brownish green eyes. They were the same color as Primm's but not hidden behind a pair of spectacles.

"I'm glad." His fingers stroked her cheek.

The caress was surprisingly intimate.

"And you? Is your heart broken?" She suddenly wanted to know much more about him than what she'd learned from Primm. She wanted to know what was inside rather than the facts that the world knew.

He shook his head without answering. "You aren't pining for him, then? This Kingsley fellow."

"Pining? No. I loved him. But not… I wasn't in love with him, I suppose." But she had cared about Lord Kingsley. Perhaps that was why it had been so easy to wish him well. She'd traded her pride for his happiness. "He was like a brother. It might have been easier if I'd realized that at the time."

Her betrothal had ended six years before, but even so, she would have remembered if she'd been even half as aware of Lord Kingsley as she was of Piers.

His voice washed over her like melted chocolate, and although he smelled of soap, the scent wafting through her consciousness was uniquely male.

Would he taste the same?

She smoothed her palms along the back of his neck.

There was nothing ordinary about their present circumstances. This was the first holiday she'd not have her aunt. And while forced to learn to fend for herself, she'd been stranded with an alarmingly handsome man.

Alone.

The feelings she'd had for Lord Kingsley had been comfortable and warm and safe.

That wasn't the case with Piers. No, these feelings were prickly and hot and dangerous.

This, she realized, was nothing more than lust.

"Why do you work for my sister then, if not nursing a broken heart?" His eyes squinted as though he genuinely cared about her answer.

Victoria inhaled, filling most of her senses with him.

She had nowhere to look but at his chiseled features and sensual gaze.

But he'd asked her a question that felt too complex to answer—too complex when it was taking all her self-control not to…

She parted her lips and leaned into him.

And she was not disappointed.

He claimed her mouth with his, firm and searching.

Coffee.

That male taste of his mingled with coffee.

It was hot and earthy and might just as well have shattered her wits into a thousand shards of glass.

This man had appeared out of a snowstorm—out of nowhere, really. And with him, he'd brought chaos.

Victoria pushed onto her toes to be closer, to deepen the connection.

He'd awoken needs she'd always denied existed—a part

of her she'd hidden from herself.

His tongue delved into her mouth—rough but soft, hard but gentle, knowing but also searching.

He clasped her jaw with one hand while the other smoothed down her side, squeezing her hip. She didn't stop him until his palm slid under her skirts, up her bare thigh. The startling touch shocked her out of the sensual fog of his kiss.

"What are you doing?"

"I'm soothing your unbroken heart," he whispered, claiming her mouth again.

She turned her head. "That doesn't make any sense."

His mouth explored her neck now. "Do you want me to stop?"

Liquid pooled at her core even as his fingertips continued grazing the inside of her thigh. A heavy ache pulsed between her legs.

Lust. This was lust.

And it was incredibly powerful.

Just a second more. She exhaled. A second more, and she would stop him.

But she'd lost her voice, along, it seemed, with her self-discipline. Did letting go of her beliefs mean she could also turn her back on her morals? Was this a trap or an opportunity?

A pounding sound—a pounding that wasn't her heart—kept her from learning the answer to that question.

"The door," she whispered.

His fingers hovered a sliver away from depravity. He didn't remove them immediately.

"I need to answer the door." Her voice was thready.

It had to be Mr. Driver. The snow had stopped falling,

and he was coming to look in on her.

Why that particular moment, though? Why now, when she and Piers had been alone for hours? Was this fate's way of saving her from herself?

Piers dropped his hands and stepped back, leaving her standing there feeling... cold. Inside and out.

"Do you want me to answer it?" he asked.

God, no!

"No!" Because then it would be known that he was here alone with her. She was willing to learn how to cook and do laundry and fend for herself, but she wasn't prepared to tarnish both the school's reputation and her own.

"Go to the parlor," she ordered at first. But Mr. Driver might peer through the window. "No, the kitchen!" Or Mr. Driver might go around and see the temporary repair to the window. "Go to Primm's room. Please?" She pushed him around the corner and smoothed her skirts, only then remembering that her gown was still damp.

"Miss Shipley?" A voice called from behind the door. "Are you in there?"

"I'm coming!" Mr. Driver's voice sounded mildly concerned. Of course, Primm would have asked him to look in on her before she'd left.

Victoria slid open the locks, and when she pulled the door open to peer out, icy cold air filled the foyer.

But she could not invite him inside.

Not that Mr. Driver was a gossip, but he would tell Mrs. Driver, who would tell other ladies who worked in the village...

Mr. Driver stood outside looking all-too familiar in his well-worn boots and a long woolen jacket. "How are you faring?" He was staring at her curiously.

"I'm washing my clothes," she replied, as though that provided an answer along with an acceptable reason to not welcome him inside.

"I've been worried, but this is the first chance I've had to look in on you." His brow furrowed. "Are you having difficulties, Miss Shipley?"

She realized that she didn't look at all like herself.

She didn't, in fact, feel like herself.

The Miss Shipley Mr. Driver knew was perfectly mannered and always put together. How could he not imagine that she was having difficulties?

"I'm doing well." Without Lord Rosewood's untimely appearance, could she have said the same? Perhaps she was, in fact, doing better than usual. "How are you and Mrs. Driver? The storm hasn't damaged your cottage, has it?"

"No, not at all." He reached up a mittened hand and scratched his head. "There's a horse in the stable. Wondered if you might know who it belongs to?"

"She is Lord Rosewood's," Victoria answered, shivering in the cold but relieved that he wasn't asking to be invited inside.

"Lord Rosewood is here?"

"Yes. I mean, no. He was. He..." She searched her mind, unaccustomed to dissembling. "He arrived in time to travel with Miss Primm. He was here, but he left." Yes. That fit. Victoria exhaled in relief.

"She should have told me." The stout and weathered gentleman scowled. "Horses require tending."

"I'm tending to her," Victoria said. "She's... skittish. So, I promised I'd see to her." And then she shrugged. Dissembling, it seemed, came easier to her than she'd imagined.

"You went out to the stable in the middle of the storm?"

"Only a few times. But if you wouldn't mind looking in on her, I'd appreciate that."

He nodded but seemed reluctant to leave. Victoria wasn't sure if she was imagining it or if his eyes had darted behind her suspiciously. "Do you need me to clean out your hearths?" He seemed to remember he'd brought something with him. "Mrs. Driver sent this over for you."

The steam rising off the basket piled on another helping of guilt. She was ashamed that others had been more aware of her deficiencies than she herself had been.

Primm had. As well as Mr. and Mrs. Driver. Had her students as well? The idea was mortifying.

She reached out and accepted the basket from him. It would be rude to refuse such a gift.

"Thank you." She felt like a fraud. She hated that she couldn't invite him inside to warm up. It was unkind not to at least offer him a cup of tea.

He stepped back. "You're always welcome, Miss Shipley. I'll take care of that horse for you. But are you sure you don't need me to help you with anything else? Bring in some wood for you? Pump some water?"

Piers had already taken care of both those tasks. Tasks she hadn't even considered.

"I'm doing well, really." She pinched her mouth together.

"Good day, then. Have a happy Christmas." He didn't look at all happy, though.

"And you!" She waved.

She closed the door and pressed her back against it. She ought to be half-frozen, but all she felt after lying to that kind man outside was scorching shame.

SHE LIKED IT

*P*iers propped himself against the wall just around the corner from where Victoria explained away Artemisia's existence. When she tried convincing Primm's maintenance man that she didn't need help hauling wood or pumping water, he realized just how horrible she was at lying.

Because in telling him what she had, she'd inadvertently created more problems for them.

Snow only fell sporadically by now and, if so inclined, Piers and Artemisia could ride into the village now and take a room at the inn. The risk of these past few days spent alone together would drop significantly.

But what fun would there be in that?

At the sound of the door closing, he stepped around the corner to find her pressed flat against the door as though the hounds from hell were trying to break it down from outside.

Piers folded his arms across his chest, ignoring the cold air she'd let in. "Don't you think my sister is going to realize trouble's afoot when Driver mentions that I traveled to Starbridge Abbey with her?" Auggie was not naïve, nor would a detail like that get past her.

Even so, Piers rather enjoyed seeing Miss Shipley looking like this—ruffled, flushed, and a little like a child with her hand caught in the cookie jar.

"I'll tell her the truth. She'll understand." But the look in her eyes gave away that she didn't completely believe that. "I didn't think of that."

Driver's visit had been her perfect opportunity to be rid of him—to put an end to all of this—her need to be taught the basics of living, along with whatever it was they'd started before being interrupted.

"That was a mistake." Her eyes were wide. She wasn't referring to lying to Mr. Driver.

"Kissing me?" he confirmed. "Kissing me was a mistake?"

If anything, her eyes grew wider. True, she'd offered up her mouth quite sweetly, but he had, in fact, done most of the kissing.

However, he wasn't about to admit that.

"But…" Her pretty brows furrowed.

If Piers had any conscience at all, he'd pack up and make his way into the village that afternoon.

"Yes," she finally answered. "It was a mistake."

"You didn't enjoy it?" Piers ignored the cold. He'd hung his shirt near the stove, but it wouldn't be dry for some time.

"Yes! No. That's not the point. The point is that, although understandable, given our unusual circumstances, for the two of us to continue with this sort of… behavior… would be unconscionable."

"You liked it, though?"

"I've already lied enough for one day." She pinched her mouth together. "Yes. I did. I liked it."

He chuckled. Damning praise indeed.

But he knew better. She'd all but vibrated beneath his touch, and she'd met his kiss eagerly.

In fact, he couldn't remember the last time he'd experienced an encounter as sensual as that one had been.

If ever.

He scratched his chin. "But it was a mistake?" he clarified.

"Yes." She stiffened her back and folded her hands in front of her. With her hair half escaped from her coiffure, and her gown listless from the laundry, she still managed to resemble a formidable teacher.

His cock stirred.

"If you don't mind, I'm going to change out of this wet gown." She wriggled uncomfortably. "I suggest you cover yourself as well—to stay warm. I just nursed you back to health. I'd hate for you to fall sick again."

Holding a basket of what promised to be a hot meal, she swept past him dismissively before he had the opportunity to compound their mistake.

Because as much as he hated to admit it, she was right.

And that made staying with her all the more tempting.

TAMPING down his less-than-proper urges toward the more-than-proper teacher, Piers rummaged through his sister's chamber until he discovered the pack he'd left behind on the last occasion he'd visited the school. Inside, he found a vaguely familiar shirt, deeply creased, of course, an older pair of breeches, and a few other items that might come in useful.

There were all sorts of reasons he hadn't left now that the storm had subsided, but he wasn't sure why she hadn't insisted he go.

Was it because of the lessons he'd promised her?

Or was it more complicated than that? Were there other skills she wanted to learn but was too straitlaced to suggest herself?

Improper skills?

After pulling on socks, his boots, and coat, he went about cleaning the laundry buckets out of the kitchen and building up the fire in the stove, careful so as not to strain the stitches in his arm.

"Thank you," Victoria said from the open door.

Piers kept right on mopping the floor.

"I was just now coming in here to see about this mess. Funny how washing one thing creates another chore entirely. Like cleaning out the hearth. And cooking. Although that's not washing, is it? It's just another chore. They are never ending, aren't they?"

She was babbling. "Mrs. Driver sent two pot pies over. She meant both to be for me. Of course, she did. No one knows you are here. But she also sent biscuits. So we won't have to cook tonight. Or tomorrow, really. Unless you no longer wish to teach me. I quite understand—"

"Victoria." Piers set the mop aside, reconsidering all of this.

"Yes?"

"I—"

She stilled, staring up at him with terribly concerned eyes—her top teeth pinched down on her bottom lip.

"Show me Primm's recipes. That way I can prepare to start cooking tomorrow."

He couldn't help but notice that the gown she'd changed into wasn't all that different than the one she'd had on before.

Dreadful things, designed to camouflage the wearer.

And yet, he was intensely aware that beneath the dull-colored wool, she hid skin as inviting and silky as a butterfly's wings.

She exhaled.

And then she might as well have punched him in the gut. Because she smiled again.

This woman didn't need colorful gowns or a fashionable hairstyle. She didn't need either of those because she had the most intoxicating smile he'd ever seen.

"Are you hungry?" she asked, the corners of her mouth already beginning to fall.

"Starving," he said.

"GOOD." Victoria primly clasped her hands at her waist.

She hadn't been sure how she would be able to face him again, but he didn't seem to suffer similarly.

And although the clothing he'd donned needed ironed, or steamed, she was grateful not to have the distraction of him walking around half-naked for the rest of the day.

Her gaze landed on the basket. "It shouldn't take much to heat them up." Victoria did her best not to show how flustered she was by the way his shirt stretched across his shoulders.

"Heat what?"

"The pot pies." She opened the container and pulled out

a cloth-covered dish. They were good-sized portions, and if she'd been alone, it might have lasted her three or four days.

She stepped forward and nearly tripped over the mop. Before Mr. Driver had arrived, they'd had no difficulty maneuvering around while working with one another, but now she felt like she had two left feet. After nearly colliding with him on her way to the stove, they both stepped to the same side and nearly did it again.

The kitchen, inexplicably, had shrunk to half the size it had been earlier that morning.

He finished cleaning the floor and returned the mop to the closet while she unpacked the basket in what had become an awkward silence.

Mrs. Driver had not only packed the meals and the dessert, but she'd placed neatly folded napkins alongside sprigs of evergreen tied up with a red ribbon.

Was that because Victoria was one of the school's directors? Or was that something Mrs. Driver would have done for anyone? The decorations were not necessary, but they reminded Victoria that Christmas was in just two days.

They reminded her that not all days were the same. They reminded her that she had something to look forward to. Christmas was full of traditions and music and family.

She hadn't experienced one of those magical Christmases since before Margaret had died.

The thought struck her.

"My heart wasn't broken when my betrothal ended." She returned to the subject as though a few hours hadn't passed since they'd had this discussion. "But I learned how foolish it was to believe in dreams." Not the dreams that were out of her control, anyhow. But the dreams that depended on the promises of others.

Or on anything other than herself, really. "I ought to have learned that lesson earlier."

"How old were you when he… when you ended it?"

"Two and twenty."

But his attention was on something behind her. "You can't leave the towel sitting on the stove like that." He reached around her. "You're more dangerous than I thought."

She knew better. And yet, she bit her tongue to keep from apologizing. Because at least half of her distraction was his fault. First, for having flaunted himself earlier, and now, for looking equally striking in a wrinkled shirt and tight breeches.

Furthermore, she'd been pouring out her feelings to him, and all he could do was chastise her about where she set the linen.

She'd keep quiet from now on.

But then he proved he hadn't been ignoring her. "What's wrong with believing in dreams?"

"Do you believe in them?" she countered.

He seemed to weigh his words carefully before answering. "I hadn't really thought about it. When I've wanted something, I've simply gone after it."

"Precisely. It is not your dreams you believe in, it's your own abilities."

"Is that why you're here?" He indicated the school. "To replace your dreams with a career? Is working for my sister, managing a school of spoiled girls, so very satisfying, then?"

"No. Yes. It was a dream I could achieve. And I did." She glanced around the kitchen sheepishly. "I may not be accomplished in here, but believe it or not, I'm extremely efficient at my job. I'm an excellent teacher. My students enjoy my classes, and upon graduation, they are confident and poised to enter society."

She hated that something she'd always believed to be valuable now sounded inconsequential—insignificant—to her own ears. But she was *good* at it. And whether anyone liked it or not, *it did matter.*

Not for the first time, she wished she could read his mind.

"What did you give up on?" Piers had a way of turning the conversation back on her. It was more than a little disconcerting that she allowed it.

"Of having—or being part of—a large family." Victoria grimaced. The school was a family of sorts, but it wasn't the family of her dreams. The family of her dreams had siblings and parents and grandparents and cousins. "You ought to have gone home for the holidays. You have all of that, and yet you pretend they don't matter. I know your mother is known to be dramatic, but what if this time really is more serious than the others? Are you willing to take the chance that it isn't?"

Most of the time, Piers looked at her with amusement or casual interest. But at her words, something flashed in his eyes.

She'd obviously touched on a raw nerve. Because that flash was anger. And if she were to take a guess, his anger stemmed from fear.

"Will you be able to live with yourself if she's not there when you do finally go home?"

"It won't be the first time." He almost convinced her he didn't care.

"Because of Elijah?"

Piers glanced away from her as though she was boring

him, and then folded his arms across his chest. "He fell off his horse. Managed to survive until right before I arrived."

And then he shrugged.

That was one thing he'd not been able to control.

"I'm sorry."

His throat moved. "But as you said before. People die."

"Is that when your dreams died?" She could easily imagine he and his twin dreaming of taking great adventures together.

He was bent over now, reorganizing a few tools in the closet. "I didn't say I believed in dreams. I said I went after the things that I wanted. They aren't at all the same."

These were things she wanted to know about him. What he wanted. Why he wanted them.

Victoria set her hands on her hips and watched him, her attention nearly diverted by the muscles flexing in his legs and thighs. "You're in line to inherit a marquessate. What more could you possibly want?"

She wasn't prepared for the darkness in his expression when he turned to face her.

"I don't give a damn about my father's title. And I never asked to be Rosewood. Rosewood was my brother. Rosewood is the creature my brother became after allowing his dreams to die." His harsh laugh was as dark as his look. "Do you really want to know what my dreams are? What I want?"

"I do."

"Not to be swallowed by a title."

She mulled over his retort. Rosewood was… the creature his brother had become *after allowing his dreams to die…*

She'd opened a wound as surely as if she'd torn the stitches out of his arm.

Primm had told her he was irresponsible, cavalier, and a little immoral, but there had always been love and concern in Primm's voice.

And respect.

But Victoria had mostly only heard the criticism. She had disliked him for causing her friend pain and chalked Primm's affection for him up to loyalty. And yet... Primm wasn't the sort to give respect where it wasn't deserved.

This man's character went deeper than his rakish reputation.

"The pie should be warm now." She pointed to the stove. "I'll set the table." She'd allow him a moment alone

She was curious to know why Piers felt he'd be swallowed up by the title, but she was also a little frightened to ask.

Not frightened that he'd ever hurt her in any way, but that he would...

Leave.

She carried a basket of napkins and place settings into the dining room. Once there, she lit the hearth and set out candles and all the decorations provided by Mrs. Driver.

Christmas was only two days away. And since she had no idea what the future held, she would be festive when she could.

Piers could very well leave tomorrow.

He should.

Any longer, and they were inviting trouble. She could adjust her beliefs regarding formality and decorum, even adjust the curriculum so she could improve upon the skills she taught her students, but she wasn't nearly as confident that she could ever sacrifice her virtue. That was one lesson that might be best unlearned.

She shivered, recalling just how close she'd come to doing that. When he'd pressed up against her, she'd kissed him like a woman starved. His hair had felt soft and springy threaded through her fingers, and passion had spiraled through her veins when he touched her thigh.

She'd wanted to cry when she'd heard the pounding on the door.

But it was good Mr. Driver had come when he had.

He'd saved her. But some newly awakened voice taunted softly in her mind.

What if she hadn't wanted to be saved?

A MASSAGE

*D*espite their tense conversation in the kitchen, dinner turned out to be a surprisingly enjoyable affair. Piers complimented the table, the food, and when they wore through the obvious subjects, they'd discussed their favorite books.

Occasionally, he offered insights from his travels. Where had he kept this proper gentleman hidden so far?

Was he playing the part in hopes that she'd refrain from prying into his private thoughts again?

This genteel side of him was not ingenuine. It was different, but it also seemed to come naturally. And although she took pleasure in his intelligent observations, Victoria wished he would open up again.

After they finished eating, the two of them washed up together and then retired to the parlor.

Victoria took up her small journal and pencil and sat at one end of the settee, making notes regarding her lesson plans. Piers sat at the other and read.

The entire scene ironically resembled the most innocent sort of domestic tranquility.

Care of one's clothing, she wrote and then underlined. She then added *baking, medical emergencies,* and *necessities.*

Victoria ignored the thought that this was one of those dreams she'd rejected. Because, although it felt real, it was only temporary. The old dreams she'd locked away had involved a lifetime.

"You don't have any family? None at all?" Piers turned to face her, breaking into her thoughts—thoughts that persistently returned to him anyway.

"No one who wants to claim me." She didn't feel sorry for herself. It was simply the truth. "I have cousins, I suppose, but Father's heir wasn't interested in us once he took possession of Victoria Park." After he'd kicked her and her mother out of their home.

"Victoria Park?" He cocked a not-quite-incredulous brow.

"It was so named long before I came along."

The new viscount had allowed them thirty days to vacate the premises. Victoria had often wondered if it hadn't been illness but the loss of their home that killed her mother. "My mother and I went to live with her sister until Mother passed, and then I lost my aunt in August." Victoria swallowed the sadness rather than let it creep into her voice.

It happened to everyone. Eventually, everyone died.

She reached down and rubbed her ankles. Washing the clothing had been tiring work. She was tempted to remove her slippers.

"Up." He gestured to her feet.

"Why?"

"Just give them to me."

It was easier to comply than it was to refuse him. Before she'd barely lifted one off the floor, he'd taken hold of both her ankles and was untying her laces. "You normally spend holidays with your aunt?"

"Yes." She eyed him warily. At least she was wearing stockings. "Aunt Delia owns—well, she owned—a townhouse in Mayfair. There were always a few parties to attend, but we usually simply sat by the hearth together in her drawing room on the nights we didn't go out. She liked to knit while I read out loud." Victoria welcomed the warmth of the memory. "We put up decorations on Christmas Eve, and on Christmas, we'd sit down for dinner with two of her widowed friends. It doesn't sound all that exciting, but it was... peaceful."

At the time, Victoria hadn't appreciated how soothing those times had been. She hadn't realized what it would feel like to lose the one person in her life who belonged to her.

"And with no family to pester you now, you are convinced I must appreciate mine."

"Aunt Delia did not pester me."

He removed one of her slippers and proceeded to roll his thumb down the center of her foot.

"Oh, dear." She wanted to tell him to stop. She couldn't remember the last time another person had touched her so intimately.

Aside from this afternoon.

She barely stopped herself from groaning.

"Laundering requires muscles you aren't accustomed to using. How does your back feel?"

Her back felt tight, but... "Oh." She tipped her head back when his fingers performed magic on the arch of her foot.

What was it they'd been talking about?

Family.

She had decided earlier not to poke into his personal life but seeing as he got his way more often than not, she changed her mind.

"Primm is your sister. And she loves you. Surely the others love you as well." But then it struck her. Despite hearing all sorts of complaints about this brother, Victoria knew next to nothing about the original heir.

"Familial love." He scowled. "Is that what it's called?"

"And loyalty."

"Like that of your uncle when he evicted you and your mother from your home?"

She scowled. "That isn't the same. I hardly knew him."

"Isn't it?"

"No." He was doing it again. Turning the conversation on her. This time, she wasn't going to give in, so instead of arguing, she closed her eyes and allowed him to work the tension out of her feet.

"Familial love." He laughed. "Is simply manipulation in disguise." His voice broke into the silence. "You asked me about dreams. My brother had dreams. Dreams shattered by... familial love. He was only a few minutes older than me. Did you realize we were twins? Physically identical."

She watched him, but he didn't look up at her.

"I believe you mentioned that."

"Elijah was always meant to be Rosewood."

"But you didn't resent him." Piers wasn't a person who would ever seek position and power. He wouldn't need them because they were already ironed into his character.

But his answer surprised her.

"I hated that Eli was Rosewood." At her confused expression, he explained. "Not because I wanted any of it for myself, but because it gave my father the excuse he needed to mold—to train—my brother. After we turned twelve, we were separated. Everything changed.

"Your father took him away from you." Victoria nodded. It wasn't unusual for an heir to have a separate upbringing from the siblings who followed.

But she was missing something—some vital detail. The look on Piers's face darkened, and he pushed both thumbs deep into her arch. "Not only from me. He took Eli away from Eli."

His words had her considering her and Margaret's training.

The first day their new governess brought in the back-straightening device, Margaret had fought. She'd yelled and screamed and cried until Victoria had calmed her down.

"Fighting only makes it worse," their governess had told them. They had believed her.

Before that, the two girls had experienced relative freedom. They'd been allowed to explore their father's estate, both inside and out. They'd been allowed to explore the attic, climb trees, and play with neighboring children.

But when Victoria turned ten and Margaret ten and two, they had been required to begin acting like little ladies. Victoria had never questioned any of it. But had it been worth it?

Because, all too soon, death had stolen her sister from her.

Piers's father had stolen Elijah from him.

"Your brother changed?" she pressed.

"He changed."

. . .

Piers stared at Victoria's feet. Petite, like the rest of her.

He coaxed away the tension with the heel of his hand. His own wasn't so easily resolved.

He never talked about Elijah, not with strangers but especially not with anyone who knew him. And as much as Piers hated his father, discussing private family matters felt disloyal.

It felt disloyal to criticize something Eli had never once complained about. Eli had been the one to endure the strap of their father's belt. He'd been the one to stand at attention for hours at a time, the one who'd been forced to fast regularly—not Piers.

In fact, whereas Piers's loathing for his father had grown, Eli had accepted their father's training as his due. He'd once even tried explaining to Piers that the lessons were necessary.

They'd taught him self-discipline, Eli had claimed. He was a better man for it. As Rosewood and the heir to the Starbridge Marquessate, Eli had insisted that duty to honor was the price for being blessed with a title.

Piers had wanted to hate his brother for forgetting the adventures the two of them had imagined, but he couldn't. So instead, he'd mocked Eli at every opportunity. He'd taunted him with stories from his travels, always hoping to see something of his brother come back to life.

But it hadn't worked.

Eli had transformed from Piers's twin into the spitting image of Piers's father.

"His training was rigorous?" Victoria asked. "Ouch!"

Piers eased the pressure and then bit out an ironic chuckle. "It began when we both turned twelve. He didn't have a choice."

"Did he turn out as to be as good of a man as you have?"

"Don't," he answered. "Don't pretend you approve of me. How many times have you already said otherwise?"

"True," she surprised him by answering. "Although, my feet are coming to think differently."

She grinned.

With nothing more than a smile from her, the frustration of this conversation ceased to matter.

He exhaled, startled. "You have wise feet."

"I hope they are not my most intelligent feature." She laughed, and this time, his breath caught in his throat. Her eyes squinted, and he could see her tongue just behind her lips.

Her laughter felt like a reward.

Working his fingers up her gently rounded calves, he only knew he wanted to hear it again. In fact, as he slid his hand beneath her skirts, he wondered what other sounds he could draw from her.

Victoria's laughter caught, and when her lips parted, her smile dropped away.

He squeezed the flesh just above her knee. "Tell me to stop, and I will."

Her mouth moved, but no sound came out.

Piers wrapped his hands around her knees and, with a jerk, tugged, so she was lying flat on the settee. With her feet planted into the cushions on both sides of his hips, she presented a most intriguing invitation.

Her gaze fixed on his, and she stayed silent. She was skittish when it came to her own pleasure, but she was also curious.

"I'm going to touch you." Piers would allow for no misunderstanding. She was a woman—alone with him. He might be many things, but he refused to take advantage of her trust.

He coasted his palm along her inner thigh, and she trembled.

"Do you want this?" He'd have more than her silence before going any further.

She nodded.

"Do you want me to touch you, Victoria?"

"Yes," she whispered.

"Yes, what?" Neither of them was laughing now—or arguing. Sitting with her like this, Piers's heart thundered in his chest. She affected him like uncharted territory.

"I want you to… touch me."

"Right here," he said, fluttering his fingers over silky curls. "And here."

Piers stroked the tip of his thumb along silken arousal. Her mouth was the only part of her that moved. But not to speak—simply to tremble.

Her eyes darkened, and even in the dim light of the fire and a few candles, he could see the pink flood her neck and cheeks.

"Did your betrothed touch you like this?" The questions were crass, but something deep inside of him wanted to know—needed to know.

"No," she whispered. "Never."

"Do you touch yourself like this?"

She didn't answer, so he took that to be a yes. "Every woman should touch herself like this."

She shook her head.

"No?" Piers stroked his fingertips around her center, rubbing her with his thumb and then applying pressure with his palm. "You don't like this?"

He stopped, and she frowned. "I... do."

Those two words on her lips had him harder than he'd been in months.

Piers pushed inside and then stretched her with a second finger. "So fucking sweet."

VICTORIA SHOULD HAVE BEEN OFFENDED by his words but instead, she parted her lips.

He wanted her to move. But if she gave in to that urge, what else would she give in to? Would she invite him to lie between her thighs?

Although sprawled on the settee, she was fully clothed and for all intents and purposes, safe. Allowing him to touch her like this was safe so long as she didn't let go.

But perhaps she could only let go a little.

"Move with me, Victoria." His voice sounded harsh rather than coaxing. She didn't want him to stop.

She wanted to feel more of his hand. Deeper. Everywhere. She tilted her hips just enough...

His lips curved up in approval, and she felt him inside. Even as he'd trapped her gaze with his, all her thoughts, feelings, blood, and emotions focused on his hand moving between her legs.

This was wrong. This was a mistake.

She tilted her hips again. Just a little more.

"The softest oil, the richest velvet," Piers said. "I want to look at you. I want to see if you're as pretty as you feel." He pressed deeper, exploring.

Victoria dropped her knees wide, breathing hard and goading him. It was just as she feared because already she wanted this to go on and on.

She wanted him to go on and on. She trusted him completely.

He was leaning over her now, keeping her from trembling onto the floor, holding her so she didn't fall off the edge of the earth.

Victoria stared into his eyes, writhing against his hand but holding tight—holding something back.

"It's okay." At first, she didn't hear the words. How could she when a storm raged through her person? "It's good, Victoria."

She shook her head.

"It's good." Piers leaned forward, clamping his mouth onto her breast through the fabric of her gown and—

"Ahhh!" Victoria let go of whatever it was she'd been protecting.

Not her heart. Relating this to her heart made it seem more romantic than it really was. Whatever she'd been protecting was far more basic than her heart.

This was… desire.

It had been creeping up on her since the moment Piers arrived.

Lust.

It felt improper, dirty, and wicked…

The throbbing between her legs slowed in the aftermath, and she raised her hands and covered her face.

Both of them remained fully clothed. And yet, what he'd done had been exceedingly improper.

No, not improper. That was too mild of a word for it.

It had been scandalous. Indecent. Immoral.

And it was also perhaps the single most incredible moment of her life—or one of them, anyway. All she could think was… *More. I want more.*

What else had she been missing? The temptation was too much.

"You will take your leave first thing in the morning." She exhaled.

He withdrew his fingers from inside of her. She kept her eyes closed, hidden behind her arm.

"Is that really what you want?" His voice was temptation. His departure wasn't what her body wanted.

She shook her head.

"You don't want me to leave?"

"No." But what remained of her propriety—of her morality and dignity—did. She needed him to leave. Otherwise… "Yes. You must leave."

She clenched her fists together when his fingertips grazed her skin, retreating from beneath her skirts.

She squeezed her legs together.

"You want me to leave?"

Keeping her eyes closed, she nodded.

All that could be heard was the ticking of the clock on the mantel.

And then, "I'll be gone before breakfast." He did not sound relaxed or pleased. She waited for the sound of his footsteps to abate before opening her eyes.

It was for the best that he go right away. This was the best decision. She tidied the parlor and snuffed out all but one of the candles. She couldn't trust herself if he stayed. It was a difficult admission to make, even in her own mind. She'd always prided herself on her self-discipline, which for the most part had been unapologetically absent.

She shuffled into her chamber, deep in thought, and then set her flame to the fire she'd laid earlier. As she watched the blue and gold flicker, catch, and then spread, she shivered.

If Piers were to stay, that was exactly what would happen to her. The flame would catch, flare into something she couldn't control, and when it burned out, she would be the ashes.

Cold, dirty… ruined. And dust.

And yet, although she dreaded the idea that he would be gone before she woke—she ached at the possibility of never seeing him again.

She *liked* him.

How would she feel about him when it was all over? She'd thought herself different than other women, but what if the unthinkable happened and she fell in love with him?

Her heart skipped a beat. She hadn't even been in love with Kingsley when he'd cried off, but that had nearly broken her.

Would a physical connection lead to an emotional one?

She climbed under her counterpane and hugged her knees. He'd promised to be gone by the morning. Her life could almost return to normal.

She'd learned enough that she could fend for herself until Primm and the other teachers and students returned.

A single tear escaped, and she swiped it away. She'd done the right thing by telling him to leave. If the roads weren't passable, he could take a room at the inn in the village. It wasn't as though she was sending him out into another blizzard.

Sleep did not come easily, and when she finally began to drift off, a crashing sound had her sitting up.

Was he leaving already? The fire had burned itself out,

and the room was cold and uninviting in the cool light of the moon. Not morning yet, then.

But she had definitely heard something. Had his fever returned? Was he fumbling around the kitchen to make a midnight cup of tea?

If he was ill… She kicked her feet out from beneath the covers and stepped into slippers. At the same time, she slid her arms into her dressing gown.

Someone was moving about. Was the noise coming from the kitchen? Or from somewhere more distant? Without Piers here, she'd be paralyzed in fear. But she wasn't alone. Not yet, anyway.

A thumping sound this time.

If it wasn't Piers making the ruckus, then who? She expected to glimpse him in the corridor or see lights flickering from inside the kitchen, but the only light came from the moon filtering lazily through the various windows.

"Piers?" She stepped into the hall. "Is that you?"

The answering crash made her jump. It was not coming from the kitchen, the parlor, or Primm's room, where Piers was sleeping.

It was coming from the school!

Vagrants? Criminals? Murderers?

She froze at the possibility that any second a villain was going to charge the door that separated the school from the residence.

When another crash sounded, she flew across to Primm's chamber and threw open the door.

"Piers!" she called out in a loud whisper. Seeing a lump on the bed, a wave of relief swept through her. He had not left yet.

"Piers!" He didn't answer right away, so she scurried inside to shake him awake. "Wake up! I need you!"

"Victoria?" He rolled over. She could barely make out his frown in the shadows. "What's the matter?" His arms reached out from beneath the quilt to curl around her waist. "You're shaking."

"I know!" She would have examined how great the temptation to fall into bed with him was if a murderer or worse wasn't waiting to attack. "Someone has broken into the school! You need to wake up!"

He let go, folded his arms behind his head on the pillow, and stared at her. The sight of his bare arms and shoulders made her heart flutter—until he flashed a smug smile.

"You changed your mind? Is that what this is about?"

She nearly slugged him. "No, you buffoon!"

He was smiling—laughing at her—and they were both about to be killed.

"What is a buffoon, anyway?" He obviously did not recognize the seriousness of their situation.

"A ridiculous person—a clown. But that hardly matters right now! There. Is. An. Intruder. In. The. School!"

When he only grinned again, she reached for his uninjured arm and tugged.

And then the sound came again—thumping and cracking. It was as though someone was running through the halls of the school with a cricket bat.

Or worse.

Piers finally shot up and jumped out of bed. "What the devil?"

Victoria averted her eyes away from his naked chest. Not because of any belated modesty but because the sight of him significantly diminished her intelligence.

Wearing only his breeches, Piers didn't stop to pull on his boots or cover up in any way but pushed around her with the agility of a Scottish wildcat.

"Stay here," he shot over his shoulder.

But Victoria wasn't about to wait alone while he was shot, stabbed, murdered, or worse! She hurried to follow him. Even now, the school could be overrun with a band of highway robbers establishing their latest hideout.

If there was more than one, Piers wouldn't stand a chance. She all but flew into the parlor, located the poker, and rushed back to the door Piers had disappeared through.

The temperature difference between the school and the residence was considerable—at least ten degrees cooler in the vast and empty halls.

"Piers!" Catching sight of his silhouette, she ran to catch up with him.

"I told you to wait in the residence."

"I thought you might need this." She extended the poker toward him.

"Shh—" He touched his fingertip to her mouth. Bright moonlight unfolded from the windows near the ceiling when a cloud drifted past.

Victoria stood motionless, her heart in her throat even though she wasn't nearly as afraid now that she was with him.

This was something else.

Thumping sounded from above, and Piers took the poker from her. "If I ask nicely, will you please go back to the residence?" he whispered.

"No."

Her heart raced, not just because of the unknown, but because he was touching her.

He made a growling sound. "In that case, be prepared to make a hasty exit. If we come upon something dangerous, get yourself back to the residence as quickly as possible and then lock yourself in. Do you hear me?"

"I promise."

Piers shook his head but then led them into the small stairwell.

"The sounds seem to be coming from the second floor," she said. "I think."

But he'd probably guessed that for himself. Six classrooms and most of the teachers' quarters were set on the second floor. The first floor was mostly classrooms, and the third consisted of the large student dormitory.

Piers clasped her hand and shuffled both of them into the service stairwell.

The thumping grew louder when they arrived at the second-floor landing, but it sounded less violent now.

"Will you please stay here?" Piers whispered.

Victoria shook her head. "I'm coming with you."

She wasn't about to leave him to fight off the threat alone. She dropped his hand and gripped his waist.

His skin was silky and warm, and... Hugging him from behind, she slid her palms downward over hard, sinewy planes to the top of his trousers. "I'm coming," she repeated.

"I can't very well defend you if you're wrapped around me." He shrugged her off but hooked her hand into the back of his waistband.

It seemed unnaturally reckless, but Victoria couldn't remember ever feeling so... alive? Was this because danger lurked around every corner, behind every shadow? Or was it because she was facing it with Piers?

"Look there," Piers whispered, pointing to one of the

open classroom doors—the door to *her* classroom. Various gashes and scuff marks lined the walls that paralleled the trail of mud dragged from the main staircase.

Holding the poker in front of him and with Victoria attached to him from behind, Piers crept closer to the door.

"Stay here," he commanded. His tone allowed for no further arguments.

Victoria reluctantly released him and held her breath.

What if—? If something was to happen to him... Terror struck her heart. Not for herself. But for him.

The idea of a world without Piers Primm suddenly loomed dark and empty.

"Be careful," she urged as he disappeared into the room she'd entered a thousand times. Then, when no sound erupted, she followed.

Desks were overturned, papers were strewn around the floor, and the sweater she'd hung over a chair had been shredded into a thousand pieces.

But the most alarming sight by far was the two-horned bearded beast, white hair shining in the moonlight, standing on top of her desk with part of what had once been her favorite sweater hanging from his mouth.

A piece of the wool dropped onto the floor.

"Maaaaaaaahh." Both she and Piers jumped at the sound.

"Is it a...?"

"Goat."

GERTRUDE

*P*iers pushed her behind him again. "I take it this isn't a school pet?" He seemed more tense now than he had when she'd imagined it was highwaymen tearing through the school.

"It is not." Victoria returned. "Are you familiar with them?"

"Unfortunately, yes."

The goat, which had seemed as shocked by their appearance as they'd been to see him, leaped off the desk and ducked his head, pointing those horns. The twisty tusks had initially seemed harmless in comparison to pistols or knives, but aimed at Piers now, they were ominous indeed.

The goat tilted its head and—smiled? —with part of its tongue hanging out.

"So, what do we do—?"

Just as Victoria relaxed, the goat charged Piers. He pushed Victoria away and, using the poker, steered the animal into one of the desks.

"Get behind something!" Piers's eyes all but glowed in

the moonlight as he stared down the presently not-so-harmless farm animal.

He lurched for the goat but the little devil was too quick for him and jumped over the desk and onto a table near the window. Silence echoed in the classroom while the two of them faced off.

"Not so fast, you little fiend," Piers warned as he prowled toward the table, teeth flashing.

If Piers hadn't been roused from sleep in the middle of the night, Victoria guessed that he'd almost be enjoying this.

He waved a hand for Victoria to get back and she edged around the wall, trying to make herself invisible.

But not invisible enough.

Because their feisty intruder then flew off the table, jumped over an overturned chair, and charged Victoria.

For an instant, the farm animal almost resembled Pegasus.

"Roaaaar!" Piers reached Victoria in the nick of time, bellowing outrageously and resembling an injured bear.

She wasn't sure who was more startled—her or the goat, who reared and then shifted backward at the sight of Piers waving his hands above his head.

"Get back!" Anyone within ten miles would hear him. "Go on now!"

The nanny stared at him with wide eyes. Good lord, Piers had scared the poor thing senseless.

"Go on now!" Piers repeated.

Backing away, the goat bumped into a shelf, sending the items tumbling onto the floor, which seemed to only scare it more. Unfortunately, the bookcase was the one Victoria had chosen to display her aunt's porcelain nativity scene.

The sounds of shattering statuettes distracted their

short-haired intruder so that Piers, who'd pounced with surprising grace, was finally able to secure it.

Holding tightly onto a horn using one hand, Piers grasped a leg with the other. After a little skirmish, he trapped the animal against the wall.

"Hand me the rope." Piers's teeth flashed. Was he grinning? "She's domestic, apparently. Escaped. Must have wanted out of the cold."

Victoria swept her gaze around the destroyed room until she located the end of a shredded rope, which when she followed, was indeed attached to the goat. She pinched the end between her finger and thumb with a grimace. It was wet and filthy, and she hoped the brown crust was only mud.

"Will it bite?"

"They can, but that's the least of my concerns."

Seeing the goat trapped by Piers's hulking weight, Victoria almost pitied the poor thing. But before she got too distracted admiring his show of strength, she realized his feet were bare. And he was standing in the middle of what was left of her shattered heirloom.

Thousands of shards of broken porcelain.

"Don't move."

"She's fine, Victoria. Just hand me the damn rope."

"It's not her, but…" She gestured toward the floor. "Mind your feet."

"Oh," he answered.

"I have a small broom in here…" Dropping the rope, she picked her way around the ruined desks and then rummaged through the storage closet until she had what she needed.

If the kicking and grunting sounds were anything to go by, the goat was not appreciating being man-handled.

"Waiting over here." She could hear the smirk in his voice when instead he ought to be thanking her.

"No need to be rude." But she was, in fact, hurrying to clear a path out of the room. "Is she trying to bite you?"

"I'd rather not give her the chance."

"I think it's safe now." She picked up the only piece that hadn't shattered—a tiny baby Jesus. A few twigs and hay clung to the delicate piece. She'd put off putting it away, and now the set was ruined.

A set her aunt had treasured for decades was now… trash.

But… she plucked off the pieces of grass.

"Wait. Hold on a moment." She gathered up a handful and held it up for Piers to see. "Will this help?"

But the goat saw it first and miraculously twisted free of a man who was at least five times its size.

Rather than attack again, however, the belligerent guest deftly tore the hay out of Victoria's hand and proceeded chomping as though it hadn't a care in the world.

"It needs a name."

"I believe this annoying little beast is a she. And she likely has one already." Piers ran a hand through his hair and glanced around. "What a God-awful mess."

But the goat didn't look annoying. In fact, eating out of Victoria's hand like this, she seemed downright lovable. Almost like a pet.

"Gertrude. Until we know otherwise, I suggest we call her Gertrude."

Piers met her gaze, trying to look stern but not quite

succeeding. "Gertrude the Goat?" Piers's expression could only be described as bemused.

"Unless you can think of a better one?"

"No, Gertrude is fine."

PIERS DID, in fact, have several other names he wouldn't mind calling the goat, none of them fit for a lady's ears.

"What should we do with her now?" Victoria scurried behind as he dragged the goat—*Gertrude*—down the stairs.

After stepping on yet another sharp something or other, Piers cursed. "I should have put on my boots."

"But you didn't know. Gertrude might just as well have been a highwayman, for all we knew," Victoria placated him from behind. "Or a wild boar!"

Which was all the more reason that he ought to have put on some blasted footwear. Unfortunately, by the time Victoria had roused him from sleep, most of his blood supply had surged to the single part of his anatomy where he'd least needed it.

After she'd ordered him to leave first thing in the morning, the last thing he'd expected was for her to barge into his bedchamber.

And damned if he hadn't fallen asleep dreaming of the surprisingly enchanting spinster. When he'd opened his eyes to see her staring down at him, he'd all but questioned his sanity.

His instinct had been to pull her into the bed with him… under him… around him—

"We can't just send her back outside." Her hands drifted over his back, most likely because she was still feeling the fear of being woken by sounds of an intruder.

But he liked being touched by her.

He more than liked it, by God, and she'd ordered him to leave.

Meanwhile, he had a blasted goat to deal with.

"I'll take her out to the barn." Artemisia would appreciate the company. "But then I'll need to go through the school to see where she got in."

"I hadn't thought of that."

"You don't want any more uninvited guests," he muttered. "Especially after I'm gone."

"Oh." Had she forgotten? "Put on your boots first."

"Right." And if he was going to be trampling around outside on what was perhaps one of the coldest nights of the year, he was going to have to don a few other layers.

He wasn't all that happy with Miss Victoria Shipley at that moment. Not because she'd done anything wrong. But having skimmed her fingertips down his back, she'd again dropped them inside the waistband of his breeches, keeping close.

And he liked it that way.

He had intended to take his leave in a few hours, at her request, and all he could think about were the throaty little sounds she'd made on the settee earlier that night, or wonder what she'd taste like, and what she'd feel like—

"Thank you." Her voice brushed softly over his spine. The warmth he felt was her breath on his back. "For... saving me."

"I hardly saved you. She would have left on her own, eventually."

"But I didn't know it was a goat. It could have been anyone." She was practically plastered against him now.

He reached back and untucked her hand from his breeches.

"Go back to bed, Victoria."

He had a goat to secure somehow and then the school to investigate.

"Are you sure you don't want my help?"

In response, he laughed. He'd suffered enough of this woman's help to last a lifetime.

Trouble was, although she had casually dismissed him from the residence, he had not succeeded in dismissing her from his thoughts.

Improper thoughts—*depraved* thoughts.

She was right to tell him to go. She was open to learning new things, but that didn't mean she was prepared to reject a lifetime of piousness instilled in her.

She had been raised to be a lady.

Which, in all seriousness, could potentially place Piers in dangerous territory. If he had any hopes at all of preserving his bachelorhood, he'd make haste to get as far away from this school and Miss Victoria Shipley as possible.

But first—the goat.

And then he needed to shore up wherever she'd gotten in.

No way in hell was he leaving until he was certain Victoria was safe.

Then, and only then, would he take to the road.

Because if he pursued this attraction any further, he'd find himself in the worst kind of predicament.

And that was the last thing he wanted.

VICTORIA DID NOT LOCK herself away in her bedchamber as he'd ordered. She was too keyed up to fall asleep.

So in the wake of quiet after hearing a door slam, she took a cup of tea into the parlor and lowered herself onto the settee.

Once Piers left, she'd never see him again.

Although, that wasn't necessarily true. He was Primm's brother, and there would always be the possibility of their paths crossing.

But not like this.

Not so intimately.

Despite his resisting the duties required by his title, he would marry eventually. He might then even bring his future daughters to the school.

Why was the thought of meeting his wife such a horrifying one?

Horrifying, but not impossible. Because this was her home, the students and teachers were her family. The school was her future.

Drawing her feet up, she tucked them under her gown to hug her knees.

Had she been right to demand he leave? If not for Gertrude, she might not have been provided with this opportunity to rethink her rash decision.

Was the nanny goat's intrusion fate's way of giving her a chance to rethink what she wanted?

Earlier that night, she'd fallen asleep feeling empty and hopeless. But then later, searching the school with him, she'd felt just the opposite.

She felt vibrant when she was with him. More alert— more alive.

Sounds of the kitchen door opening and then closing heralded Piers's return.

He'd told her to go to bed. He was angry with her, and she deserved it.

Right after he'd touched her... she had commanded him to leave. He had every right to be irritated with her and yet, it was the best decision for both of them.

The door between the residence and the school slammed shut. Rather than wait until morning, he was going to repair the opening Gertrude had found tonight.

For her sake? Yes. But also to protect his sister's school.

Piers Primm could be arrogant and presumptuous.

She hadn't wanted to like him, but...

Inside existed a man of good character—a man who was more sensitive than he'd ever let on. But he brought out the worst in her. Around him, she became klutzy and tongue-tied, undisciplined and...

Wicked?

But he'd also helped her cook, clean, and keep the residence livable without the assistance of a housekeeper.

He'd rubbed her feet, and she'd all but handed him her virtue—on a silver platter—without a single thought about possible consequences.

Heat shot to her core, and she squeezed her thighs together.

Tomorrow was Christmas Eve and because of her, he would spend it on the road alone.

And she would spend it in this little residence—alone.

She should return to her chamber—go back to sleep. He would be gone in the morning and none of these doubts would matter.

Victoria curled deeper into the settee and closed her

eyes.

She didn't want to wake up to an empty residence.

She didn't want him to go away.

Not yet.

⁓

THE COLD STIRRED Victoria from sleep. She drew her arms and legs closer for warmth, reaching for a quilt that wasn't there.

Wait, what—?

Opening her eyes, she sighed into the bitter cold. She'd fallen asleep in the parlor—with no fire, no bed, no blanket.

With sunlight filtering through the drapes, she ought to feel happy to face the day. But a cold dread wafted through her veins.

It was morning!

Panic replaced the cold.

Piers had told her he'd be gone in the morning.

No-no-no! She swung her feet to the floor and rushed to the window, squinting as she looked outside, half expecting to see him riding away on his magnificent horse.

But there was no horse, no rider, just pristine snow. Which meant he was either long gone or—that he hadn't left yet.

"Piers?" Her voice came out rusty from sleep. Not pausing to think, she raced from the parlor to Primm's chamber. "Piers?"

And the same as she had the night before, she threw it open and...

Breathed.

"You're still here." Victoria tiptoed across to the bed.

He groaned. "I'll go. After I sleep." The covers muffled his grumbling. "Damned goat broke three windows trying to get in. Took me forever to close them up." He rolled over and stared up at her. "I'll go now, if that's what you want."

Circles etched beneath his eyes, and when he blinked away the sleep, his lashes looked thicker than usual.

"Do *you* want to go?" she asked. Perhaps he didn't mind leaving. Perhaps he was happy to rid himself of her.

"You want me to go." He shrugged, laying against the pillow. "So, I'll go."

How could she tell him that she'd changed her mind without seeming pathetic? It wasn't all that complicated. So why did it feel like it was?

"How do you do that?" she asked.

"Do what?"

"Make me feel like one of my students on the first day of school."

"Nervous?"

"Just… green." And senseless, and befuddled, but also excited. Her gaze trailed to where his neck and shoulders peeked out of the covers.

Drat and tarnation. If she knew any other curse words, she'd summon them as well. Because her resolve escaped her.

Again.

He reached out from the blankets and wrapped his hand around her wrist. It felt hot, not fevered, but strong and full of life.

"You're an icicle."

A war waged between the teacher in her and the woman. He laughed and tugged. "Come here."

She should have resisted rather than allow him to pull

her onto the bed. She should have rolled away rather than slide under the blanket beside him.

She ought never to have entered his chamber to begin with.

But she had. She had gone looking for him because she wanted to.

And he felt so warm and comfortable and soft and hard at the same time. She melted into him.

"I fell asleep in the parlor." She spoke into his chest. "And when I woke up, I was afraid you'd gone." She inhaled his fragrance. Woodsy, earthy. And a little like… "You smell like a goat."

His chest rumbled beneath her cheek. "Blasted little beast."

Piers wasn't like any man she'd ever met. He was both a gentleman and a rogue. He was wild but also protective. He didn't mind that people thought he was purposeless, when in fact, he was simply running.

"Piers." Every inch of her skin was suddenly alive and… yearning. She flicked her slippers off her feet even as she slid one hand up his chest.

She wanted to feel him.

Closer. All over.

"Victoria?" His arms tightened around her.

"I don't want you to go." Not yet.

He dipped his head so his mouth was near her ear. "What does that mean?"

"I'm not sure."

His hands moved down her back, searching and soothing. "What do you want?"

If she gave herself to him—if she lay with him—she would be ruined. Ruined for what? She was a teacher. She'd decided years ago that she needn't have a husband and family to live a satisfying life.

When she'd made that decision, she'd inadvertently made the choice to deny herself... this.

"More," she said.

One of his knees slid between hers—the texture of his calf and thigh was rough and foreign feeling. Her heart beat so loudly she could hear it in her head. But she could also feel it deep inside. She felt it in her chest, in her womb, pulsing between her legs.

She clenched her inner muscles.

Piers's mouth latched onto her shoulder as his hands glided over her skin.

"So sweet," he murmured.

But Victoria didn't feel sweet. She felt wanton and wild.

Could she let go? Just for a while? Would it even matter?

"Make me feel good, Piers. Please?"

He'd made her feel so much more than good the night before. She directed his hand to the spot just above her apex.

"You want me to touch you?"

"Yes."

"You want me to taste you?"

"Yes."

It was a miracle that she wasn't mortified by her neediness. But she already felt the same sense of adventure as when they'd searched the school together in the dark.

Only better.

So much better.

She would have a taste of something new—a taste of something she'd convinced herself didn't even exist.

His head disappeared under the heavy quilt. And she

inhaled a sharp breath.

Was this what she wanted?

"Yes," she gasped, parting her legs and shifting so he could move her gown out of the way. As Victoria stared at the ceiling, the thought occurred to her that not only was she breaking every rule she'd ever known, but she was doing it in Primm's chamber.

In *Primm's bed.*

Would she ever be able to look her friend in the eyes again?

All thoughts of her employer fled when his hands pushed her legs wider, and his mouth pressed low on her belly.

He was touching that place again—parting that tender flesh put there to hide her desire from herself.

Or so she'd always believed.

She moaned at the exquisite pleasure.

"Oh." She had difficulty imagining what he was doing— with his tongue? His fingers? His lips and...

Ahhh... tugging and then...

He was inside. How?

"Piers, Piers," she found herself whispering. She reached down and clutched the sides of his head. "Don't go. Stay. Please." *Make this last forever. Never leave me. Claim me. Be mine. Love me.*

Love me.

Love me.

"So sweet." His voice rumbled against her flesh, and white fire exploded behind her eyes. She arched her back, vibrating against him, her fingers threaded through his silky hair.

She jerked, and then euphoria flowed from her head all

the way down to her toes. How was it possible to feel like this?

"Piers," she breathed.

"An angel." His mouth moved to her belly. Leaving his hand between her legs, he shifted so he was lying beside her again.

His lips were shiny and parted, looking almost soft, and his eyes were hooded, almost as though he'd found the same satisfaction she had.

But it was his hair that made her smile—sticking out in all directions from where her hands had messed it up but also from the static from the blanket.

"Good morning," he said.

"Good morning."

Victoria Shipley represented all sorts of trouble, but staring down at her, Piers admitted to himself that she was worth it. With her taste in his mouth, and his hand soaked with forbidden juices and tucked between her legs, how could she not be? He rubbed gently, and she gazed at him in a way that stole his breath. His last ounce of blood had long left his brain, his heart, and his lungs, making him hard as hell.

Piers should feel guilty but he didn't. All he felt was pleasure at giving her this. Which was ironic, considering the almost painful state of his cock.

But there was no guilt—no regret.

Victoria had been raised to be the perfect lady, but she knew herself. She hadn't been afraid to ask for what she wanted.

"How old are you?" Her eyes widened with mock disapproval that he would ask her that. "Five and twenty? Thirty?" He persisted.

She scowled, and he couldn't resist dropping a kiss on the little wrinkles between her expressive eyes.

"Eight and twenty," she said. "And you are one and thirty. Two years younger than Primm."

"And I was seven minutes younger than Elijah."

It was a strange conversation to have after ravishing her in the most delicious manner possible.

"Why do you ask?"

"To assuage my conscience, I suppose. To assure myself I'm not ruining some naïve English miss." A shadow crossed her face but then just as quickly disappeared.

"I'm beyond anyone caring whether I'm ruined."

To be working for his sister, she would have had to purposely choose spinsterhood. "Does that bother you?"

"No." But she didn't sound all that convinced.

Piers stroked one finger along her center, pleased that he'd maintained this connection. "But there are advantages to that."

Her breathing was becoming shallow, and so he stroked her again.

"I hate that word," he said. "Ruined."

He rolled sideways and settled between her thighs.

"It's atrocious." He shifted.

"Atrocious," she parroted in a throaty voice.

Covering her, he braced himself to keep from crushing her beneath his weight.

He could make love to her. She wouldn't stop him. And God knew he needed the release.

"You're a virgin," he said instead and wasn't surprised when she dipped her chin. Yes.

"But you don't plan on marrying."

This time, she shook her head.

"Do you want to die a virgin?" Was she going to whip herself with regrets when he left?

"No." Her voice sounded almost surprised. "I didn't think it mattered. But… No."

When had she come to this decision? Five minutes ago?

He inhaled, clenching his teeth. She could change her mind in a week or two. Hell, she could change her mind in a few minutes.

She could change her mind the very instant he buried his cock in her folds. He inhaled again and, exhibiting self-control he ought to be applauded for, rolled off her and dropped his feet off the edge of the bed.

Her disappointed cry mirrored his own feelings. "Are you leaving?"

"We have too much to do today," he answered, rising from the bed but only turning around when his libido was under control.

Her gaze was not on his face, but on the bulge of his breeches. Well, almost under control.

Hell and damnation. She wasn't making this easy.

"Victoria?"

She finally met his gaze.

"Do you know what day it is?"

As though emerging from a fog, she nodded. "It's Christmas Eve."

"Get out of bed, Miss Shipley, and dress warmly. If we're going to do the holiday up proper, we have a long list of chores to complete."

DOMESTIC PREPARATIONS

*P*iers hadn't exaggerated when he'd said there was much to do.

After dressing in a woolen gown, a thick shift beneath it, and a very serviceable pair of woolen stockings, Victoria didn't waste any time in cleaning out the hearths so Piers could set up the wood for new fires. And by mutual agreement, they split up the various tasks involved in the baking she'd deliver to the less fortunate on Boxing Day, along with beginning preparations for the meal the two of them would share on Christmas.

Which meant he was staying for at least two more days.

Two days.

How many rules could they break together in forty-eight hours?

"Fetch your coat, woman. We need evergreens for the parlor," Piers laughed while he brushed his hands together.

Victoria would have thought she'd feel awkward with him, or that he would look at her differently after going down... but he seemed to be enjoying himself.

As was she.

When the knowing look in his eyes threatened to turn her knees to jelly, she swept her gaze around the kitchen, which he'd shown her how to keep clean while they worked.

Dough rested on the table near the stove to rise beneath clean linens and what felt like hundreds of vegetables, chopped and sliced now, had been placed in the cold storage.

But he hadn't forgotten the one thing she longed for the most.

"Evergreens?"

Decorating for all manner of festivities was something she knew. It was something she was good at. And even though it wasn't at all practical, she was grateful that it mattered to him. And although she knew he took issue with his father, she risked asking, "Will they be gathering vines and mistletoe at Starbridge Abbey?"

Decorating the school was something Primm had happily delegated to Victoria.

"My brother, Theo, will insist on it." The affection in his voice was unmistakable.

"Theodore is the youngest?"

"My sister didn't leave much out about us," he commented wryly, but without any ill will.

They'd strolled through to the entryway, and before she could reach for it, he was holding her coat behind her.

These occasional flashes of gentility were more intoxicating than having the most sought-after bachelor tend to her every whim at a Mayfair ball.

Although not as intoxicating as what he'd done under the quilt. Her cheeks flamed at the memory.

"Your sister and I have spent a good deal of time in one

another's company." She ducked her head, forcing herself to sound normal. But as much time as she and Primm spent with one another, Victoria thought they ought to know one another better than they did.

The one thing the school head mistress rarely spoke of was herself—of her childhood or her feelings. Some of the students joked that she lacked the latter, but that couldn't be true. She was simply better at containing them.

Victoria had once imagined herself to be the same sort of woman her employer was, but the past few days had proven her wrong.

Because when he smoothed his hands down the sleeves of her coat, she didn't resist the urge to lean into him.

She had all but begged him to make love to her, and he'd instead chosen to make preparations for Christmas.

Half of her was charmed by that, and the other half frustratingly insulted. She ought to be mortified.

His arms wound around her from behind, and her heart swelled at the intimacy of his whiskers scratching the skin near her ear. She made a low humming sound and lingered in his embrace.

"Do you have a hat?" His voice rumbled.

Not what she expected him to say. "And a scarf and mittens." In the cupboard just behind them. But she had no wish to move from that spot. "Do you?" Was that her voice sounding so deep and almost hoarse?

"Umhmm…" His inhale was so close that it could have been her own.

She drew in a breath for courage. "Why did you stop this morning?" She'd told him what she wanted. It was only fair that he explained himself to her. "Was it because you don't trust me not to demand an offer of marriage?"

It was the first thing that had come to her mind. There were too many women who would do almost anything to win a title. Tricking a man into marriage, however, was something Victoria would never do.

"You could demand one," he said. "But I'm a rake, remember? Rakes don't follow the same rules honorable gentlemen do."

He walked her forward, and as though to prove his point, lifted her hands and held them flat against the wall.

And behind her, his shaft surged against the curve of her spine.

"Do you feel that?"

She dropped her forehead to the wall. She wished she wasn't wearing her coat. She wished…

"Yes," she whispered.

"I don't want you to have any regrets. I'm giving you time." His hands slid inside the front of her coat, cupping her breasts so that his words barely registered.

Her head was light and heavy at the same time, and when he squeezed her through the layers of her dress and shift, she was glad the wall was there to support her.

"I don't need time. I won't have regrets."

Well, she might.

But with her body screaming for his, she didn't care.

"I'll regret it more if we don't." It was something no lady should ever admit. But she didn't care.

He dropped a kiss on the edge of her jaw. "I'll take that into consideration."

And then he released her, leaving her cold and aching and pressed against the wall.

Alone.

. . .

PIERS KNEW he'd left her frustrated and annoyed. It had been his intention.

He didn't want her imagining a great love between the two of them. He didn't want her imagining that despite everything he'd said, despite everything she'd heard about him from Augusta, that he would propose marriage.

By God, his father would love her. Not the woman Piers was coming to know her to be, but the lady—the façade—the persona she'd cultivated practically since birth.

Victoria Shipley would make an excellent countess and an even better marchioness. But if that was something she was secretly hoping for, she was going to be disappointed.

And he couldn't make love to her until he was certain that was all she wanted from him.

At the front door, he rubbed the back of his neck and watched her. It wasn't that he wanted her to feel humiliated but his reasoning was sound.

And so he said nothing while she pulled a knit hat over her head, awkwardly wound a colorful scarf around her neck, and then jerked on two ridiculously fluffy mittens—all while refusing to look at him.

Piers swallowed the ache at the back of his throat, dropped his gaze, and didn't move until she marched past him. It was for her own sake. She might even thank him someday.

She opened the door, let in a cold whoosh of air, and then allowed the door to slam behind her.

Or perhaps she wouldn't.

Piers pulled it open again, following her with less enthusiasm than he had for anything they'd done all day.

The sun had shone bright earlier but while they'd been busy in the kitchen, thick clouds had gathered.

"The woods are over here," she said without turning around.

If he hadn't been such an ass, she might have smiled at him. She would have smiled, and that would have been the end of it. The end of what, exactly? His bachelorhood? Her virginity?

Both?

Watching her trudge her way through the snow, he realized he could not allow her to remain in foul spirits. It was, after all, Christmas Eve.

Piers bent down and scooped a handful of snow up into his gloved hands. Rising, he shaped it into a soft ball, took aim and...

Whomp! He got her right between the shoulder blades.

"You!" She turned around finally, eyes blazing.

Which was almost as good as a smile.

No. Piers shook his head. Nothing came close to her smile. Except perhaps that look she made right before—

She scowled and bent down to shape a weapon for revenge.

Whack.

"Your aim is surprisingly accurate!" he shouted, brushing his shoulder. "For a girl!"

He ducked when a second missile came flying, barely missing his head this time. Victoria took a moment to enjoy her small victory, staring at him defiantly, hands on hips.

Piers scooped up more snow to make another ball and sprinted toward her.

"Stay where you are! No fair!" She was backing away from him, not looking as satisfied now that he was getting closer. But she didn't give up. Instead, she scooped handfuls of snow up, mostly only shoving them in his direction, until she tripped over something hidden in the snow and fell backward into a drift. "You! You!"

She lay sprawled in the pile of snow, still glaring up at him.

"Baboon?" Piers mocked.

"Buffoon, you idiot!" Indecision lurked in her expression. But she didn't move to get up. She simply lay in the sparkling white snow gazing at the sky.

"Truce?" He reached out a hand to assist her up. She hesitated but then took it. With nothing more than a gentle tug, Piers had her on her feet.

For such a small woman, she'd managed to create far too much havoc in his thoughts these past few days.

She moved to relinquish his hand but Piers didn't let go. Instead, he spun her around and brushed the snow off her back and legs...

Anything to touch her. Even if she was mad at him. And fortunately for him, or perhaps both of them, she didn't protest.

She should.

She surrendered fully, standing still even after he was finished. Her cheeks were flushed, and her dark brown eyes sparkled from beneath her hat.

She shouldn't be this beautiful. "Not fair," he said suddenly.

"I know. You're much larger than me. And stronger." But that wasn't what he'd meant.

He turned away from her and swallowed hard.

""If I'm remembering correctly," Piers called out as he led her in the direction of the trees, "We'll find some holly up ahead. And ivy."

"I didn't realize you knew the grounds."

"That's because I only visit my sister on holidays and summers while you are off charming patrons into opening their pockets. God forbid I visit while the school is crawling with giggling females." He shuddered dramatically.

Victoria caught up with him. "You stayed here? At the school?"

Although Augusta maintained that she was wholly independent, whenever he knew she was alone at the school, if he was in the area, he'd made his best effort to visit.

"Where else would I stay?

Her eyes narrowed. "Where did you sleep?"

Piers threw back his head and laughed. "If you are imagining that I've already been in your bed, then you would be wrong. Augusta has always respected the privacy of others. I slept in the parlor."

"Oh, dear. And yet, I haven't been nearly as considerate." Victoria winced.

"Well, I was on death's door, and I am her brother."

"But that doesn't excuse me..." She looked away from him.

"Keeping me warm?" Piers laughed. He supposed she had a point.

He couldn't even begin to discern the sound that squeaked out of her throat.

"She isn't as unsympathetic as you think," Piers surprised himself with an attempt to assuage some of her mortification.

Silence fell between them as they each turned their attention to the trees and branches overhead.

"I know. Under different circumstances," Victoria said, "Your sister would have been happy to make the visit home. She doesn't always say, but she missed you and your family."

"Likely true. She likes to run our family as well as she does the school—always has." Marching through the trees, keeping an eye out for Christmassy branches of evergreen, Piers found himself talking about growing up at Starbridge Abbey—the good parts. Times he spent with Auggie, who'd always been the most interesting of his siblings.

"Auggie's always understood me, having disapproved of my father's method herself. Hand those over." Piers wrapped his arms around the larger branches Victoria had collected. "You have plans for all of these?" He cocked a brow.

"I do, as a matter of fact." Victoria plucked a sprig of perfect greenery off some nearby brush and added it to the pile in his arms. "Perhaps that explains some of your sister's teaching philosophy. There are some schools that depend on corporal punishment. But this is not one of them."

"She never has accepted the status quo. Unfortunately, she's paid for it more than once." Piers half grinned, half winced. "And by refusing to marry the man our father chose for her, she had her revenge." It was a miracle Father ever allowed her to come home at all.

"What did she do?" Victoria's curiosity lit up her face.

Piers shook his head. "You'll have to ask her when she returns."

"That's not fair." She gave him a gentle shove. "She'll never tell me."

But his sister's secrets weren't his to share.

A bitter gust of wind chose that moment to disrupt the snow off the trees overhead, dusting them with silver frozen crystals.

Victoria's laughter compelled him to watch her.

Her nose was bright red, and her half-boots likely had

only protected her feet for the first few steps through the drifts.

"We should go back inside now." He held out the treasures she'd collected for her to hold. "Take these."

She raised her brows but allowed him to transfer the branches anyway. And in the next moment, he'd swooped her up and into his arms.

"What are you doing?" She initially suspected the worst, squealing, but then her protests turned to laugher as he carried her through the woods. "You don't have to carry me! I'm fine!"

"Take advantage of the gesture, Victoria." He didn't have to carry her. But her toes must be frozen numb by now, and he was mostly healed of his injuries.

Furthermore, he wanted to.

And that made all the difference in the world.

VICTORIA HOVERED over the ground at Piers's mercy. He ran initially, but they'd come a considerable distance and when they finally neared the clearing, he slowed to a walk.

"We don't have a yule log," she pointed out. It was easier to be carried than to try to convince him otherwise.

"We'll improvise." He marched along, undeterred. Their breaths mingled in the air between them.

Victoria tilted her head toward his shoulder. "I must admit, I could get used to this sort of treatment."

"I guessed as much." He huffed.

"Are you tired? I can walk."

"I'm fine."

"Do you always do this? Carry women across frozen meadows for no reason?"

He sent her an impatient side-eye, and she laughed.

Again, she'd gone from irritation to… liking… wanting.

"Are your feet cold?"

"My feet?" He turned his head, and their faces were so close that they were almost touching. "Surprisingly not."

He'd slowed to an almost leisurely pace. And even though his breathing was slightly labored, he turned his face forward once again but didn't set her down.

The position gave Victoria the perfect opportunity to study his profile. His strong jaw, his nose, which had a small bump on it, and… his mouth.

He'd only kissed her that one time—just before Mr. Driver interrupted them. And yet, he knew her more intimately than any other person ever had.

Victoria blinked at the realization. Piers knew her more intimately than she knew herself.

And yet, she hardly knew him at all—not in the physically intimate sense that he knew her. Was this typical? If so, she didn't want to be typical. If she was going to toss her virtue to the wind, she wanted to know him just as well. She wanted to draw back the blanket, so to speak, and learn the mysteries of the male anatomy.

While the landscape innocently bounced by, an electrical surge that was becoming all too familiar shot through her.

She shifted the evergreens and tried not to squirm as he carried her the rest of the way home.

With the clouds blocking the sun completely, darkness wasn't far off. When they reached the door, Piers stomped his feet, shouldered his way inside, and then finally lowered her to stand on her own.

In the foyer.

It immediately reminded her of the humiliating confession she'd made earlier. Had it been a confession? Or had she formed it more as a request?

"I'll take that into consideration," he'd said. As though she was negotiating with him.

His ability to turn hot one moment and cold the next was infuriating. Only, to be fair, he was not the only one.

You will take your leave first thing in the morning.

Had that been only yesterday? He'd asked if that was what she'd really wanted, and she'd insisted that it was.

Why?

Because she'd been afraid—afraid of her own feelings but also afraid of his.

Piers had already removed his gloves and was shrugging out of his coat while Victoria unwound her scarf.

"I'll light a fire in the parlor." He seemed oblivious to her thoughts for once.

She nodded and turned to hang her scarf on the hook.

This was the most time she'd ever spent in one person's company. With Primm, there had always been other teachers near—and students. When she'd stayed with her aunt, they'd given one another space.

Even so, Victoria hurried to change so she could sit by the fire with him. What was different about Piers from other men?

The answer was obvious when shivers jumped along her skin. She was intrigued by him as a person but there was something else.

Something exciting and… irresistible.

After returning her mittens to the shelf, she unbuttoned her coat with shaking fingers.

From the cold.

No. Not the cold.

The things he'd done to her that morning had been... fantastic. But there was more to these relations. She knew there was more.

Sounds of wood popping in the hearth drifted out of the parlor.

She padded along the foyer toward the warmth but stopped at the entrance. Down on one knee, watching the flames, Piers hadn't heard her approach.

He seemed deep in thought. Was he feeling guilty that he'd not rushed to his mother's side? Was he remembering his brother?

Was it possible he might be wondering about her?

"What are you thinking?" she asked, doubtful that he would tell her.

Staring into the fire, he lifted his shoulders and then dropped them, as though he'd taken a deep breath.

A spiraling piece of ash floated up the chimney.

"That you are precisely the sort of gel my father would want me to marry, given the chance." His voice sounded cold. Almost angry. He turned and cocked a brow in her direction. "Ironic, eh?"

"Why would that matter?" she dared to ask.

"Why indeed?" He turned to ask. As quickly as it came, the flash of bitterness disappeared. "What we need tonight is some flaming brandy."

"Really?"

"To pluck raisins from."

Happy to move beyond his father's opinions on marriage, Victoria latched onto Piers's suggestion. "For just the two of us? I thought that was a children's game."

"Sit over here." He pointed to the nearest chair. "We can raid Augusta's secret cupboard."

"It isn't so secret anymore, is it?" She sauntered toward the fire.

Or was it him?

Before going out to gather the evergreens, she'd placed Mrs. Driver's leftover pot pies on the stove. "The pies ought to be warm by now. And I saw raisins in the larder." Crouching down, she unlaced her boots and removed them. Too tired to do anything beyond that, she lowered herself onto the chair beside Piers and held her toes near the hearth. "Just let me warm up a minute, and I'll fetch—"

A warm hand captured her ankle. "Your stockings are wet."

"They'll dry—" Victoria exhaled while he slid both hands up her leg and then rolled her stocking down. When he reached for her other foot, his gaze caught hers. The knowing behind his eyes confirmed that he, too, was remembering what had happened in this room the night before.

And in his bed early that morning.

He took his time rolling down the second stocking, soothing his palms along her calf.

But then he pushed himself up and draped her stockings near the hearth. Rather than make for the door in search of his sister's brandy, he planted his own stockinged feet flat on the rug and faced her.

His primal stare tied her in knots.

"Have you changed your mind?" he asked.

He didn't seem as though he wanted to depart from the school just yet. He was leaving the decision up to her.

However, she hadn't taught social skills for nearly a

decade for no reason. Good communications involved give and take, and she had already shared her thoughts on this issue.

It was his turn.

"Tell me your concerns." If this was a negotiation for him, she'd treat it the same.

One side of his mouth lifted. "Fair enough." He narrowed his eyes. "But not until after we've eaten. You stay there. I'll fetch the pies."

He turned and left the room.

Victoria shot off the chair, buzzing in anticipation of...

Something she wasn't quite sure of.

Regardless, she dashed down the corridor to her chamber. Because if they were going to have the conversation she imagined, she was going to look her best.

IRONING OUT THE DETAILS

*P*iers returned to the parlor to find it empty. For a moment he thought she'd changed her mind, but when he stepped into the corridor, and heard her rummaging about behind the door to her chamber, guessed she was changing for dinner.

Returning to the Parlor, he set the hot pies onto the low table, lowered himself onto the settee and stared at her stockings.

Dull blue wool, they looked to have been made for a grandmother—or the spinsterish woman Piers had imagined from Augusta's letters.

Victoria was interested in learning his concerns. Nothing between them was conventional. He doubted there was another woman in all of England willing to discuss the prospect of an affair so openly.

He'd always thought mystery was attractive, but there was something about the honesty of this situation—about Victoria Shipley—that enticed the hell out of him.

"I'm starving." She appeared in the threshold, one arm

propped against the frame, two wine glasses dangling from her fingers. In her other hand, she clasped a bottle of wine.

Piers exhaled a long, slow breath.

The dress she'd changed into was nothing like any of the serviceable gowns she'd worn since his arrival. Puffed sleeves draped lazily on her arms, leaving her shoulders bared, glowing alabaster in the firelight. A delicate rose shaded the swells of her bosom, of which the low décolleté revealed plenty. He watched her throat move before she strolled inside.

She'd not come to these negotiations unarmed.

Piers rubbed his hands together. Another side of this woman to appreciate, a side that was dangerous, exciting. It showed she was willing to take risks for something she wanted.

Piers licked his lips. Because that was sexy as hell.

His gaze pinned on her, Piers took the bottle and easily removed the cork.

"We could move to the dining room." He gestured toward the two bowls on the table. "But it's cozier in here— warmer." Piers had weapons of his own but bowled over by hers, at that moment anyhow, couldn't recall what they were.

"No, this is lovely." She stepped around to the settee and stood the glasses on the table.

The gown, a scarlet silk, nipped in at her waist, and the skirt, which flared out from her hips, swooshed when she walked.

No wonder Augusta sent this woman to raise funds. In less than a minute, she'd entranced him.

Taking the seat beside her, Piers filled the two glasses with wine with hands that weren't as steady as he'd like.

A lesser man would have admitted defeat before she was halfway across the room.

And what would define such a defeat?

Sex?

Marriage?

A lesser man wouldn't have cared—he only would have wondered why some other gentleman hadn't snatched her up.

Victoria opened a linen napkin and smoothed it on her lap.

Piers trailed his gaze over her bare shoulders. "Aren't you cold?"

She answered with a pretty little shrug. Who was this woman?

Good Lord in Heaven, she was smiling at him now.

"When I was just a girl," she said, "Decorating required all the servants most of the day. We'd thread ivy up the banisters, around the railings and columns, and above all the hearths." She shook her head. "I haven't thought about that in a very long time. But I remember that it was… magical. Christmas Eve and Christmas Day. They felt… magical."

"Didn't your aunt decorate?"

"The servants were responsible for most of it. But it's not the same as when we are children, is it?" She tilted her head. "Did your family observe traditions around the holiday?"

"A few. The Yule log, of course. And a few games of Snapdragon," he smiled at the memory. There had been some magic—long ago. So long, though, that he could barely remember it.

"Is Starbridge Abbey as grand as it sounds?"

"Grander. But old. And in winter, the walls and floor

might just as well be made of ice." Piers dug into his dinner and proceeded to describe the ancient abbey that was his childhood home.

It was odd to realize some of the fond memories he had. Memories from before their father had snatched Eli out of their midst for his training.

In turn, Victoria talked about her only sister. "Margaret would have turned thirty this year. But in my mind, she'll never be older than ten and eight."

"She never married?" Piers topped her glass off.

Victoria shook her head, and an enchanting curl escaped her coiffure. "She was betrothed to the Marquess of Brockington's son but died before they even met." She grimaced. "I was six and ten at the time. The day after the physician diagnosed her, my father sent me to Mayfair to live with my aunt. Diphtheria. Since then, I've read about it, and although I'm grateful I didn't have to watch her suffer, I wish I could have been there to comfort her in the end."

"It's easily passed from person to person," Piers pointed out. Her parents had done well to protect her. "Eli died after falling off his horse."

"I know." She lifted her glass as though to toast the flames in the hearth. "To Margaret and Eli."

"To Margaret." Piers lifted his glass. "And Eli." He brought the glass to his mouth and drained the contents. By the time he'd received word of his brother's condition, it had been too late. Piers had barely arrived home in time for the funeral.

Victoria leaned back on the settee beside him and patted her belly in a most unladylike pose. "This conversation is far too serious for Christmas Eve." They'd finished off both pies and the entire bottle of wine. "And we've yet to put up the decorations."

"No." He turned and his gaze locked with hers, placing his arm along the back of the settee. "We can put them up tomorrow."

~

THAT THRILL SHOT through Victoria again.

In a matter of days, this man had ripped apart the layers of propriety she'd cloaked herself in for most of her life. He had her questioning why she'd put them there to begin with.

Had she donned them for protection? If that was the case, then what exactly had she been protecting herself from? Disappointment? Shattered hope?

Or the temptation to believe that her world couldn't fall to pieces in the blink of an eye?

Because when the pieces began cracking, there was no glue strong enough to put them back together.

Piers was going to leave in a few days. Although the attraction between them was unlike anything she'd ever felt, she knew better than to build any hopes on it.

It had nothing to do with hope or faith in the future. These feelings were rooted in nothing but the present.

But they were real. They were as real as the storm that had brought him to her.

Her gaze was trapped by his. She should have stopped after her first glass of wine.

Piers stroked a strand of her hair with the tip of his finger. He hadn't touched an inch of her skin, and yet she felt it all over.

"You asked about my concerns." His voice was low.

Victoria cleared her throat. "You feared I would regret it."

"Not right away." He flashed a smug smile for an instant. "But later."

"I have no expectations." He would need to know this.

Piers Primm was not simply Piers. His title could be found in Debrett's, and his family lineage in John Burke's dictionary of the peerage. His name meant something to not just England but the world.

He was the Earl of Rosewood. He was the future Marquess of Starbridge. In a nutshell, he was *exceedingly* tempting husband material.

If that was what she wanted.

Piers turned somber again. "I won't take a wife until after my father's death—especially not one like you. Not only because it would provide him with immense satisfaction. But I don't want my wife—or our children—to have to endure his manipulations. And, unfortunately, last I heard, he was healthy as a horse."

He was warning her... but his gaze had dropped to her mouth.

Victoria licked her lips. "I've no plans to marry. Ever. Even if I couldn't teach, I have means enough that I'll never be in want—I have my aunt's townhouse sitting empty in Mayfair if I ever need it." And if that wasn't convincing enough, she added, "I'm very lucky. I realize this. Because I don't *need* a husband."

He edged closer, and his arm slid behind her shoulders. The warmth of his powerful thigh pressed against hers. "I like you, Victoria. If I didn't, none of this would matter."

"You like me?" She'd always considered the word anemic, but coming from his mouth...

"You're not like other ladies." His smile was a rueful one.

Some locked up feminine part of her wanted to hear more. But she swallowed questions that might lead him to believe she wanted…

Love?

"You have to know you are beautiful." His throat moved. "You're also endearingly open-minded and brave. However…" His voice turned stern. "You will always be a lady."

"I've acted less like a lady these past few days than any other time in my life."

"Doesn't matter. Being a lady is not what you do. It's who you are." He shrugged and then grimaced. "My father would love you."

Which, she realized with a stabbing sensation, was a mark against her. He'd been quite clear about his feelings for the marquess.

"Come here, Angel." He leaned forward, his hand at the back of her neck. And then his lips caught hers softly, like a web catching a butterfly. She opened her mouth, wanting more. She wouldn't escape this kiss. She didn't even want to.

His breath was hers. And his taste, a potion that weakened all her defenses.

Dizziness consumed her.

"What else?" she whispered. "What else concerns you?" If her heart beat any faster, it would leap right out of her chest.

She was going to lie with him.

She wasn't going to deny herself that.

Which made it all the more important that they get everything out in the open now.

"I won't spend inside of you," he mumbled against her lips.

Her eyes widened. Not in her wildest dreams could Victoria have imagined having such a conversation.

"I'm going to pull out." His mouth left hers to create a tingling trail of fire along her jaw, her neck.

"G-good. That's good." She clutched his shoulders. She didn't want to wait a second more. She wanted…

Him.

She wanted…

This.

Now.

"We're good, then?" His words vibrated against her skin at the same moment the hair at her nape loosened. He was removing her hairpins.

"Yes."

Why did his fingers threading through her hair feel so incredibly naughty?

"It's the color of scotch or the sun at twilight. Damn, Victoria."

"I didn't realize you could wax poetic." Her voice hitched.

"Only when I'm inspired."

He had a hand on her bodice, cradling her breast over the material. And then he was squeezing and rubbing. "This is good?"

"Yes."

He drew the material down, exposing her, and then dipped his head to claim one tip with his mouth. This was good. This was *so much more than good.*

"You're welcome." He peered up at her with a wide smile, his lips glistening, and she realized she'd spoken aloud.

She couldn't help smiling back at him.

He tensed, and his eyes glowed with something fierce.

"What's wrong?"

"That smile. It's dangerous."

Her smile was what...? She didn't take the time to consider his meaning before all thoughts returned to Piers's mouth on her, grazing his teeth over very, very sensitive skin.

"I want you in bed." His arms curved around her waist, the other under her knees, lifting her off the settee.

She'd never been carried by anyone, and now he was doing it for the second time that day.

It made a lady feel... cherished, dash it all.

It made her feel loved.

"You shouldn't keep doing this." She buried her face in his neck.

"Why not?" She felt him shake his head, chuckling.

"Because it's dangerous as well."

But he didn't put her down. And when he stepped into the chamber he'd been sleeping in, she nearly stopped him.

It was Primm's bedchamber.

Was it better she have her own bed as a reminder of her wickedness after he left?

No. She might never sleep again.

Inside, he lowered her feet to the floor and stepped back. He then shot her another questioning glance, and at her nod, crossed the room to set flame to the fuel in the hearth.

As it roared to life, excitement roared silently between them.

How was it possible that a man could touch her with nothing but his eyes?

"I want to see all of you." He hitched his chin, his stare

dropping to where she clutched her bodice in front of her. "Undress for me."

He wasn't asking. He wanted her full participation.

Yes, this was her first time, but it might also be her last. She was mortified at the idea of standing before him unclothed, but desire won out.

She allowed the bodice to fall, where it caught around her hips. Not giving herself a chance to change her mind, she reached around her back to unfasten her skirt.

She could only pretend his eyes weren't burning into her when the silk gown fell to the floor followed by her short stays. Once she'd dispensed of all those, she stood before him, holding her chemise at her waist, clutching tightly to her last ounce of modesty.

"Your turn." She swallowed hard.

PIERS DIDN'T NEED to be asked a second time. She was curious. And she wasn't afraid to tell him what she wanted. He moved his hands to unfasten his falls and proceeded to undress without ceremony.

When he drew his shirt over his head, a curious tingling slid up his spine to settle at the back of his neck. He was...

Nervous. He'd not been nervous with a woman since... in a very long time.

But this woman... Miss *Victoria Shipley.*

Since that day he'd first touched her, hell, since she'd opened the damned door for him, looking like an angel sent from heaven, he'd imagined this.

He wanted her hard and fast, but he also wanted to draw it out, like a banquet or sipping fine scotch. This would be her first time. He realized she imagined it might be her last time, but he seriously doubted that.

He tossed his shirt over a chair, and he thought he heard a small sound of appreciation from where she stood. She did not avert her eyes.

Piers climbed onto the center of the bed and stretched out—one leg straight, the other bent. "Victoria. Come here." He patted the space beside him.

He would encourage her to take this at her own pace.

She dropped her chemise and, looking like a Roman goddess, scrambled up beside him. Kneeling and resting on her heels, she did nothing to hide her hesitancy. Not second thoughts, but indecision as to what part she would play in this.

Piers took her hand and placed it on his chest. "What do you want?"

She was so serious—so damned earnest.

"I want to touch you."

"Touch me, then. Touch me wherever you want."

She bit her lip as she dragged her hand down his sternum to his navel. She swirled her fingers around the hair on his belly while Piers clutched his fists at his side.

"What do you like?" She flashed her eyes up. "Where do you like to be touched?

"Anywhere." Piers swallowed hard. "Just don't tickle me."

"I won't." She was studying him again, stroking his abdomen with both hands now, making his mouth water and his cock painfully hard. "I wanted to touch you like this when you were ill. It made me feel guilty—wanting something like that."

"But you didn't?"

"No. It would have been wrong."

"That was... considerate of you." Piers wondered if he'd ever been this aroused before. At the same time, the thought of her soothing his heated body while he'd been ill... it filled his heart. When had his heart become involved in any of this?

"You were sick." Her hand moved dangerously low.

"I'm not sick now." Piers exhaled, aching for her to wrap those pretty little hands around him. By God, with his cock dancing and waving like that, it was no wonder it hadn't reached for her itself.

"I'm glad," she said.

"Touch me, Victoria." In case she had any doubts as to what he wanted. "Please."

She pushed up on her knees, her breasts partially hidden by her hair, and took hold of his cock with both hands.

Piers resisted the urge to thrust his hips off the bed. *Use me. Ride me. Fuck me.*

But this was for her.

"It's hot." She sent him a shy glance, licking her lips. "And soft, but hard." She laughed softly to herself. "So, this is the secret mystery of man."

"Never laugh at a man when he is at your mercy, Miss Shipley."

She slid him another glance, not nearly as shy this time, before leaning forward and kissing the tip.

"Victoria." Her name on his lips was little more than a choking sound. "You don't need to do that."

She turned her head to the side and stared at him. "You said whatever I wanted."

"Is it, though? What you want?"

"Yes."

Was he even breathing now? He inhaled. "By all means, then."

Her fingertips swirled around the tip, spreading the pearl of seed he'd had no control over. When she kissed him again and swirled her tongue down one side, Piers fought not to embarrass himself.

"Sit on me." And lest she not understand, he added, "Straddle me."

She sat up and then, in a surprisingly graceful motion, had both her knees bracketing his hips, hovering her center over him, her brows furrowed.

Piers reached between them to ensure that she was ready.

She was… so wet.

"You have all the control," Piers said. "You determine how deep; you determine how fast. And you determine whether you want to stop or keep going."

"Like this?" She lowered herself just enough that he skimmed her entrance. He struggled to keep from pushing deeper.

"Yes," Piers answered through gritted teeth.

"It'll fit?" A little concern this time.

"It'll fit. But it might take a moment for your body to adjust."

"It's supposed to hurt. I know that much." But a brave, determined look marked her expression. It was an image he instinctively knew he would never forget.

"That's what I've heard." Was that a tremble in his voice?

It trembled because Victoria was slowly, incredibly slowly, taking him into her body. It was the sweetest torture tied up in the most exquisitely painful anticipation.

"You're…" Piers felt tongue-tied. "Incredible."

"Farther?"

"If you want." *Dear God.*

Leaning over him, her mouth inches from his, she relaxed, filling herself to the hilt. A soft gasp from her—a groan from him. Crimson velvet encroached his vision even as she froze and then dropped her head.

"Are you all right?" he asked.

She nodded, her forehead barely touching his chin.

"Victoria?"

Soft, fluttery exhale. And then she raised her head to meet his gaze again.

"I'm good."

"Good?"

Silence except for the crackling sound in the hearth.

"Very good." She shifted, and then lifted and lowered herself again. This time, Piers moved with her—with deliberately aching restraint.

He caught her mouth, thrusting his tongue into hers in cadence with the rhythm that was exciting and exhilarating but also natural and wonderful and...

Right.

At some point he'd clasped her hand with one of his. His fingers tightened on her hip. He didn't close his eyes. He'd have been a fool not to watch this woman move, not to watch the place where they joined as he moved in and out of her.

Glistening. Kissing. Sucking. Piers reached for her breast, holding one and watching the other bounce as her confidence increased.

"Piers?" His name on her lips was a question. *Is this right? Is this real? Am I safe?*

"Good girl. Whatever you want—sweet mother of God."

He lifted her up and off so she could drop down again, grinding, and tightening and swiveling her hips. He matched her energy, keeping his jaw clenched when his release threatened.

Exquisite tension grew, and Piers held himself in check.

"Perfect," he soothed. "Just like that, Victoria. You're so good. You feel so good." He found himself reciting a litany of encouragement. Just… "Don't stop."

And then she threw her head back, clenching around him.

Thank God because he couldn't hold back forever.

He lifted her off and jerked back just in time to keep his promise.

VICTORIA LAY LIMP on the bed, lazily watching Piers, who'd gotten up but quickly returned with a clean linen in one hand. And when he wiped away his seed, which was cooling on her belly, wave after wave of conflicting emotions rolled through her. Appreciation for his gentleness, and that, for the most part, she need not worry about consequences. But also… regret. Not regret for what they'd done, but a different kind of regret. Something deep inside of her.

The spilled seed was a reminder that having her own child was not in her future. She shouldn't be upset.

She hadn't contemplated motherhood for a very long time.

Furthermore, her heart seemed to have taken over all her other organs. Was that something lovers felt after joining? After sharing such a primitive and intimate act?

She shivered. Feeling this vulnerable, she might very well have placed her actual heart directly into his hands.

With his hand splayed over her belly, Piers met her eyes. "That was... You are..." He shook his head. "Beautiful."

Her gaze locked with his. What were these feelings? Not love.

They could not be love.

"Is it always like that?" she asked.

His throat moved. "No."

He tore his gaze away from hers and tossed the linen onto the floor.

It was over.

Victoria moved to climb off her side of the bed, but his strong arms caught her waist. "Where are you going?"

"I should go... to my own bed."

But he pulled her into him. "Is that what you want? I have so much more to show you."

"More?" Relief, followed by a thrill, shot through her. She chose to ignore the hot feeling in her chest that may or may not be a warning.

Because she wanted more. She wasn't ready for this to be over.

She turned into his arms, sliding hers up his chest and around his neck. "Show me, Piers."

And since he'd said it was dangerous...

She smiled.

A NOT-SO-PRIVATE AFFAIR

"Miss Shipley!" The high-pitched noise sounded from far away.

Victoria huddled deeper into the covers. Sleep hadn't come until dawn and only after Piers had thoroughly exhausted her.

The first time… had been a deliverance.

The second time… She felt light-headed at the memory.

Piers had made love to her slowly at first, covering her, holding her wrists into the mattress. She'd felt owned but oddly protected with his weight bearing down on her. His mouth had captured her cries while his member filled her in the most perfect way imaginable.

And the third time—

"Victoria!" More urgent. "What are you doing in Miss Primm's bed? And who is this man with you?" The voice was more insistent now, and the covers moved when Piers sat up beside her.

The voice? Who? What?

Victoria's eyes shot open, and she stared down the

length of the bed, horrified to imagine that voice could actually belong to who she thought it did.

Lady Priscilla, known at the school as Miss Fellowes, also happened to be her former betrothed's sister.

But none of that mattered at that moment—only the fact that Prissy was here, standing in the threshold of the doorway to Primm's chamber.

Where Victoria lay in bed with…

Primm's brother.

Both of them naked.

Another girl appeared behind Miss Fellowes. Allison Meadowbrook looked more intrigued than horrified.

Victoria stiffened and checked herself. "Miss Fellowes? Do you mind…? Could you please…?" Her voice failed her. What was a lady supposed to do when discovered in such a horrifically compromising situation? She searched her brain for the answer, but her brain had ceased to function. "Please…?"

"Close the door?" Piers provided.

Priscilla covered her face with her hands. "Yes. Of course. Dear God, Allison, what are you doing here?" She dropped one hand from her own eyes to cover the younger lady's behind her. And then, turning away and corralling Miss Meadowbrook, propelled both of them backward and then closed the door.

Leaving Victoria…

Horrified? Shocked? She shouldn't be surprised, and yet… *Dear God*…

She dropped her gaze to her hands, where she clutched the quilt so tightly her fingers were turning white. But she couldn't move. She couldn't speak.

What had just happened?

Piers's hand rubbing her back finally brought her back to life. Because he was rubbing her *very naked* back... Naked!

Naked!

She lurched off the bed. "I need to speak with her. I need to tell her..."

But again, she was at a loss.

Piers was sitting up but looked resigned, rather than panicked.

"I'll marry you." His voice cut through the tension in the room. "You can tell her we're betrothed."

Victoria stopped dressing long enough to send him a scathing glance. "This is no time for jokes. I'm serious. It's not Prissy I'm worried about. It's—" Victoria closed her eyes. "Dear God, I cannot imagine a worse gossip than Allison Meadowbrook."

"I'm not joking." He climbed off the bed while his gaze searched the room, presumably looking for his breeches. "We took a chance, and we got caught."

"I told you I wouldn't expect an offer. And I didn't. I don't." She fumbled with the laces on her gown... a ball gown, for heaven's sake. She was going to have to face her colleague and a student wearing a *wrinkled ball gown*. She might as well begin drafting her resignation over her first cup of tea.

"You told me you had no expectations, but that was based on the premise we kept matters private. When it was just between the two of us." Piers effortlessly fastened his falls. "Victoria." His voice forced her to look at him. "We don't have a choice. We got caught."

But she was shaking her head. "No. I'll come up with something. You have no wish to marry and I have an established career." She wound her hair in a knot at her nape. "I'll bribe the chit myself if I have to."

But this was a catastrophe.

She smoothed her gown and inhaled a calming breath. Piers would rethink his proposal once he was fully awake. "We'll talk later. Just... Let me speak with Prissy first." Because he didn't want to marry her, and although that wasn't something that would bother some women, it would bother Victoria.

It would more than bother her. Such a marriage wasn't worth both of them giving up their lives.

Although...

A contrary thought niggled at her that she could have many, many nights like the one she'd just had. But how long before they tired of one another? How long before she longed for the classroom and his feet itched to travel again?

And that didn't even begin to consider his feelings for his father. Just last night he'd insisted he'd not marry until the man was dead. *"I won't take a wife until after my father's death—especially not one like you."*

She was the daughter of a viscount. She had been raised to be a countess. And she had an enormous dowry she'd tried to forget about.

And if marrying her in any way pleased his father, he'd resent the union all that much more.

"We'll figure something else out." Victoria moved toward the door.

"It's not the end of the world." Piers's voice stopped her. "Marrying me."

Not right now. But it would be eventually.

She glanced back. "I'll handle this."

~

PIERS FINISHED DRESSING, his unanswered proposal weighing on his shoulders. He and Victoria ought to have spent what remained of the morning in bed—making love again and then sleeping off the exertions of what had proven to be…

One of the best nights of his life, by God.

And it wasn't simply the sexual satisfaction. He liked hearing her talk about subjects that mattered but also subjects that didn't. And he loved hearing her laugh. He'd told her stupid things from his past just to see her smile.

So many smiles from her.

He pulled his shirt on. Primm had mentioned Miss Fellowes. From what he could remember, the woman taught history along with domestic sciences. But that was all he knew about the intruder who'd ruined the morning.

He and Victoria had planned on cooking the food they'd begun preparing the day before. He hadn't once imagined…

This.

On Christmas Day of all things.

Piers shoved his feet into his stockings and then tugged on his boots.

Victoria hadn't done this intentionally. He was one hundred percent certain of that. She'd have to be a flawless actress to pull off the horror he'd seen on her face a few moments ago. But even more than that, he *knew* her.

It wasn't something she'd do.

Because she was… good—which meant he was going to have to marry her.

Many titled men wore their honor like a cloak. Piers, as

the spare, had considered himself unencumbered by the concept.

She could deny it all she wanted, but Victoria Shipley was a gentlewoman.

He ran a hand through his hair.

He had been caught in bed with Victoria Shipley—a woman who wasn't only the daughter of a viscount, but one of his sister's closest friends.

The assistant director of the school.

He had no doubt Auggie would spit on his grave if he failed to marry Victoria.

He exhaled.

Marry Victoria.

She'd told him no, but she could not have meant it. Their compromising predicament had been witnessed by not one, but two ladies.

He buttoned his waistcoat and smoothed his hair. He needed to look as respectable as possible. For a flash of an instant, he contemplated slipping out to the stable, saddling Artemisia, and not looking back.

But in that same instant, an emptiness stretched out in front of him. And he wasn't quite sure why that was.

He shook his head, tugged on his jacket, and stepped out of the bedchamber.

Two horrified ladies stared at Victoria when she stepped into the parlor.

Rather than even attempt an explanation, she took another route.

"What are you two doing back already?"

Prissy and Allison's early return fell under Victoria's realm of responsibility as the assistant director of the school. They were supposed to remain at Mr. Meadowbrook's estate until after the new year.

"Have your parents fallen ill?" Victoria addressed Allison. "Has something happened?"

Prissy shifted an annoyed glance at the younger girl, whose pale blue eyes and curling blond hair made her appear more innocent and sweeter than she really was. Truth be told, for as long as she'd attended Miss Primm's, Allison Meadowbrook had been one of the more troublesome students. At seven and ten now, the girl's incorrigibility had become nearly impossible to contain.

However, the family not only paid tuition, but provided the school with extravagant financial gifts every time their daughter did something she otherwise might be expelled for.

"No. They are perfectly healthy. It's their daughter who needs her head examined." Priscilla grimaced. "Allison threatened to run away if I didn't bring her back to the school."

"That's only because my parents had invited *him* to visit for the holidays."

"Him?" Victoria cocked a brow.

"The Earl of Hardwood." Allison frowned.

"Mr. Meadowbrook has betrothed Allison to the earl." Priscilla turned in her seat to face the younger girl. "You will be a proper lady—a countess, for heaven's sake. It's an incredible honor for a girl like you."

The Meadowbrooks were not nobility. They were simply incredibly wealthy due to Allison's father's well-timed investments at the turn of the century in all things pertaining to steam engines.

Victoria couldn't help but nod in agreement. She vaguely recalled the man, a dark-haired, charismatic gentleman she'd met in London a few years ago. If she remembered correctly, he was quite good-looking. Although not nearly as good-looking as Piers. "He seems a kind enough gentleman."

"He is not *James*." The name came out more of a wailing sound. Allison crossed her arms over her bosom, her lower lip jutted out.

Oh, dear. "And who is James?"

"One of her father's footmen," Priscilla answered. "Or he was, rather. Mr. Middlebrook sent him away after Allison confessed that they were in love."

"I hate my father! I hate everyone!" Allison lifted her chin.

With nothing to say to that, Priscilla turned to face Victoria.

"Did you realize there is a goat and a strange horse in the stable? Beautiful horse, by the way. I assume it belongs to..." Her gaze shifted for a moment to the back hallway. "We didn't come into the residence initially. Mr. Driver let us into the school, but there are several piles of..." She frowned. "When I saw that Primm's carriage was gone, I assumed you had gone with her to Starbridge Abbey. Not for a minute would I have imagined you'd remain here alone."

But she had not been alone.

"No." Victoria shook her head. She was going to have to explain herself somehow.

"But the school is in a shambles! Mr. Driver is assessing the damages as we speak."

How had Victoria forgotten about that? And if Mr. Driver was going through the school, he'd discover the repairs Piers had made. Which meant he would suspect she wasn't alone.

"Gertrude broke in through a window and then she panicked," Victoria provided.

Both ladies stared at her as though she'd gone mad.

"Gertrude is the goat," Victoria explained. "She was roaming the school and before I'd realized what was happening, she'd already done a good deal of damage." She had assumed that she and Piers would address the mess after Christmas.

When she'd imagined he'd still be here.

"Anyway…" Priscilla turned apologetic. "In agreeing to return, I had planned on Allison and I keeping to my quarters on the second floor. But when I saw the damages, well, there was no way we would sleep in that. Your chamber was empty. I was going to put Allison in…" She pinched her mouth together.

Priscilla seemed more embarrassed than the girl seated beside her.

Victoria shot her a silencing look.

Because…

Allison.

"You may unpack your belongings in my chamber, Miss Meadowbrook." Victoria summoned all the authority she could muster.

She was surprised that she'd been capable of any at all.

"I'll find out anyway," Allison warned. "So you might as well tell me."

"Go," Prissy said, and then added, "Please?"

The younger girl fidgeted a little while gathering her valise and then finally left Victoria alone with Priscilla.

"What were you thinking?" Priscilla all but begged after the sound of Allison's footsteps disappeared. "What are we going to do? I'd never tell a soul, but..."

Victoria covered her face with both hands. "I never imagined anyone would come back early."

"Yes, but..." Priscilla was shaking her head. "Who is he?"

Victoria inhaled and then let out a long breath. "He's Primm's brother—Lord Rosewood." She went on to explain how he'd shown up at the beginning of the storm and how he'd been injured and then ill.

"But even Primm says he's a rake. Why would you...? Did he force you?" Priscilla's eyes turned fierce and her face, which was normally pale, turned even whiter. "I'll shoot him myself—"

Victoria held out a hand to reassure her friend. "No. No. It was nothing like that. It was... more along the lines of... an opportunity. For both of us." She wouldn't lie. She wouldn't make up excuses. "Primm can't find out. No one can find out."

Priscilla nodded, then shook her head. "Do you love him? Surely he has to marry you."

"That's out of the question." Victoria held firm. "I mean, I like him, very much." More than she wanted to think about in that moment. "But he's leaving. He needs to travel to Starbridge Abbey to see his mother. He and I, we have an agreement." She dare not go into any further detail than that. "But I don't know how to keep Allison from telling anyone who will listen. I need your help with that child..."

"Not a child." Priscilla corrected her. "And she isn't going to be cooperative. Although…"

"Yes?"

"If we could help her manage Lord Hardwood, she might be willing to keep quiet."

Victoria shook her head. "But how?"

"I don't know. But I'll think of something. And then I'll speak with her."

"And we can't let Mr. Driver know either."

"The fewer people involved, the better. But surely he's seen the horse?"

Victoria bit her lip. "I told him Piers left it here so he could travel in the coach with Primm."

"But he did not ride with Primm, and the one person who will know that is Primm herself. Oh, Victoria. Perhaps we should go to her with the truth—"

"No!" Victoria was wringing her hands in her lap, searching her mind desperately for some other feasible solution.

"I'll take care of my sister." Piers joined the conversation from where he stood in the open door.

Priscilla was already off the settee, but Victoria jumped up as well.

"Priscilla." Victoria swallowed hard. "May I present Lord Rosewood? My lord, this is Priscilla Fellowes, sister to the Earl of Kingsley, who also happens to be our most excellent teacher of history and the domestic sciences."

Priscilla managed a curtsey. But that, it seemed, was all the patience she had for such niceties in the face of the debauchery she'd walked in on earlier.

"It would normally be a pleasure to meet you, my lord. But unless you are willing to provide an acceptable explanation for—" Victoria's dear friend blushed and dropped her gaze.

"It's not necessary—" Victoria tried to stop her friend.

"Lord Rosewood must leave the school at once," Priscilla continued. "Unless, that is..." She shifted a meaningful glance toward Victoria, allowing the obvious question to hang in the air.

"Right," Piers answered ambiguously. "Unless."

He turned to Victoria. "Might I have a word? Alone. If you don't mind?"

Victoria hated the look in his eyes—a little angry, more than a little cynical—much like the look he'd had when he first arrived. He'd changed into different clothing than she'd seen him wearing before, and his hair was neatly combed back from his face.

Was he going to propose again, or was this going to be goodbye?

Logically, his leaving was best, so why were her palms damp? And why couldn't she fill her lungs up with air?

The sun was shining today—Christmas Day—and for some reason, she didn't want to have this conversation inside. "I'll fetch my boots and coat."

And then, too distraught to be concerned that it was inappropriate to leave Priscilla sitting alone with Piers, she swept out of the parlor, nearly colliding with Allison.

"Miss Shipley." The girl gave her a smug look. "Going somewhere? Say, Gretna Green perhaps?"

"I'm changing into a more appropriate gown." Victoria hated that she would have to make an explanation to any one of her students, let alone Allison Meadowbrook. But offending the girl wasn't something she could afford. "There are biscuits in the kitchen if you're hungry."

The thought of delaying her conversation with Piers and serving tea in the parlor was tempting but with Mr. Driver lurking about, they didn't really have time for that.

"You've lost a button." Allison pointed. Sure enough, the girl was right. Likely, Victoria had been less than careful when she'd undressed the night before.

In front of Piers.

"Yes, well…" Failing to come up with a reasonable explanation for that, she shrugged. "I'll return shortly. I imagine Miss Fellowes and er… Lord Rosewood would appreciate a few biscuits as well."

It was past noon by now. She and Piers had slept half the day away—only because they'd been awake most of the night.

She slipped past the younger girl to enter her chamber.

If only this reckoning hadn't come until the holidays were over. Better yet, if only she could turn back time—to before Piers had arrived.

But…

No.

She wouldn't trade these past days for all the king's gold.

Unfortunately, such choices came with a price. She only hoped neither of them was forced to pay it.

HAPPY CHRISTMAS!

*R*ather than attempt to make polite conversation with Miss Fellowes, Piers asked that she tell Miss Shipley to meet him in the stable.

As much as it pained him, as much as he abhorred seeing the glee on his father's face at the news, Piers knew deep inside that he and Victoria didn't have a choice.

Marriage was the only logical remedy.

He marched through the snow, his boots making crunching sounds and the air stinging his ears.

"That's your horse in there?" A stout fellow appeared from around the stable. He had to be Mr. Driver.

There was no way his visit to the school was going to be kept silent.

"She is."

"I suppose the other creature is responsible for the damage in the school. Mistress Primm is not going to be happy." The man fixed his unrelenting stare on Piers. "Mind if I ask your name?"

Blast and damn.

"Rosewood," he answered. At this point, no good could come from dissembling.

The man's brows shot up to where his hairline must have been a few decades before.

"Miss Primm's brother? The earl?"

Piers nodded. "I take it you are Mr. Driver?"

"Yes. Yes. Forgive me, my lord. I didn't realize she'd returned yet."

"She has not." Piers wouldn't provide the man with any specifics because a lack of information allowed for the possibility of a miscommunication.

His sister's loyal handyman stared at him suspiciously again.

Mr. Driver gestured behind him. "Jonesey's goat escaped again, I see."

Piers neither confirmed nor denied what he knew about the goat. "Well, then," he said instead. "If you'll excuse me."

"Of course."

Piers continued around the stable, opened the door, and inhaled, needing the simplicity of the smell of the animals. It was so much less complicated than the rest of his life.

Gertrude glanced over at him lazily.

"This is your fault," Piers groused. If not for the goat's escapade inside the school, he would have left the morning before, just as Victoria had asked him to.

There would be no need for a hasty betrothal because those women wouldn't have come charging into his bedchamber.

He never would have been caught in bed with one of his sister's most notable staff members.

Because he never would have carried her there to begin with. He wouldn't have watched her disrobe in the firelight. He wouldn't know her taste or where she was ticklish. He wouldn't know what it felt like to bury his cock—

"I take it back, Gertrude." Piers frowned.

But the goat didn't care. She bent forward and made a few digging motions with her front leg, and then lifted her head to stare at him...

Ominously.

Piers ought to have considered that she might charge him. Why wouldn't she? It was that sort of day, after all.

And with the closed door at his back, Piers had nowhere to go. "I said I take it back." Piers's life flashed before his eyes the moment before impact. At the last second, he attempted to step to the side, but the goat caught him anyway.

And although Gertrude's horn merely clipped his groin, Piers bent over in gut-wrenching, unthinkable, earth-shattering pain.

"You bloody cock-sucker," Piers growled. But the animal, having accomplished what it wanted, sashayed back into the stall with Artemisia and then made herself comfortable in the hay on the floor.

Leaving Piers clutching his manhood and barely able to move. After a few shallow breaths, he hobbled over and closed the gate behind the little beast.

His horse flicked her mane, showing no sympathy whatsoever.

"Happy Christmas to you too," he mumbled. It seemed as though all women had turned against him this morning—even Victoria, who'd considered his proposal a joke.

Piers propped himself against the gate and then, his knees weak, slid slowly until he was seated on the ground.

Being punched, stabbed, or even shot couldn't have hurt more than taking a ram to the bollocks.

He'd have cut loose with a litany of curses if not for Victoria peeking her head inside.

"Piers?" Her voice sounded as though it was coming from the opposite end of a tunnel. "Piers?"

Piers opened his eyes.

"What happened?" she asked.

Since arriving, she'd seen him at his worst. Must he add emasculation to the list of calamities she'd be witness to?

He held out one hand. Was he even breathing? "The goat," he managed.

"The goat?" He could practically hear her thoughts click into place as she processed his meaning. "Did she...ram you?"

"That's putting it mildly," he agreed. The pain may or may not have subsided, but was overall too acute for him to notice any improvement.

Victoria closed the door behind her, then crossed to lower herself to sit beside him against the closed gate.

"Oh, Piers. I'm so sorry."

She wasn't talking about the goat.

"It's not your fault." This wasn't the conversation he'd envisioned. He needed to gather his composure and propose again.

"I had no idea anyone would return before the new year." She slumped beside him. "I ran into Mr. Driver on my way over here. I take it the two of you met."

"Yes." And then he added, "We don't have a choice, Victoria."

She was silent for a moment, which Piers appreciated, because it gave the throbbing a few seconds to die down.

And then she tipped her head backward, banging it softly against the gate.

"Is there nothing else—" But she ought to know better than anyone else.

"We got caught," he said.

She dipped her head forward this time. "I know. I was just so sure that if we could keep everything quiet... but... I know you're right."

He grunted. Piers normally enjoyed hearing those words.

"I'm not sure the school could weather a scandal like this. Just last year, your sister had to fire a teacher when word got around that she was born on the wrong side of the blanket. If Allison decides to talk..." A small cry tore out of her. "Primm wouldn't have a choice." She dropped her head onto her knees. "I'm going to miss teaching. I'd already started my new lesson plans..."

Feeling less like he was being turned inside out from the groin area now, Piers reached across the space between them to take hold of her hand. "She'll have a difficult time replacing you, if that's even possible."

She waved a mittened hand through the air. "Everyone is replaceable."

Not her. But Piers didn't think she'd believe him.

"The teachers are like a family—they are sisters. I'll miss them dreadfully. And now I won't be able to teach anything I've learned this week." She caught his gaze and scowled. "*Not that.*"

"I should say not." But she was in no joking mood, so he turned serious. "Tell me."

"I wanted to teach these girls, these young women who come to us to learn to be ladies." She laughed. "I wanted to teach them… how to survive—how to keep a house warm and prepare a meal. Little things that aren't so little at all. Because one never knows when—"

"When she will be stranded alone in a vacant school over the holidays?"

"I suppose it sounds more than a little foolish. I'm no expert, that's for certain, but I was thinking I could pay some of the more capable women from the village to perform demonstrations…" She turned to stare at him, and then made a faint grin. And even though it wasn't her most vivid, it still twisted something in his gut. He winced, and she dropped her gaze to his lap. "I am sorry about Gertrude. Is there anything I can do to help?"

This woman.

If he was to be tied to one woman for the rest of his life, he could certainly do worse.

And despite nearly being castrated, his injured organ jumped to life.

"Later, perhaps." His words summoned a pretty flush up her neck—in addition to the pink in her cheeks from the cold. "But we need to marry." Remembering himself, he turned to face her.

She bit her bottom lip and stared around the stables as though she'd find any other answer to their problem. She exhaled. "We hardly know one another."

"More than most."

Victoria had put the notion of marrying behind her a very long time ago. Because although she'd once anticipated being a wife and mother, the events that were supposed to lead up to it had been painful and humiliating. She couldn't help but resist the idea of marriage after enduring four postponed ceremonies and then being jilted.

That betrothal had come from an arrangement between her and Lord Kingsley's fathers. She'd held on because she'd believed it would eventually lead to happiness for both of them.

Piers's proposal, on the other hand, was a necessary result of their decision to reject societal norms—no, more than that—of their decision to ignore the tenets of basic morality.

"What will happen after? Will you leave the continent again? Where will we live?" All valid questions, but also her attempt to delay the inevitable. Because there was no chance on earth that Allison wasn't going to tell the first person who would listen that she and Miss Fellowes had caught Miss Shipley in bed with Miss Primm's brother.

In Primm's bed no less! For some reason, that particular detail made it at least twice as bad in Victoria's eyes.

Was Primm ever going to forgive her?

"We'll travel together to Starbridge Abbey, where you can meet my brothers and mother. Primm, at least, will be familiar. We'll make our announcement. We'll make this work. As for the other details, we can work those out later. I'm not without funds. We can buy a small estate and live wherever you wish. There's no way in hell I'd leave you to the tender mercies of my parents." He wasn't as pale as he'd looked when she first came in. And she could tell he was doing his best not to seem overly miserable at the thought of marriage.

An institution he'd firmly rejected only twenty-four hours ago.

She mulled his words over in her mind. "I can't leave

Prissy here—Miss Fellowes—the two of them would flounder more than I did."

"We can bring them along as well. All the better to provide you with a chaperone."

Victoria nearly snorted at the irony.

But instead, she nodded.

And as though he sensed exactly what she needed, Piers leaned over and pressed his mouth against hers. This kiss was gentle at first—solidifying their agreement. Without even thinking, Victoria opened her mouth so he could deepen it.

"Mmm," he sighed, his hand coming up to clutch the back of her neck. How was it possible that her body could come alive so easily, sitting on the floor of a barn in freezing temperatures?

Victoria arched her back. "Are you...? Is your...?" She wanted him again.

If she was going to have to pay for her indiscretions, she dashed well was going to take advantage of the benefits.

Piers broke their kiss. "You've brought on a miraculous recovery, Miss Shipley." He stroked himself through the fabric of his trousers. "I believe I'll muddle through."

He pulled her to her feet but bent forward and wrapped his arms around her thighs. Before she realized what he was doing, he'd thrown her over his shoulder.

Did she protest?

No. The ground bounced in front of her eyes as he carried her through the breezeway and into an empty stall.

This was so bad—so very, very bad.

When he lowered her onto her feet again, she couldn't be sure whether she was dizzy from anticipation or because all the blood was rushing out of her head.

"Is there time for this?" Her heart raced, and that ache between her legs was hot and demanding. "Prissy is bound to come looking for me."

"Then we'd better be quick."

Piers spun her around suddenly and pinned her hands against the gate. "Hold on." He roved his hands over her front, down her hips, and his mouth made fiery trails around her neck and shoulder.

"Victoria." Her name was a gasp on his lips. He placed one booted foot between hers, edging them apart at the same time he lifted her skirts.

Yes.

She arched her back, inviting him to fill her again.

His hands touched her everywhere that she wanted—her breasts, her hips, the curve of her behind, and finally her center. These weren't caresses. They were more of a desperate search. The tenderness of the night before gave way to something more urgent—something almost angry.

When he entered her from behind, Victoria braced herself. She forgot who she was—where they were—and why anything other than this even mattered. He made low guttural sounds, penetrating, gripping her hips so tightly it hurt.

Her own gasps and sighs matched each thrust as the two of them soared above the rest of the world.

And this time, when the stars exploded into a light brighter than the sun, Piers did not pull away.

This time, as completion rolled through her, she welcomed the heat of his release.

Piers's arms tightened as he half leaned, half supported her from behind. The frost of their breath hovered in the air between them.

"So, we are engaged?" His voice caressed her cheek.

She allowed herself to smile. "We are engaged."

"And you will come with me to Starbridge Abbey?"

"Along with Priscilla and Allison, yes."

He shifted his mid-section back, sliding out of her and allowing her skirts to fall back into place. Speechless, but thoroughly satisfied, Victoria fussed at her gown while he tucked himself away.

"You'd best wipe that expression off your face, Miss Shipley, or your friend and your student will guess precisely what you've been up to."

"What *we've* been up to," she corrected him. Because he had, in fact, done most of the work.

Piers handed her a handkerchief, and when Victoria wiped at her legs, her hands were shaking.

It was best, of course, that she did not return to the residence with his seed trailing down her thighs. The thought didn't even make her feel like blushing. Where had her modesty gone? Who was she?

The lines of propriety hadn't only blurred, they'd been wiped clear away.

"It isn't all bad?" she asked, facing him again. "I know you didn't want to marry—"

"That was before." He dropped his hands to her waist and then gave her a kiss that was long and slow and lingering…

"We should go inside," she finally whispered into his mouth.

"I suppose we should."

UPHOLDING TRADITIONS

$\mathcal{P}$iers and Victoria found Priscilla bustling in the kitchen, wearing the apron Victoria had used and pulling out the vegetables they'd prepared the day before. Allison stood in the corner looking morose.

When Priscilla caught sight of them, however, she turned, hands on hips, and eyed them both suspiciously.

"Well?" Priscilla cocked an eyebrow.

Victoria glanced over at Piers, who'd taken her hand in his, and for the first time in as long as she could remember, felt as though she was the young girl in need of chaperoning.

"Will you wish us well, Miss Fellowes? Miss Shipley has agreed to become my wife." He sounded quite matter-of-fact.

"I should hope so," Allison grumbled from where she stood. But Priscilla clapped her hands together in front of her and then burst across the room to embrace Victoria.

"I am so happy! What a perfect event to celebrate on

Christmas Day!" she said. "We have so much to do. We need to roll out and bake the biscuits for the baskets. And begin cooking dinner. Allison, take those evergreen cuttings I found and decorate the parlor and the dining room. I'm sure Lord Rosewood would be more than willing to assist you. There's another apron hanging in the larder… Victoria?"

Victoria was a little jealous of Priscilla's obvious competence, but more impressed than anything. Furthermore, she was happy to allow her friend to take control of the preparations for the day.

"You know your way around a kitchen?" Victoria asked while she processed the fact that she was entangled in another betrothal. If she dared dwell on the other… event that had just taken place in the stable, she doubted she'd be fit for conversation.

Piers hadn't moved, however. "We can celebrate today, but tomorrow, Miss Shipley has agreed to travel to Starbridge Abbey to make our announcement there and to inform my sister of the… situation."

"You mean, the happy occasion?" Prissy corrected him.

Victoria dropped Piers's hand and reached out to Priscilla.

"I cannot travel alone with Lord Rosewood."

"A little late to think of that," Allison murmured.

Victoria continued on as though the younger girl hadn't spoken. "We cannot leave the two of you here, either, so would you be willing to come along?"

"To Primm's home?"

"Yes. Starbridge Abbey."

"But we only just got here—" Allison began to protest.

"Of course we are willing to come along," Priscilla cut in, answering for the both of them. "But first, we celebrate."

"Christmas," Victoria dipped her chin.

"And your betrothal to Lord Rosewood," Prissy added.

"Yes." A betrothal. The mere idea of being betrothed again was an unsettling one. Her hands shook as she tied the apron behind her.

"Now off with you two!" Priscilla shooed Piers and Allison out of the kitchen.

After they had gone, Priscilla handed Victoria the rolling pin. "We need to shape the dough," she said. "And while you do that, I want you to tell me everything."

"Oh, really?" Victoria took the pin, happy she'd learned this particular skill already. "I doubt there's much you don't already know." The embarrassment was beginning to wear off—with Priscilla, anyhow.

She scooped out some flour to begin dusting the work-table and her hands.

"I realize that after things ended with my brother, you said you'd never marry, But… That was a long time ago. Are you in love with him—with Lord Rosewood?" Priscilla, as Kingsley's sister, of course knew the truth about Victoria's long, drawn-out betrothal that had never come to fruition.

She was asking not as Victoria's subordinate, but as the girl who had once believed they would be sisters.

"You're not wrong. I had decided it wasn't for me," she answered. She didn't need to explain the disappointments she'd experienced already. "But we don't have a choice."

"You always have a choice." Priscilla was mixing up some fruit and sugar. "But you must have feelings for him—to have gone so far as to…"

Oh, yes. Victoria thought. I have feelings for him.

But she, more than anyone, realized that a betrothal was nothing but a beginning. And such beginnings could easily go sour.

"I believe that he and I will get along well enough." They certainly had managed well enough in the stable.

Victoria eased up on the pressure she was using with the roller when the dough began to tear.

"I hope so." Priscilla sighed.

Victoria decided they needed a change of subject.

"How did you learn all of this?" She hadn't realized her younger friend was so efficient in the kitchen.

"I do teach domestic sciences, you know."

"Yes, but I thought you limited that to overseeing staff and household budgeting?"

"I couldn't very well understand those two areas if I didn't understand the basics, could I?"

"No, of course not." Victoria wondered how she'd gone so long not realizing this. "How did you learn them? I never would have guessed." Because everywhere else except for the school, Priscilla was known as *Lady* Priscilla. She was the daughter of an earl and had been raised in a castle that was centuries old—Sky Manor.

Priscilla slanted Victoria a wince. "I didn't grow up learning them," she said. "But after all that business… with Lord Lockely, I needed some… purpose."

"No need to explain." Lord Lockely had been the reason for Priscilla's ruin.

"Anyway, since I was confined to Sky Manor and Olivia was taking over Mother's responsibilities, I found myself spending more and more time in the kitchen—learning from Cook."

"How very clever of you."

And although Victoria had no idea what her own future held; she began explaining some of her ideas about the curriculum changes she'd been contemplating to Priscilla.

"It is all well and good for our students to be successful in society, but if they can't lay a fire, or prepare a meal for themselves if the need arises, we've done them a disservice." Her words were a bitter reminder of the disservice she'd done to herself by never bothering to learn these skills.

Priscilla added some lard to a pan on the stove and then turned around, looking sympathetic.

"Primm must have been terribly worried about her mother to have left you here alone. Did you have a difficult time of things?"

Had she? Victoria mentally looked back on the past week.

"I would have managed well enough. But that's about all. After a few days, one grows tired of eating stale bread and cheese. If Piers hadn't arrived..." She laughed. "I have never appreciated a hot meal as much as the egg and cheese bread he taught me how to make."

Something in her voice must have given away more of her feelings on those days, because Priscilla's eyes welled up as she stared at her. "Oh, Victoria!"

"It wasn't that bad." Victoria suddenly felt the need to share more of what had transpired—using catgut to sew Piers's wound, nursing him through the fever, the night they'd had to chase after Gertrude, and even the laundry. She did not share the more intimate details but she did go so far as to confess the doubts she'd had about the value she'd placed on the subjects she'd been teaching.

"Decorum has its place. It always will, but I think perhaps we need to find a better balance."

While Priscilla moved from task to task, putting biscuits in the oven, sauteing food for the meal, and packing the fruit mixture in jars, Victoria had retrieved the notes she'd made and the two of them discussed ways they could improve on each of their prospective subjects.

And by the time the last pan of biscuits was cooling, they'd sketched out a plan to present to Primm.

And that thought, unfortunately, reminded Victoria that she might very well not be at the school to implement it.

Thinking of all she was going to miss, she sighed. Not wanting to dwell on that, she turned to the baskets.

"If we wait until after the break to deliver these, the biscuits will be bricks by the time they get them."

"Well then," Priscilla pursed her lips. "At least that way, Mr. Watson could add another room onto their cottage." She grinned. "Did you hear Mrs. Watson gave birth to a girl just before term ended?"

Priscilla added the warm jars of fruit to the three baskets Victoria had decorated.

"I did," Victoria smiled. She'd been looking forward to meeting the newest little citizen of Warstone Crossing. "The other two are for the Joneses and the Smiths. Are you acquainted with them?"

Priscilla smiled. "Mrs. Smith is in the knitting club that Miss Fortune, Miss Addy, and I established last spring."

Victoria knew of it. It wasn't really a knitting club, but a weekly get-together where some of the local village women were learning to read.

"How is that going?"

"Splendidly. Although the ladies lack time to practice. But I think they enjoy it." Priscilla rubbed the side of her nose, leaving a trace of sugar. "We cannot wait to deliver these until we return. Would you be willing to go now? Perhaps your fiancé could locate our driver and have the carriage readied. Allison can help me finish cooking the dinner and we could sit down to enjoy it after you've returned."

Her fiancé.

She might as well get used to that. "Let me find Piers." Victoria shrugged out of the apron. But then she reached out and took Priscilla's hand. "Thank you for not making this difficult, Prissy. I am so very sorry you had to witness…"

Priscilla nodded. "What are friends for?" And then she laughed. "But for what it's worth, I'm not all that worried about you marrying Lord Rosewood."

"Why not?" Victoria was genuinely curious.

"I've never seen you look happier."

SHE LOOKED HAPPIER?

Overwhelmed and disappointed in herself was a more apt description of how she ought to appear. And yet, she had to admit to herself that she was different. A lady—a woman—couldn't possibly share the sort of night she'd shared with Piers without undergoing some sort of inner transformation.

But that would imply there had been something more to it than sexual gratification.

Wouldn't it?

She strolled into the dining room and then the parlor, pleased to see the decorations were hung in the manner she'd imagined. But the man whom she was seeking was noticeably absent.

As was Allison.

Victoria had nearly given up on finding him when the sound of bells ringing outside caught her attention from the window.

He had hooked up his beautiful horse to, of all things, a sleigh!

And he had taken Allison along. For the first time since arriving back at the school, the girl was smiling. More than that, she was laughing when Victoria met her in the foyer.

"Lord Rosewood wants to know if the baskets are ready."

Priscilla must have heard the commotion as well, for she was already carrying all three gifts toward the door. "What a marvelous idea!"

"But do you want to come? I could stay here and work on the—"

"Oh, dear me, no. You're hardly to be trusted with my Christmas pudding." Priscilla was all smiles. "Besides, I think a sleigh ride is the perfect outing for a newly engaged couple."

Victoria wanted to argue, seeing as this wasn't the romantic engagement Priscilla implied, but the sleigh was, in fact, an excellent idea.

"Tell Lord—tell my fiancé that I'll be out shortly," she told Allison, who surprisingly nodded and disappeared outside again with no grumbling whatsoever.

"I don't have any flour on me, do I?" Victoria turned to Priscilla even as she touched her hair self-consciously.

Priscilla brushed at Victoria's gown and then stepped back. "You're glowing."

Victoria rolled her eyes heavenward, donning her coat. "I don't suppose it matters. Seeing as I'll be covered from head to toe with wool." She tugged on her hat, and then wrapped the scarf around her neck.

With mittened hands, Victoria slid her arm through the basket handles.

"Take your time," Priscilla waved. "Dinner won't be ready for a few hours yet."

Allison was returning inside. "Be sure to pull the lap blanket over you. The wind was colder than I imagined." The girl's cheeks were pink and her eyes sparkling.

"I will… Thank you."

Victoria hadn't realized snow was falling again. This storm was nothing like the previous one. But it was perfect.

Thick flakes danced lazily as they fell from the overcast sky.

The sleigh sat only two passengers, and Piers took up most of the seat where he waited, reins in hand, wearing a tall hat and scarf and the coat she'd assisted him out of when he first arrived.

"You aren't going to stand there all day, are you?"

PIERS HAD REALIZED that if they didn't want the baking to go to waste, they would have to take those baskets around before leaving. He'd spied the sleigh earlier, and after a few repairs, had no trouble whatsoever making it drivable.

After allowing Artemisia to stretch her legs with a quick run, his not-so-docile mount was tolerant enough that he could hook her up to the contraption. It was Christmas, after all.

And all the while, without intentionally doing so, as he wiped the sleigh down and then located a lap blanket, he'd imagined Victoria's response.

Hoping, of course, for a smile.

"You aren't going to stand there all day, are you?"

She didn't scowl or frown at his teasing.

He got his reward, indeed, and it was all the more brilliant in the waning light of day.

She tilted her head, her teeth showing and brown eyes shining. "Are you going to sit up there all day waiting for me, or are you going to help me load these baskets?"

With a surprisingly light heart, Piers jumped off the sleigh. Only a few hours had passed since he'd been with her, and yet she'd taken up most of his thoughts since he'd left her working in the kitchen.

"Thank you." She smiled up at him as he relieved her of the baskets. "I didn't think anything could lift Allison's spirits."

"What did I tell you about doing that?" he mock scowled at her.

"About what?"

"That smile, Victoria." The effect of it was visceral.

She simply shook her head. "Foolishness."

After he had the baskets stowed away, she allowed him to assist her onto the seat and then he strolled around the back to join her.

"Where did you find this?" She asked as he arranged the lap blanket over both of them. He did not think he was mistaken that her hand lingered on his thigh longer than was necessary. "You certainly are full of surprises."

"Beneath a canvas behind the stable. More practical than the carriage, don't you think?" Although some of the snow from the earlier storm had melted, plenty still covered the roads.

"Definitely," she sat up straight beside him. "Practical. Especially the bells. That's the first thought that came to mind when I saw it."

"Then we are of like minds." Piers took the rein in one hand and slid his other beneath the blanket to take hold of hers. It felt natural, riding with her like this, but despite the intimacy they'd shared, an awkwardness existed between them.

Or perhaps that was *because* of the intimacy.

She gave him directions for their first stop but fell silent afterward.

She did, however, squeeze his hand.

He was in uncharted territory. Before meeting Victoria, he'd been adamantly opposed to marriage. He'd felt that way right up until this morning.

"Your father is going to love me," she broke the silence. "I am so sorry. I didn't mean any of this to happen." Her words were meant to console him, but she herself seemed to lack enthusiasm.

Which left him in a most unlikely position—thinking she might be the one to need consoling.

"You don't want to marry me?" The question came out sounding more incredulous than he'd intended.

"I hadn't planned on marrying anyone," she answered and then exhaled, as though she'd resigned herself to the inevitable.

"It doesn't have to be as bad as you're imagining." He was

a little offended. Served him right for doing the honorable thing.

Another sigh. "It's not you." She squeezed his hand again.

This was not the scenario he'd envisioned when he'd planned to take her out in the sleigh. And then the irony of it hit him. Not only was he being honorable, but he'd made an attempt at being romantic.

What had she done to him?

"It's the betrothal part," she said. "I… told you before that I was betrothed."

"Are you pining for him? Is that it?" Was she harboring some notions that—

"No. Not at all. I was betrothed to Lord Kingsley for twenty-two years—my entire life. And I didn't end it. He did. But before that, we postponed our wedding four times."

"Why?" Piers made his best attempt to follow her train of thought.

"First, it was because of Margaret's death. A year later, my grandmother passed away. Then it was my father, and the last postponement was so I could mourn my mother."

Piers had known she had no family left, but he hadn't asked her for any of the details.

"People didn't seem to stop dying until we'd broken it off —until this year."

People die, she'd told him. "You know there's no real connection."

"Of course I do. I understand the difference between correlation and causation. It isn't rational at all. But," she shrugged. "I hadn't thought about it for ages. But being engaged, I suppose, brought it back up."

"Are you more concerned with the betrothal than the wedding itself?"

"I know it sounds foolish…"

Her fears would have been laughable if they weren't so… So damn sad.

He pulled the sleigh to a halt and turned to her. "But you realize this is different."

The gaze she had pinned on him was serious, indeed. "It is, isn't it?"

"And no one is holding a pistol forcing us to do this. It was our decision."

She nodded.

"It's true that there would be a scandal if we decided against marriage. If we choose that route, it will tarnish the school, and you'd have no choice but to resign. But these things pass. A year from now, no one would care. But I think…" He touched the side of her cheek. "That despite all my prior reservations, we've made the best decision—for my sister, for the impressionable ladies who walked in on us, but most importantly, for you and I. Because after everything is said and done, when it comes to this particular rule…"

"It matters," she said.

"But you know that." Artemisia was bristling at waiting, so he dared not relinquish the reins to take Victoria into his arms. Instead, Piers settled for leaning forward to press his lips against hers.

Cool and sweet—not unlike the person herself. When he drew away, her eyes were closed and she exhaled a soft sigh.

"Better?" he asked.

Her lashes fluttered open. "I think so." Her lips were shiny and soft—relaxed.

Of all the potential disasters they faced, there was something—*an undefinable force*—that just might hold them together.

He hadn't been looking for a bride when he came to the school. Marrying had been the very last thing on his mind.

But the most precious gifts in life didn't necessarily come along when one was ready.

She nodded, eyes shining, and then made a little self-conscious sounding laugh. "I will try not to worry, then. Which is problematic, isn't it? Because as soon as we resolve ourselves to *not* do something, we want to do it even more."

"I suppose that explains it, then," Piers said.

"What?"

"Why I'm constantly wanting to kiss you." Piers winked, and since Artemisia was growing restless and they had deliveries to make, his urges at that moment had to go unsatisfied.

AFTER LEAVING the baskets on the doorsteps of their intended recipients, Piers took Victoria for an extended ride. And a few times he gave into the horse's desire to fly across the countryside. By the time they returned to the school, the horse had worked off her restlessness and Piers had dropped an arm around Victoria's shoulders, holding her snuggled up against him.

The sky was growing dark so he pulled to a stop at the entrance, gave her a scorching kiss, and sent her inside while he put up the horse and sleigh.

. . .

INSIDE, Victoria found Priscilla looking flushed as she stirred a pot on the stove and Allison seated on the work-table, swinging her legs.

"I'm back. What can I do to help?" Victoria asked.

"Nothing," Priscilla smiled. "Did you enjoy yourself?"

"I did." She glanced around the room. "How did you accomplish all of this?" Several dishes had been readied: chestnut stuffing, mashed potatoes, roasted carrots, and slices of roast beef and goose... "A roast and *goose*?"

"Mr. Driver brought the goose over shortly after you left. In return, I had him take some of the beef back for him and Mrs. Driver to share."

"We'll never finish all of it!" But the savory scents had her mouth-watering.

Priscilla wiped her hands on a towel. "Oh, but we will. I'll pack what's leftover in a basket so we'll have good food to eat for the drive to Starbridge Abbey."

The domestic sciences teacher most certainly had everything in hand. "It all smells positively delicious. Do you need help with the table?"

"I've set it already," Allison offered. "We're mostly just waiting for you and Lord Rosewood to return."

At the reminder that Piers would be back at any moment, a very silly buzzing anticipation had Victoria backing toward the door. "He's putting the horse up. I'm going to change out of this gown, but I'll be right back."

Because she wanted to look *pretty* for the evening. Good heavens, she wanted to look pretty for Piers.

"I'm going to do the same," Priscilla announced. "Allison, can you stir this until I return?"

And surprisingly enough, the girl jumped off the table and did as Priscilla asked.

Victoria had not expected this Christmas to be all that enjoyable. Memorable—yes. But by the end of the evening, she admitted to herself that it had, indeed, been both.

After all the cleaning up was finished, Priscilla assisted Victoria in laying out a makeshift bed for Piers on the settee.

It went without saying that alternate sleeping arrangements were necessary now that there were four of them sharing the residence. Piers had suggested he sleep in the school, but even Priscilla had declared it was too cold, and Victoria had quickly agreed.

God forbid anything happen to Piers. Not because she hated the idea of another failed betrothal but because he was... Piers.

And he was...

Growing on her.

It had been decided that Victoria would sleep in Primm's chamber and Priscilla and Allison would share hers.

"I don't know how to thank you," Victoria smoothed the quilt while Priscilla plumped a pillow. "For cooking and for understanding and for... everything."

Priscilla shrugged. "I don't mind cooking. And I'm glad everyone enjoyed it. But." She met Victoria's stare. "I do understand. At least I think I understand. But do be careful, please? And I saw how you looked after you came in earlier. And I know you're my employer, but I beg of you, please, please promise me that you'll refrain from..." She shifted her stare away from Victoria. "Any additional... well. Allison doesn't need any reminders of what she saw this morning. Of course, it goes without saying that she's going to tell the first person she sees, but the less fodder she has, the better."

Antics.

Victoria knew Priscilla meant well—in fact, the younger woman was justifiably concerned. But the fact that a teacher would have to censure her, *Victoria Shipley,* in such a manner was… humiliating. It was mortifying.

Shame slammed into her.

"I'm sorry, of course you mustn't worry." It was one thing to break the rules while alone—quite another with innocent young ladies under the same roof. "Rest assured, there will be no more *antics.*"

TO THE ABBEY

*V*ictoria stared out the window where Piers rode beside and slightly behind them on Artemisia. Victoria, Priscilla, and Allison were comfortable in the same carriage they'd used to return to the school two days before.

"Primm is certainly going to be surprised to see us," Priscilla announced vaguely, staring out the window from where she rode facing front.

Allison, who sat snoring softly beside Priscilla, had insisted she'd become ill if she weren't facing forward, and so Priscilla and Victoria had agreed to take turns sitting backward.

"I'm not sure whose reaction I'm more worried about—Miss Primm's or Lord Rosewood's parents. I'm not exactly in the blush of youth." Victoria spoke softly so as not to wake the younger girl.

"You're a catch. Don't fool yourself. His parents are likely to jump for joy." Priscilla's words, however, had the opposite effect of what she intended.

Victoria couldn't help remembering the scathing tone

she'd heard in Piers's voice when he'd mentioned how pleased his father would be if Piers were to settle down with *someone like her.*

Yesterday with him had been... incredible. It had been exciting and romantic and festive but... that didn't mean he'd change the way he felt about his father. How was Piers going to feel if they greeted her with open arms?

How was she going to feel if they did not?

When she'd been betrothed to Kingsley, their future together had been planned out in great detail. Where they would live, the duties she would step into. She'd been well acquainted with his mother, both his younger brothers, and of course Priscilla.

She'd known where she would sleep after they married. She'd known that Lord Kingsley was going to do his best to be an attentive husband. They'd decided to fill their nursery in the first year of their marriage.

But with Piers...

She knew nothing.

And too late, she'd realized he hadn't answered her question as to his inclination to travel. He said they would find an estate... Somewhere. But where would they live in the interim?

And she had no idea if he intended to remain in England to help raise their children.

Children!

Victoria settled her arm low on her belly.

The trouble with breaking rules was that while breaking them, consequences seemed...

Inconsequential.

She raised her fist to pound on the ceiling, and just as

the carriage drew to a halt, she pushed open the door, jumped out, and vomited.

THE FIRST TIME the carriage stopped, Piers heeded Miss Fellowes's advice to ride ahead. She had insisted that his fiancée was fine and wouldn't want him to witness her under such embarrassing circumstances.

But by the third time, he pushed the well-meaning teacher aside. Discovering Victoria bent over, he'd held Victoria's scarf out of the way and soothed his other hand along her back.

It was the first time he'd touched her since sending her off to sleep alone the night before, and she leaned into him.

"Travel sickness?" he asked, and she made a slight nod.

"I don't suffer from it." Her voice was low. "Normally."

He squatted down and studied her face, which was parallel to the ground. A few tears lingered on her cheeks, and she held a handkerchief against her mouth. "Could it be something else? Are you ill?" He touched his hand to her forehead but she shook her head.

"Not ill." She spoke just loud enough for him to hear. "Terrified."

"You're nervous?" he asked, and she nodded again. "About meeting my family?"

Piers held back a chuckle, more than a little amused that Miss Victoria Shipley was anxious at the prospect of meeting the Marquess and Marchioness of Starbridge. To offer his reassurance, he pressed his forehead into hers. "They're going to love you."

"That's the trouble. If they love me, how are you going to feel?"

Which had him at a loss until he recalled the harsh words he'd said to her on Christmas Eve: *"You are precisely the sort of gel my father would want me to marry."* Piers had not hidden how he felt about his father.

"Ironic, isn't it?" She parroted his own words back to him.

It was difficult to argue with oneself, especially when it had been his opinion just two days before.

And truth be told, he did, in fact, wish that his engagement wouldn't bring his father such pleasure.

Piers shook his head. "I suppose the joke's on me."

Disappointment flashed across her face so quickly he wondered if he'd imagined it. But he had not. That had not been the proper response for him to make.

"It's not a joke," he corrected himself.

"I know." She rose, shrugging his hand off her back, swiping the linen at her mouth. "I hate that you've seen me like this."

This was the polite Miss Shipley speaking. Propriety demanded a lady be mortified for her betrothed to witness something so base—so primitive.

Nevertheless, if she were ill, he would be the one to comfort her.

He was coming to know this woman's body by heart—every intimate detail—and the only thing about her casting up her accounts that bothered him was her discomfort.

He didn't give her a chance to step back before pulling her into his arms. "Everything is going to be fine. You'll see. I like you well enough. And you like me, don't you?" He dipped his chin to meet her gaze.

She didn't smile, but she wasn't scowling either. "Yes." A dry laugh escaped her. "Unfortunately."

That had been nearly six hours ago.

Piers smoothed a hand over the hair along Artemisia's long neck.

Victoria's nerves had ignited his own uneasiness. Not to mention a real fear that his mother's illness was more than he'd presumed it to be.

Piers shifted in his saddle, pleased to see the Abbey rising in the distance. Torches glowed at the entrance, and lanterns burned in various windows.

Nearly two years had passed since he'd ridden up this drive. He experienced a familiar combination of homecoming and dread.

Typical where his father was concerned. Because, unfortunately, he was going to have to face the man.

But Eli wasn't here anymore. Melancholy joined the cauldron of emotions brewing in his gut.

And guilt.

Because he'd failed to come home in time to say goodbye to Eli. And after, he'd failed to step into his brother's shoes.

No, he hadn't failed; he'd chosen not to.

When he did, *if* he did, it would be on his own terms.

Was his betrothal to Victoria the catalyst? He'd put off marriage, but he'd known he couldn't do so indefinitely. And Piers would always know that Victoria had not been chosen by his father.

Piers had offered for her of his own volition. He'd been obligated by honor, but fulfilling that honor had been his choice.

There was no irate father or brother holding a pistol to his head.

As their entourage drew up to the front of the Abbey, he tugged at the collar of his coat. He was sweating, damnit. Victoria wasn't the only one suffering from nerves.

Piers dismounted and drew the rein over Artemisia's head as he watched his father's stablemaster approach.

"Welcome home, my lord. Is His Lordship aware that you are coming? He did not tell me he was expecting guests." Markey skimmed a glance down the road as the carriage approached.

Piers stretched his arms, leaning back to take in the looming tower of the entrance to what once had been the abbey's nave. The molding still crumbled, and the carvings were in worse disrepair than before he left.

He then rubbed his chest with a clenched fist, already feeling the smothering effect of being in his father's proximity.

"Artemisia's worked hard today. Ensure sure she gets a good rubdown." He handed over the reins, dismissing the man. Piers refused to answer to one of his father's lackies before even stepping across the threshold. Artemisia was warm from the long ride, having only stopped for a few short breaks. "Before the end of the century, Markey."

Being home, as usual, brought out the worst in him. It wasn't the stablemaster's fault that part of his duties included reporting all comings and goings directly to the master of the household.

Piers patted the mare's rump as she walked away, and then approached the ladies' carriage as it drew to a halt.

He didn't wait for a footman but opened the door himself. First out, of course, was Miss Allison Meadowbrook, followed by Miss Fellowes.

Victoria, he guessed, would want to put off facing his family as long as possible.

He leaned in and offered his hand. "How are you?" Although pale, she was looking decidedly better than the last time they'd stopped. Or perhaps it was because she was partially hidden in the shadows.

"Fine."

"Found your courage, I hope?"

Her brown eyes flashed at him. "Of course."

Despite her objections that they hardly knew one another, Piers was coming to understand this woman more than she gave him credit for. He knew her, not from spending days and days in her company, or having hours and hours of conversation, but from something almost... intangible.

He'd felt it even before they'd become intimate—before they'd had sex. It was as though he could feel what she was feeling.

She leaned forward and peered over his shoulder. "Primm described it to me, but I hadn't imagined it would be so imposing."

"It's only a pile of bricks and mortar." And yet, she was right. The abbey had no doubt been intended to strike awe in those who approached.

She caught his eye and raised a brow but ignored his sarcasm. "True, but that pile is, nonetheless, impressive."

He grunted a sort of agreement and then assisted Victoria out, holding her elbow when she landed on the ground.

"Piers!" A familiar voice carried over the wind. At the same time a shaft of light illuminated the area.

Victoria dropped his arm and took a step back.

A grand staircase fanned out from the entrance where the front door had been thrown open. At the top of it stood Liam, his younger brother who was closest to him in age. Damned Liam might very well have been Eli's twin. His resemblance to Eli was more uncanny than Piers had remembered.

Noah stepped through the door behind him, followed by the youngest, Theodore.

The latter two didn't hesitate in skipping down the steps and rushing to greet him. Piers returned their enthusiastic embraces even as he met Liam's stare over their shoulders.

"When Augusta arrived alone, we assumed you weren't coming," Noah said.

"I missed her at the school." But then he frowned. "How is she?" They all knew he wasn't asking about his sister. Although Piers had judged their mother to have failed on many levels, it hadn't stopped him from loving her. She'd demanded more than her fair share of attention, was manipulative and selfish as hell, and yet, she'd endured marriage to their father.

That, and she was his *mother*.

"Weak." Liam frowned. "I wouldn't have written Augusta if I'd thought she was being theatrical."

Piers nodded. Liam wasn't the sort to exaggerate.

"But you haven't come alone?" Theodore, the kindest and gentlest amongst all of them, reminded Piers he had introductions to make. "Of course, leave it to Piers to show up with three beautiful ladies in tow."

Piers moved to make formal introductions before any untoward assumptions were made. When he gestured toward Victoria, a bitterly cold wind gusted along the drive.

"Let's go inside, shall we?" Noah suggested over the wind. "And make introductions out of this cold."

"Not that it's much warmer inside," Theodore added with an apologetic grimace.

The eldest of his brothers pivoted without comment. Whether eager to get out of the cold or simply bored already with the greetings, Piers didn't know, but Liam disappeared inside while Noah offered Victoria his arm. Theodore gestured for Miss Fellowes and Miss Meadowbrook to follow.

Piers stood rooted, taking one last moment of fresh air.

He was home. Why did his arrival have to feel so... complicated?

Victoria had landed a few subtle reprimands for his lack of appreciation for his family. But having been here for five minutes, he recognized his father's influence on Liam.

It was in the arrogance of his bearing—his cold demeanor. The condescension that dripped from his voice.

Would that be the case if Piers hadn't kept himself away for so long? A voice niggled in his mind. But, no, Piers cut off the thought. Because his father would have done his best to pummel those traits into him instead.

Straightening his shoulders, Piers climbed the stairs to enter. Once inside, almost-forgotten memories slammed into his awareness—some bad, but some good as well.

Augusta approached from the end of the lengthy foyer, and seeing her here brought even more nostalgia.

"Piers! You came!" But her brow furrowed when she realized he had not come alone. "Miss Shipley? What...? Has something happened at the school?"

"A goat!" Miss Meadowbrook offered up before anyone else could speak.

"A goat?"

As Victoria and Miss Fellowes explained and updated his sister on the condition of the school that was her life's work, two others arrived to stand beside Augusta. His mother and a younger, familiar young woman.

The mahogany door to the left opened, and his father stepped out.

"Rosewood." Piers didn't turn to answer the clipped, cold voice that never failed to churn his stomach.

"You missed Christmas, but you have come after all." His mother reached out her hands.

This woman, who had been on the plump side for as long as he could remember, was a shadow of her former self. Piers schooled his features to hide his shock. But over the past two years, she'd all but wasted away.

"Mother." He stepped forward.

In the wavering light of the sconces, shadows danced over her hollowed cheeks. Although her dark hair was swept up in the style she'd always favored, her scalp was visible through dull strands that were more silver than brown.

"My dearest Piers," she said. Even her voice, thready-sounding, had weakened. Piers embraced her, something stinging in his chest, and then leaned down so she could kiss both his cheeks. Her shoulders felt brittle and frail beneath his hands. "Liam said you wouldn't come when you heard—that he doubted you would even read your mail. But you are here to make good on the contract, just as I assured him you would."

"So, you are not altogether without honor." Lord Starbridge's voice echoed in the stone foyer, and Piers finally turned to acknowledge the man.

If anything, his father appeared more robust now than when he'd left.

But what contract were they referencing?

Piers sent a questioning look at Liam, who stared back at him as though Piers was the devil himself.

"You've come to reacquaint yourself with your betrothed," his mother said. "Of course you remember Delilah?" She drew the young woman beside her forward.

Lady Delilah—The Earl of Southwick's daughter, and also the woman who had been Eli's betrothed.

Piers froze.

He really ought to have gone through his mail before coming.

BETROTHED? Victoria glanced toward the kind-looking young woman—Delilah.

His betrothed?

Contracts?

Victoria's limbs began to tingle, and a roaring in her head drowned out the conversation.

Standing timidly beside Piers's mother, the young woman reminded Victoria of herself. Not her actual appearance, but the sadness in her eyes, the proud bearing instilled with a sense of humility.

And the uncertainty in her gaze as she stared at Piers when he stepped forward and bowed over her hand.

Piers moved stiffly as he greeted the woman.

When he stepped back, he shot Victoria a glance that held a myriad of emotions.

She's seen a similar expression on Lord Kingsley's face numerous times before he'd expressed his desire to end their betrothal, but she had not recognized it for what it was.

Confusion, guilt, and *regret.*

Victoria stiffened, and the young gentleman who'd escorted her to this point covered her hand with his. At his youthful appearance and gentle demeanor, she guessed him to be Theodore.

She couldn't meet Piers's eyes and dropped her lashes to stare at the granite floor. Primm's curiosity and Allison's smugness prickled her awareness. But it was the pity she felt rolling off Priscilla that reminded her who she was. She straightened her shoulders and lifted her chin.

Primm turned the conversation. "Piers has gallantly escorted my colleagues here to spend the remainder of the holiday, along with one of our students. I understand there are damages at the school, and it would have been a trial for them to reside there until repairs could be made."

Although Primm provided the excuse for their unexpected appearance to her family, when she turned to draw Victoria forward, her narrowed gaze promised that there would be questions later.

When Primm, rather than Piers, made the introductions, the marquess and marchioness were kind but dismissive. Victoria, Priscilla, and Allison might just as well be servants.

"Miss Shipley is the daughter of the late Lord Whitley," Primm provided. "And Miss Fellowes is the Earl of Kingsley's sister."

"I am not without connections, either." Miss Meadowbrook lifted her chin.

"But of course you are not." Lady Starbridge murmured before catching the eye of the most formidable of all the servants lined up against the corridor's stone wall. "Have Mrs. Snead prepare three guest chambers at once."

"Only two will be necessary. I will share with Miss Meadowbrook," Priscilla spoke up.

The marchioness nodded.

"Have all of you eaten dinner?" Primm asked.

"We stopped at an inn several hours ago." Again, it was Priscilla who answered.

"In that case," Lady Starbridge addressed the butler again. "Trays must be sent up at once." The older woman swayed slightly, and Primm rushed to her mother's side.

"I'll handle everything, Mama. You shouldn't be standing out here in the cold."

A maid rushed over to join them. "Lady Augusta is quite right, my lady." The maid agreed with Primm even as she placed an arm around the frail marchioness.

Victoria met Priscilla's gaze in surprise. They had known Primm was the daughter of a marquess, but no one had ever addressed her as a lady. It was…

Disquieting.

"Rosewood." The marquess had his gaze pinned on Piers, obviously annoyed by such trivial details. "We have much to discuss."

Piers made to move toward Victoria but she stepped back, shaking her head. Now was not the time for their announcement. In fact, she wasn't sure they ought to make one at all.

His mother was happy to see him, as were at least two of his brothers.

This was his homecoming, and she had no wish to increase the strain between him and his family.

This was *his family.*

While Lady Starbridge was being led away, Primm gestured toward a door opposite to where Lord Starbridge had appeared. "The four of us can take tea while your chambers are prepared." With a nod, she dismissed the line of servants who then meekly scurried away.

The marquess, along with Piers's three brothers, disappeared into what was presumably his study.

Piers caught Victoria's hand before she could follow Primm, and for the moment, anyhow, the two of them were, incredibly, alone.

"*I didn't know.*" He squeezed her hand and stared down at her. His eyes looked tired, but there was no mistaking the sincerity behind them. "Lady Delilah. She was my brother's betrothed. But..." He ran his other hand through his hair. "This is the first I've heard of any contracts."

"Then don't say anything about us tonight," Victoria said. "Just listen. Don't make any decisions."

This was his family.

"No." He didn't hesitate. "I need to set this straight."

"Please, Piers. Just wait. Let me speak with Primm first. You and I will talk in the morning. Your mother is happy for now..." She'd looked so pleased that he'd returned.

A bleak expression darkened his face. "She doesn't look well."

But Lady Starbridge hadn't hidden the affection she had for Delilah. A woman she'd been denied once already as a daughter-in-law.

"Wait until morning, Piers, please?"

Suddenly, Victoria wasn't sure about anything. Both of his parents were alive. And although they both had faults, they were his *mother and father.* He had brothers! He was the heir. He was the oldest.

He had responsibilities, but most of all, he had *family.*

And that girl… Lady Delilah. She had expectations. Had the young woman's wedding been postponed more than once? Victoria understood all too well what it felt like when a betrothal ended—like the world had flipped upside down.

Piers's mother had said there was a *contract.*

"Miss Shipley?" Primm peered out from the drawing room, and Victoria guiltily shook off Piers's hand.

"I'm coming." She stepped away from Piers, backing toward her friend.

"Please wait," she mouthed to Piers, but he only tightened his jaw in response.

COLD FEET

*A*lthough a fire burned in the hearth of the drawing room, the high ceilings and large windows kept the room from feeling much warmer than the foyer had.

Priscilla and Allison huddled together on a high-backed velvet settee, still wearing their coats.

Victoria took the space beside Allison before Primm lowered herself into the chair that faced them.

"Tell me." Primm looked rather fierce. "Is my school still standing? Has it burned to the ground? I want all of the details."

Victoria shook her head. "It was a goat who broke in. Not marauders."

"Truly?" Worry strained her friend's features.

"A few broken windows and holes in walls. An over-turned desk and more than one steaming pile, which I'm sure Mr. Driver has already taken care of. But the school is intact." Victoria schooled her features to be as reassuring as possible. "Truly."

At that, Primm exhaled a loud breath and then scrubbed

her hand down her face. "Not that I'm not happy to see the three of you. But if the school's condition isn't that bad, then why have you come? Is one of you in trouble?" Her gaze landed on Allison, specifically.

But now that Victoria was getting a good look at her friend, she realized that Primm looked less than herself.

"How are *you*?" Victoria unintentionally deflected.

Beneath Primm's ever-present spectacles, Victoria noticed dark circles. And her mouth was more pinched than usual.

Primm closed her eyes, and when she opened them, she had regained her composure. "Much better. Now that Piers is here. Delilah has cared diligently for our mother in my absence. Mother was starting to become frantic that he wouldn't come."

"But what about—?" Allison began but Victoria dropped her hand on the girl's knee before she said anything about what had happened before they'd left the school. When the girl turned to her with a frown, Victoria squeezed.

Very hard.

"Lord Rosewood was not aware," Victoria said. "Of the nature of your mother's illness, or… about an arrangement with Lady Delilah." Indeed he would have told Victoria if he had been! Wouldn't he?

Primm made a face. "He must have suspected. A union between ours and Lady Delilah's family has been planned for decades. Her father was killed just before Eli passed— and her mother died years before. We are all she has left. Now that Piers is Rosewood, upholding the contract is his responsibility. A wedding between the two of them is just what our family needs to… heal." She made a sad smile.

"Perhaps it is what my mother needs to return to good health."

So much show of emotion was quite out of the ordinary for the school headmistress.

Priscilla's and Allison's concerned gazes made Victoria squirm.

"Does, she—does Lady Delilah love Piers?" This was important. *This mattered.*

"She doesn't know him, really. But I think she is just the sort of wife he needs. She'll make few demands on him but be supportive. I already think of her as a sister. We all have for years."

Victoria's heart skipped a beat. "There is something you must know."

At this, Primm's brows rose, and she once again appeared every inch the stern school director.

"We did not come here because of the damages to the school. We could have just as well stayed back at the residence." Victoria thought her next words out very carefully. "But we came because… Your brother arrived the night of your departure. He was injured and the storm… I couldn't turn him away."

"Of course you couldn't."

"I had hoped I could nurse him back to health and have him on his way without anyone being the wiser, but even if the storm had passed quickly, he really was quite ill…" Victoria allowed her gaze to drift sideways to Allison and Priscilla. "Miss Fellowes and Miss Meadowbrook arrived, and then he was seen by Mr. Driver."

"And—" Allison attempted to speak again. Victoria squeezed the girl's knee with all her might.

"How long?" Primm's hard swallow was visible. "How long were you alone with him?"

"Long enough." Before Victoria lost her courage, she leaned forward. "I know what this could do to the school's reputation. As does your brother."

Primm nodded slowly.

"He was willing to marry me, Primm," Victoria said. "But—"

"That would ruin everything with Delilah." Primm could not have sounded more disappointed.

"He needn't go through with it. I'll tender my resignation. It's not as though I'll be destitute," Victoria said.

"What would I do without you, though?" Victoria could already see her friend's mind hard at work.

"We haven't a choice. Look at what happened when the circumstances of Miss Jones's birth got around." Nearly half the parents had threatened to pull their daughters out of the school. Victoria and Primm had had no choice but to fire the young woman.

Which, in the long run, turned out fine for Miss Jones, who had been hired to teach French and Latin. She had since become the Duchess of Bedwell.

"I don't want to lose you, Victoria." Primm turned to address both Allison and Priscilla. "Don't mention a word of this to anyone until we speak again in the morning." At their stunned expressions, she added, "Is that understood?"

Primm's uncompromising authority had both of them nodding.

Was it possible that Miss Meadowbrook could be induced to keep quiet? For a few seconds, Victoria very nearly believed she could. But...

Mrs. Driver knew.

Parents relied on the school's stellar reputation. There was no way Victoria could stay on in the wake of this sort of scandal.

"Pardon me, my lady." A maid appeared at the door. "We have a chamber readied for the two ladies now. If they're prepared to be shown up."

Priscilla glanced at Victoria, who nodded. "It has been a very long day. And I, for one, long for nothing more than changing into my nightclothes and some of that dinner promised by the marchioness," Priscilla said. "Come along, Allison."

The younger girl did not argue, and they both followed the maid out of the parlor. When the door closed behind them, Victoria slumped a little in relief.

But Primm, it seemed, wasn't finished asking questions. She leaned forward, her hands draped together over her knees. "You spent four nights alone with my brother?"

"Yes. Miss Fellowes and Miss Meadowbrook arrived on Christmas Day." Victoria hated that her voice shook.

She'd been terribly nervous about meeting Piers's parents and brothers, but once the shock of having to marry him wore off, she'd experienced an unexpected disappointment.

She'd actually been looking forward to winning them over. An ache cramped her chest, and her head felt heavy. How naïve of her to imagine such a possibility!

"I sewed up the wound on his arm—if you can imagine that." Victoria met Primm's gaze. "I realized after you left that I'm rather clueless when it comes to taking care of myself. Without any servants, that is…"

"I'm well aware of this." Her friend dipped her chin in agreement. "That's part of why I was so reluctant to leave you alone. But I knew you could always turn to the Drivers for help if need be."

"I managed, though." With Piers's help. She'd been so proud of those simple little achievements, but in light of all the upheaval she'd caused, they suddenly seemed relatively insignificant.

"Four nights alone with my brother." Primm watched Victoria carefully.

This part was very tricky. "Yes. He was burning up with fever initially."

"And after? I know Piers, and he isn't one to be felled by any sort of sickness for long."

"No." Victoria recalled his determination to make himself useful even though, in her opinion, he'd narrowly escaped death.

A knock sounded, and Victoria was permitted a slight reprieve while a different maid entered carrying a tray of tea.

The aroma was almost enough to soothe Victoria's wounded spirits.

Almost.

Primm poured and fixed both cups. After handing Victoria one of them, she asked, "Did anything… untoward happen? If so, then…" She frowned. "That would over-shadow his responsibility to Lady Delilah."

Victoria stalled by taking a sip of the strong, hot drink. This was her opportunity to confess all to Primm.

"He was the perfect gentleman. There is no reason for me to hold him to it." Victoria would speak with Allison—offer whatever she could to keep the girl quiet until matters were settled between Piers and…

Lady Delilah.

"Thank God," Primm exhaled. "Of course you wouldn't do something so foolish as to allow my brother to compromise you…" She stared over her cup at Victoria. "I'd have had to strangle him if that was the case."

Victoria hadn't *allowed* Piers to compromise her. On the contrary, she'd all but *begged him to.*

Victoria took another swallow of tea, hoping Primm wouldn't notice her shaking hands.

"I'll go away to London."

"Let's not decide anything yet." Primm set her cup and saucer back onto the tray and rubbed her hands together. "Perhaps the school can weather this. It's not as though you could have sent him away. All you did was save a gentleman in peril. And I thank you for that. I'm not sure what I'd do if something happened to Piers. Idiot that he is, he's a lovable idiot." Primm smiled almost apologetically. "As I'm sure you've realized."

Lovable? Stinging burned the backs of Victoria's eyes. "Er, yes."

Her friend appeared more confident now. "Furthermore, I've heard from more than one parent that they regretted signing the petition demanding I sack Miss Jones last year—what with her being a duchess and all now."

"But Miss Meadowbrook isn't likely to—"

"It's not as though they found the two of you in bed together." Primm laughed, blinking at her own joke. "Really, I cannot afford to lose you as my etiquette teacher. Not to mention, you're more successful at attracting donors than anyone else."

But the truth was going to come out eventually. Victoria didn't know how she could face her friend when it did.

"I'll speak with Piers. Or, if you'd prefer, the three of us can discuss a plan tomorrow morning. No doubt, after meeting with my father tonight… He's in with my father now!"

"It's all right," Victoria said. "At least, I think it is. I asked him not to say anything until tomorrow."

"Good thinking. Now, what would I do without you? You're the most level-headed person I know." Primm tilted her head thoughtfully. "Aside from myself, that is."

"I should leave," Victoria announced. "First thing in the morning."

"You mean return to the school?" Primm didn't contradict her, but sat thoughtfully for a moment. "Piers isn't going to be pleased to break his promise to you, so I understand how it might be awkward for you." Genuine concern was evident in Primm's voice. "Let's wait until tomorrow to make any decisions, though."

"I just think it would be for the best." Victoria couldn't bear coming between Piers and his family. He would make this difficult for everyone. How would that affect his mother's health? Not to mention his relationship with his sister—Victoria's dearest friend.

And Piers himself had said marriage wasn't their only option.

"I can take the carriage we traveled in today, and Miss Fellowes and Miss Meadowbrook can return with you later. No reason for the two of them to turn around again."

"I feel terrible about it. Let's speak with Piers first."

"No." Victoria clutched her hands in her lap. "This is too important. Your family is at stake here." This might be their only opportunity to come together again.

In a startling realization, Victoria understood why she'd been so nervous about coming here. A part of her had hoped that her appearance as Piers's fiancée would help him reunite with them.

And in the deepest part of her heart, she'd hoped to become... one of them.

Delilah is like a sister to me, Primm had said.

"I'll go at dawn." Victoria stared into the giant hearth. "Please, tell Piers what we've decided. And then you and I can revisit my resignation when the holidays are over."

"You don't have to—"

"It's for the best." Victoria's bones ached from today's journey—from being jostled for hours, but also from casting up her accounts. Now that she knew the outcome, all she wanted to do was curl up beneath a pile of blankets and sleep forever. "Tell the others that I'm... tell them whatever you wish." She was exhausted.

"You are quite certain? I could send Miss Fellowes and Miss Meadowbrook with you—"

"I'm certain. They've traveled more than me, what with having returned from London early."

Primm kept silent for nearly half a minute, and Victoria hoped she didn't require an explanation as to why they'd come back early.

But she must have decided now was not the time.

"I'll inform Coachman John of your decision so he can be ready in the morning." She lowered her chin, effectively forcing Victoria to meet her gaze—and inadvertently reminding her of Piers. "If come morning you've changed your mind, we'll meet with my brother together."

Victoria was not going to change her mind. "Thank you."

ANTICS

*P*rimm showed Victoria to the room that had been readied for her. And although she stayed for a few moments, looking uncertain, she seemed relieved to take her leave when a maid arrived with dinner.

Victoria wasn't really hungry, but she forced herself to take a few bites of the meal.

That had been hours ago.

Huddled now beneath the thick quilt in the giant bed provided for her, Victoria lay awake. Whenever she closed her eyes, all she saw was his face. All she heard was his laugh.

How was that possible? She'd barely known him a week.

Even with a fire burning in the hearth across the room, she hadn't warmed up. One would have thought the thick stone walls of the abbey would provide adequate insulation against the cold.

Instead, they seemed to do just the opposite.

The single curtainless window rattled from across the

room, and Victoria was certain the wind penetrated right through the glass.

When she heard the door creaking open, she was wide awake.

"Priscilla?" She sat up.

Not Priscilla, but the silhouette of an all-too-dear gentleman.

Piers.

"You need to go," she said, denying the urge to draw the covers back and invite him to join her.

He closed the door behind him and crossed to the bed. Knowing she might never see him again, she drank in the sight of him—of his walk, the tilt of his head, the way his hair tended to stand on end.

He was still dressed in the clothes he'd worn that day, and as he stepped into the slant of silver moonlight, there was no missing the tension around his mouth.

She didn't protest when, instead of leaving, he bent over to remove his boots. And after he wrestled his arms out of his jacket, Victoria didn't stop him from joining her beneath the heavy quilt.

His body was cold beside hers at first. But after a minute of cuddling, that warmth she'd longed for all day finally eased into her bones.

"You didn't tell them, did you?" she whispered, breaking the tired silence.

She felt him shake his head. When he spoke, his chest moved beneath her cheek. "What a mess. We never should have come." And yet, she knew he didn't really mean that.

"But your mother..." She was not well. If he hadn't come, he might never have seen her alive again.

"I'll tell them in the morning. The longer they go on believing—"

"You should marry her," Victoria spoke as though it was only a suggestion. "You mustn't feel bound by me—"

He cut her off with a kiss that was more violent than tender. When he drew back, both of them were breathing heavily.

He pressed his forehead into hers. "I hate this, Victoria. I hate him."

"But you love your mother."

"And she'll love you—"

"Or she'll hate me."

"They'll have no choice but to move beyond their plans and accept what I want." He sounded fierce but also... tormented.

She was right in her decision to leave without telling him. Because if she stayed, he might not let her go.

Because he needed her? She wouldn't be enough. He needed his brothers—he needed to make peace with his parents. The marquessate was *his legacy.* He would one day be Starbridge.

"They are your family," she reminded him. "The cornerstone of your existence." Victoria, more than anyone, knew what it felt like to live without that. "Your mother is frail."

"Don't." His arms tightened around her and he buried his face in her neck. "If I'm going to marry anyone, it's going to be you. We decided—you and I."

Victoria ran her fingers through his hair, torn and more confused than ever.

Why did her decision to leave hurt so much? Was it because their all-too-brief engagement had allowed a little light to shine on the dreams she'd abandoned years before?

Or was there more to it?

She didn't want Piers to estrange himself from his family. He was a good man—a sensitive man—and he loved his brothers more than he wanted to let on.

He'd lost Eli, and now they stood to lose their mother as well. He needed his brothers. And they would need him.

Primm would need him.

It shouldn't matter that every nerve in her body craved him. She crushed the desire to wrap her legs around his waist.

I need him.

"You can't stay in here." She waged a war with the part of her that wanted to insist the opposite.

A part that involved all of her body and a good portion of her heart.

He soothed her sides, the backs of her legs. And with each stroke of his hands, her resolve melted away.

"I need you, Victoria." In all the times they'd been together, he'd never indicated feeling anything more than physical desire for her. He'd said she was beautiful. He'd said she was perfect. But even when he'd proposed, he'd never admitted to anything other than *liking* her.

But tonight…

He *needed* her.

His mouth claimed hers again. Rough but, unlike his last kiss, this one was desperate… And as he found solace in her arms, that desperation melted into an odd… peace.

Victoria trailed kisses over his face—along the length of his jaw, over the coarse texture of his whiskers, cradling his jaw as she did so.

And when he settled between her legs, nothing in the world could have convinced her to send him away.

Because this joining was more than any lesson in lovemaking. It was more than the unexpected pleasure of passion.

It was goodbye.

She watched his face as he rocked above her—noticing every crease, every expression—and memorizing them.

"Victoria," he whispered. "My angel." He hovered over her, his arms shaking from holding himself up.

How could she live without this?

She pushed the thought away. She was his, for now—he was hers. She tightened her legs around his waist and pulled him closer. And unable to bear her own emotions, she closed her eyes.

His arms collapsed and the pace of their joining increased.

Allowing her other senses to take over, she absorbed every sensation—the sounds of his breath, steady as his body moved in and out of hers—the painful pleasure from the stretching and stroking as she invited him deeper.

Her urgency increased and he matched it. "Piers, please."

The world spun out of control, her soul cracked and although she felt as though she was falling, she was not afraid to land, she relinquished her heart and completion consumed her.

Afterward, Victoria burrowed into him, lingering in the comfort of his embrace and never wanting to let go.

But morning would come all too soon and the house would come awake early.

"You need to go," she finally told him.

"I know." He caught her lips and, after a thoroughly tender kiss, drew back. "I'm going to marry you."

"Get some sleep," was all she said, trailing her hand down his arm and grasping his fingers.

"Goodnight, Victoria." He squeezed and then relinquished her hand.

After he'd quietly exited her chamber, Victoria huddled into the warmth of the mattress, inhaling his scent—imprinting the memory so she would never forget.

But she didn't cry.

Her life was on the precipice of significant changes. Changes she'd never imagined. She'd done this once before, when she'd agreed to break her former betrothal.

It had been the most challenging thing she'd ever done. And now, she found herself doing it again.

She would survive, but she was going to need all her strength to get through it.

And yet sleep never came.

When the black of the night sky turned dark blue on the eastern horizon, she quietly climbed out of bed and changed back into the wool gown she'd traveled in the day before. Then, wooden inside and trying not to shiver from the cold, she packed up her valise, shrugged into her coat, and after one last look at the bed, tiptoed to the door. She was lucky to make only one wrong turn before locating the stairs and then the foyer that led to the entrance.

"Coachman John is outside waiting for you." The butler stepped out from the wall, causing her to jump.

Thankfully, she would not need to go searching for the driver in the bitterly cold morning. This part of leaving, anyhow, was going to be easier than she imagined.

The stoic servant opened the door and waited.

"Thank you." She stepped outside and onto the front

step and jumped a second time when the door behind her snapped closed.

The horizon had turned a lighter color of blue, and the air itself might have been frozen. She glanced up at the majestic structure behind her. It wasn't all that hard to imagine nuns hiding from the world inside.

Was she doing the right thing? She'd truly made a mess of her life and, unfortunately, involved people other than herself.

Along with the school.

Her leaving like this was best for all of them.

So why did it feel like she was running away?

Coachman John approached, his eyes peering from beneath his hat and over the scarf wound around his neck and face. "Miss Primm asked me to ask if you had changed your mind."

Had she?

No.

"I have not."

He nodded. "Have a care not to burn yourself on the brick," he warned as he opened the door and then lowered the step for her to climb in.

"Thank you." She climbed through the door, but before he could close it, she held out a hand. "But we aren't going back to the school," she informed him.

His brows shot up.

"I need to go to London," she added. "I want to go to my aunt's home, to London, please."

This particular coachman had delivered her to her aunt's for the holidays more than once. "Very well, Miss Shipley." He closed the door, and seconds later, the carriage rocked as he climbed onto the driver's box.

Driving away from the abbey, Victoria held her breath—half-expecting Piers to come out and stop her, or Primm, or even Priscilla.

She must be delirious from not having slept.

Only after the abbey disappeared in the darkness did she settle her feet on the hot brick, unfold the heavy lap blanket, and slump into the seat for her journey.

Her life at Miss Primm's was over, but that was only part of why her heart was breaking. She could establish a meaningful existence in Mayfair, but there was something else she could never replace.

Not something, she corrected herself. *Someone.*

"YOU'RE UP EARLY, AUGGIE," Piers acknowledged his sister as she crept into the morning room. With the full sun shining through the windows, this was likely the warmest any chamber in the abbey ever was.

"I've been up for three hours now." Pouring herself a cup of tea, his sister attempted to daunt him with the same tone she no doubt used on her students.

It didn't work with him, of course.

He wrapped his hands around his half-empty cup of coffee. "I'm not marrying Delilah—"

"She left."

"Delilah left?"

"Miss Shipley," his sister clarified. "Miss Shipley is gone."

He blinked. What the devil was she talking about?

"She departed for the school this morning," Auggie added in a gentler tone.

But that made no sense at all. Piers rubbed his chin, watching her. "I'm going to marry her," he said. "Victoria."

His sister was shaking her head. "She asked that I inform you that she's changed her mind. She cannot bear the thought of giving up her freedom. She doesn't want to give up her career." Auggie held up a hand. "I know you want to protect her, Piers, but she'll have all the protection she needs with the backing of the school."

"You mean from you? Did you send her away? Damnit—"

"I asked her to stay here but she insisted on going."

"But I…" He frowned. Victoria had said nothing last night. In fact, she'd welcomed him most enthusiastically. And they'd not done much talking.

No, she'd vaguely suggested that they abort their plans. She'd suggested he ought to marry Delilah for his family's sake. But when he'd refused, she'd not argued the point.

Even now, the vivid recollection of their lovemaking sent flames licking through his veins.

"When? When did she tell you this?" he asked.

"Shortly after all of you arrived. While you were in with Father."

That heat turned cold as he considered what his sister was telling him. Victoria had already known she was going to leave when they'd made love in her chamber.

One last rule to break? A final fling? It hadn't felt like that.

He'd been too caught up in his own troubles to pay attention.

His sister set her cup onto its saucer. "You may not realize it now, Piers, but you need this family. Even Victoria recognized that. By marrying Delilah, you can begin patching things up with Father—and even Liam, Noah, and Theodore. And nothing would make Mother happier. They need you to take the reins away from him. You're the only one who can put an end to Father's... ways. Don't use my school as an excuse to turn your back on us."

"Your school?"

"I can protect Miss Shipley. Even if she has to leave the school, we'll both weather this. So you needn't feel compelled to marry her, Piers."

Piers stared down at his fists, clenched where they rested on the table. "It isn't a matter of honor." For all intents and purposes, he had no doubt Victoria could protect herself. "But I'm going to marry Victoria."

It ought to be a matter of honor. He'd more than dishonored her in the physical sense. But that wasn't what compelled him now.

"Why would you pursue this, then? To embarrass Father?"

"It has nothing to do with Father." The truth swept in like the afternoon sun.

"Then what, Piers?" Auggie's mouth turned down as she leaned forward. And then her jaw dropped. "Surely, you don't—"

"I love her."

Silence.

His own words shook him. He *loved* her. Feelings from the night before welled up in his heart. His chest swelled and the truth of what he wanted clicked into place.

He loved her. The concept had just taken a while to catch up with him.

But he did.

I love Victoria Shipley.

It didn't matter how, when, or why. He just did.

"But you can't!" His sister threw her arms into the air at the same time the door opened.

"He can't what?"

Delilah stood in the opening and glanced between the two of them. She was very pretty and very sweet. Some might consider her beautiful.

But none of that mattered.

Because she wasn't Victoria.

"Sit down, Delilah." He gestured toward the chair. "We need to talk."

A NEW BEGINNING

*A*lthough Victoria had not closed her aunt's townhouse, she'd only kept a skeleton staff employed—one manservant and the housekeeper, an elderly lady, Mrs. Dinkers, who'd worked for her aunt longer than Victoria had been alive.

But the door was locked and if not for Coachman John's persistent knocking, Victoria wondered how long she would have been ignored, standing in the rain, locked out of her own residence. When Martin, the lone footman, finally did open the door, she stepped into the foyer which could not have been cleaned since before the funeral. A thick layer of dust covered the pedestal and statue to her right, the molding, and the ordinarily gleaming balustrade.

But the most noticeable of all was the musty odor that hung in the air. She climbed the stairs, astonished that Mrs. Dinkers had allowed circumstances to come to this.

And when she entered the parlor where she'd spent so many nights sitting with her aunt, the room felt nearly as cold as the chamber she'd slept in at Starbridge Abbey.

"I'll lay a fire if you like," Martin offered.

"Thank you. But would you first inform Mrs. Dinkers that I have arrived?"

Martin rubbed his forearm across his mouth and then dropped his gaze. "Mrs. Dinkers is, er, indisposed."

That was the moment Victoria caught sight of what had once been her aunt's liquor cabinet. It had been fully stocked when Victoria was last there, but the doors had been left open, and the shelves held what appeared to be mostly empty decanters.

"I would have made more preparations," the young man apologized. "We weren't expecting you."

"I can see that," Victoria murmured. She drew a line in the dust along the table set behind the settee. Before leaving town in August, she'd left instructions and provisions for all the furniture to be covered for protection.

Numb, she exited the parlor, disheartened by the disheveled state of her aunt's lovely townhouse. It was the middle of the day, and a housekeeper with any conscience at all would be anxious to greet her employer.

Victoria turned to Martin. "Where is she?"

The young manservant twisted his mouth into a grimace. "Sleeping."

Victoria raised her brows. "Is she ill?"

He shook his head.

But when Victoria turned toward the stairs to make her way up to the servants' quarters, Martin's voice stopped her. "You will find her in… the mistress's suite, Miss Shipley."

Victoria inhaled through her nostrils, pinching her lips together.

Ten minutes later, she'd given the woman her notice. And although she'd ordered the woman out of her aunt's once-lovely suite, she hadn't the heart to send her packing into the cold. The weather outside was dismal, wet and muddy, and the housekeeper's drunk and slovenly state wasn't conducive to surviving under such conditions.

After the confrontation, Victoria stood at the top of the stairs, feeling extraordinarily…

Displaced.

"Do you plan to stay, Miss Shipley?" She hadn't realized Coachman John had remained waiting for her in the entrance foyer.

Victoria bit her bottom lip, staring down at him. "I'll need to hire staff." Her eyes met the coachman's knowing ones, and his pitying look was nearly her undoing. She'd held herself together for the entire journey, but now…

She'd known, practically speaking, of course, that the townhouse would be empty. But at that moment, the pain of losing her aunt struck her acutely. Standing in that foyer, exhausted through and through, she had never felt more alone.

"Can I send a note to the agency for you? No one will miss me at the school if I don't return right away."

Victoria forced herself to focus on Coachman John's words.

He was not needed back at the school because there would be no one to drive for a few weeks.

Primm and Priscilla, and even Allison, would be celebrating Piers's engagement and possibly even planning for a wedding.

Because Lady Delilah was like *a sister to Primm*.

Victoria dipped her chin, hating that she felt bitter for something so petty. "If you wouldn't mind. The sooner I interview candidates, the sooner I can..." *Move on with my life? Forget about teaching?*

Pretend her heart hadn't splintered into a million pieces?

She pictured her heart shattered like the pieces of her aunt's nativity statuettes. How long would it take to sweep it up?

"I'll tend to the horses first and then go right over."

"Of course." The horses would need a thorough rubdown. "And John?" She reached out, faltering to address him with such familiarity. "Thank you."

He tipped his hat and nodded, and then the helpful manservant, who was her last tie to Miss Primm's Private Seminary for the Education of Ladies, disappeared out the door.

Which was a ridiculously dramatic thought. He wasn't leaving London yet. She rubbed both hands down her face.

Sleep. She'd feel more like herself if she could get some sleep.

Instinctively, she dragged her feet until she arrived at the room that had always been hers. She was grateful to discover that Martin had deposited her belongings there.

The furnishings in this room, at least, had been adequately covered.

The hearth sat empty, but she was too tired to do anything about it. Instead, she tore the large sheet off her bed. But, of course, it had been stripped bare.

At least she didn't need to go searching for linens, which were kept in the chest at the foot of the bed.

She would come up with a plan. Make a list. Set goals for herself.

Tomorrow.

She mentally broke down some of the challenges ahead.

First, she must hire a staff. But she also needed to contact her man of business and advise him of the changes she'd made. With her inheritance from her aunt, and the wages she'd been saving, she had more than enough money. She'd need to make a withdrawal, however, if she were going to live in London.

Tomorrow. She would consider all these things tomorrow.

Moving around with an unusual weight of melancholy, Victoria forced her arms and legs to make the bed, piling on all three of the quilts she'd found in the chest.

She would write to Priscilla and Lord and Lady Kingsley and let them know she was here. And the few of her aunt's acquaintances who resided in London throughout the year.

But not until she was settled.

The thought of talking to people and making explanations for her departure from the school was too much to bear.

More tired by the second, Victoria removed her coat and half-boots with fingers that were numb from the cold. Then, still wearing the gown she'd traveled in, she climbed beneath the covers.

If she wasn't so tired, she mused, she would cry. But the instant she closed her eyes, exhaustion took over. And for the first time since she'd arrived at Starbridge Abbey three days before, she was finally able to sleep—not nap, or nod off for ten or fifteen minutes at a time, but fall into a sleep that was deep, heavy, and, thankfully, dreamless.

Time ceased to have any meaning. She'd open her eyes and notice that it was dark outside or that the sun had come up again. But then she'd roll over and succumb to unconsciousness.

All her life, she'd gone through her days following a strict schedule. She never slept in.

The mattress absorbed her boneless form. This was her life. Sleep, cold, and… nothing else.

And she might have gone right on sleeping if not for the sounds of male voices outside the door.

"It's been two days." A young man—familiar.

Where was she?

Her chamber at her aunt's townhouse.

Not her aunt's. Hers. She had come to London. Alone.

And the voice belonged to Martin, the footman.

Go away.

But the door flew open.

"Miss Shipley."

She had no choice but to peel her eyes open.

Coachman John stood at the foot of her bed, cap in hand, brows furrowed, and shuffling his feet. Upon seeing that she was awake, he lifted his chin. "When Miss Primm instructed me to drive you, she also charged me with your safety and wellbeing. Are you ill? Do I need to send for a doctor?"

Was she ill?

She was weak, and… thirsty. But she was not ill. She licked her lips, which were dry and a little cracked. "I'm not ill." Her voice sounded more like a croak than anything human.

"You have an applicant waiting downstairs. Two more will be arriving shortly."

"Applicant?" Victoria pushed her hair out of her eyes.

"To replace Mrs. Dinkers." The coachman's voice wavered between concern and disappointment. Anyone who'd known her before this had every right to be disappointed.

"Will you hire the best one for me?" She wasn't ready to face the world. She just wanted to go back to sleep.

"That, I'm afraid, Miss Shipley, is not within the realms of my expertise."

Victoria buried her face in the pillow. He was going to be stubborn.

"Pardon me if I'm out of line. I don't know what happened with those people at that abbey, but you are a better person than this. You are *Miss Shipley, Assistant Director of Miss Primm's Private Seminary for the Education of Ladies.*"

Victoria groaned.

"Come on now. You need to eat and move around. You'll feel better after, mark my words."

What had her life fallen to that she was being reprimanded by the coachman?

And yet, he was the only person at the moment who cared.

No one else even knew where she was. A coachman and a clueless manservant were the only two people in the world who would know if she lived or died.

That was the thought that jolted her awake.

She nodded slowly and then licked her lips, her tongue nearly as dry. "Would you mind asking Martin to send up some water for me to clean up? And tea?"

"I'll fetch the tea myself, Miss." Coachman John sounded more than a little relieved. "And I've a fire burning in the parlor."

"Thank you." Before she could apologize for her slovenly behavior, he'd already disappeared.

An hour later, after washing up with some very cold lavender water, dressing in a clean but wrinkled gown, and twisting her hair into a neat knot at the back of her head, she felt slightly more herself.

The fire blazing in the hearth in the parlor made her feel even better. While she'd been asleep, someone had cleaned it.

She inhaled. She could do this. She could go on.

But the ache in her heart remained. How long was she going to have to live with it?

Coachman John came up behind her. "Are you ready to proceed with the interviews? Do you need a few more minutes?"

Victoria shook herself. She was going to make it a priority to provide this gentleman with a well-deserved sizeable bonus. He had, indeed, gone above and beyond his duties.

"I'm ready now, thank you."

Two hours later, Victoria had hired a new housekeeper, a butler, an additional footman, a cook, and three maids—one for the kitchens, one for the upstairs, and one who would do a little of both.

And last but not least, she hired a lady's maid for herself.

Her initial inclination had been to keep the staff to a minimum, but that would only mean more work for those she hired. Since she could easily afford to pay the wages, she hired all the applicants she liked, sending only one of them away—a young man who had reeked of gin.

Victoria glanced up from her list to see Coachman John standing in the open door of the parlor. "He was the last of them, Miss Shipley."

"Thank you. I imagine you're anxious to return to the school." Her throat felt thick at the thought.

She'd hired servants to staff the house, but she didn't really know any of them.

Coachman John was familiar—and trustworthy.

"Indeed. There will be work waiting for me there." But she sensed he wouldn't leave until he trusted she wouldn't retreat to her chamber again.

"Students will be returning soon," she said. Another pang of loss. She wouldn't be there to greet them—to hear all their news from their brief holidays. Victoria stiffened her back. "Will you thank Miss Primm for me? And tell her that I am well-settled here?"

He studied her for a moment, and then nodded. "I'll be on my way, then, Miss. Best of luck to you." He took a step back.

"Thank you. For everything."

"It was my pleasure."

Then the last familiar face from her old life walked out the front door, leaving her truly alone in the middle of Mayfair to forge a new beginning.

She set her mind to the future. There was plenty to keep her busy. If her mind were focused on bringing the house back to order, then she wouldn't have time to dwell on what she'd lost.

Specifically, a most impertinent gentleman who'd wheedled his way into her affections.

She couldn't dwell on the fact that this broken engagement, unlike the first, had actually broken her heart.

Ironic, in that it had lasted for all of forty-eight hours.

Rather than return upstairs to her chamber, Victoria descended the stairs to the kitchen. Upon inspecting the larder, she found cheese and dried bread to eat while making up a list of needed supplies.

Her new housekeeper, butler, and cook would return to begin work the following day, and the others the day after.

Which meant that she was mostly going to have to fend for herself for a few more days, anyway.

But this time, she wasn't clueless.

And when she fell into bed that night, her room was warm from the fire she had laid out. The water she cleaned herself with was water she'd fetched herself, and the tea and egg and cheese bread tasted all the better for having cooked it on her own.

But despite her successes of the day, when she slid under the covers that night, Victoria buried her face in her pillow and finally allowed the tears to come.

Her heart physically pained her. If she hadn't known what it felt like to have a broken heart before, she certainly did now.

She missed the way his whiskers scratched her cheeks and jaw, the teasing look in his eyes whenever he'd caught her staring at him.

The comfort of his hand on hers. His laughter.

The list went on and on.

How was it that she missed him even more than she missed the school?

CONFRONTATIONS

*T*he Marquess of Starbridge slammed his fist onto the desk.

"Liam isn't the heir, by God! This is an abomination! It's an insult to the ancestors who've held the marquessate together for centuries!"

Piers, Liam, Noah, and Theo stood in the high-ceilinged hall of their father's study in an unusual show of unity.

"Liam is the best man to oversee Starbridge Abbey," Piers stated.

He should not have been surprised when Liam grudgingly admitted that after running the abbey for two years now, he hated the idea of giving it up. But that issue had only partly explained his brother's animosity.

"He is also the best man to marry Delilah." Piers turned to meet his brother's gaze.

Liam nodded before turning back to face their father. "I —not Piers—am going to marry Delilah."

Lady Delilah, Piers realized, had been the more significant reason for his brother's animosity. Apparently, after

Eli's death, Liam had been the one to offer her the most comfort. The two of them had fallen in love but, refusing to defy her dead father's wishes, Lady Delilah had forbidden Liam to say anything.

She'd only agreed after Piers had informed her that he had no intention of upholding a contract that had been entered into decades ago—a contract that would ruin both of their lives.

"I won't have it!" Their father's complexion appeared more ruddy than usual.

"You have no say." Piers faced the man he'd run from for most of his life. Not just for himself but for all of them. And for their mother. And, in a way, for Eli.

"I am *Starbridge*." He emphasized his authority by slamming his fist a second time. "As long as I live, I'll damn well control what happens under my roof."

Liam scowled, but it was Piers who dealt the last blow. "If that's the case, there won't be anyone living under your roof to control."

The threat was only a partial bluff. But when the four of them and Primm had sat down together earlier that day, they'd all agreed that they could not go on like this.

Their father had always been a cruel and controlling man—but as he'd aged, his demands and expectations had only gotten worse. Liam had gotten to the point where he'd feared leaving their mother alone with him.

And so, with some guidance from their level-headed sister, they'd made some decisions together—as a family.

"And you won't have anyone to manage the tenants or the investments," Liam added.

"You won't have anyone to go over your books or implement the new machinery we've purchased." This from Noah.

"You would be all alone, Father," Theo said softly. "When you don't have to be. Let us go forward with your blessing. Liam is more than capable of taking over your duties."

"I've been doing most of them anyway." Liam's voice was sure.

Their father's response was a snarl. "And what of my heir? Will you abandon all your responsibilities once again so you can continue rutting around the world?" He turned to face Piers with mean, cold eyes.

Piers took an unconscious step backward, feeling singed by the pure hatred directed at him.

"I'm not Eli," he answered. "I may look like him, but I am not him. I have other plans for my life that don't include stepping into your shadow." Plans that involved one very improper school teacher.

He was not abandoning his responsibilities. He was giving them to the man who deserved them—who truly wanted them.

"Liam will take over here." Piers again locked eyes with his brother. "And I will be your proxy in the House of Lords in London." And one day, he would be Starbridge. In that, anyway, he had no choice.

But for all intents and purposes, Piers was handing Starbridge Abbey over to Liam.

As they'd ironed out the details before meeting with their father, the four of them had spent the rest of the afternoon catching up.

He had his brothers again. Eli was gone, but they still had each other.

He'd even told them his plans with Victoria—whom he was eager to track down first thing the following morning.

His first instinct had been to go after her right away. But Auggie had pointed out that if he did that, without first resolving the issues with their family, Victoria might just as well send him away.

But he would follow her to the school—put her concerns for Lady Delilah to rest and promise her he hadn't ruined his family—and then ask her again to marry him.

He'd beg her if necessary.

He loved her, damnit.

But first, they'd had to deal with his father.

ONE LAST APPLICANT

"Thank you for your service, Mrs. Dinkers."
Victoria used her teacher's voice as she handed
the former housekeeper an envelope that contained enough
money for her to find lodgings for a month, longer if she
was frugal. Victoria had been tempted to send her away
without a recommendation but decided the woman needed
a second chance and provided her with one anyway—even
if it was somewhat lukewarm.

"I don't know how you'll live with yourself, Miss Shipley. Turning your aunt's most loyal employee out like this.
Poor Mrs. Beasley is likely rolling in her grave."

"I highly doubt that," Victoria exhaled. "And I'll live with
myself just fine. And for the record, I wish you well."

"If I die, it'll be on your conscience." Mrs. Dinkers
snatched the envelope out of Victoria's hand and, with a
scowl, marched out the front door.

Stunned by the woman's contempt, Victoria gently
closed the door behind her, relieved at finally having taken
care of that solution.

With the new butler, Mr. Hill, running errands to replace some well-needed supplies, while Mrs. Teller, the new housekeeper, met with the cook who'd just arrived, Victoria had nothing substantial to prevent her from entertaining doubts about her decision to leave Starbridge Abbey without telling Piers goodbye.

The quiet also gave her time to analyze the reasoning behind that decision.

Because, yes, it was important that Piers and Primm's family reconcile. They would find comfort with one another, and their mother would have peace. Furthermore, Victoria had felt more than sympathetic for Lady Delilah. The young woman must have been devastated by the death of her betrothed. She would have experienced all the disappointment of so much more than a canceled wedding. Victoria remembered how the very reason for her existence had disappeared.

But Delilah would have been bolstered by the knowledge that Piers would step in—that she would still become a countess and eventually a marchioness.

Which was as it should be—because when a lady was raised for that single purpose, it defined her.

Although...

She mentally checked a belief. Because over the course of her career at the school, her opinion on this had shifted. Ladies must not allow themselves to be defined by society.

They needed to define themselves.

Victoria strolled along the foyer, realization coursing through her veins.

If Victoria had remained at Starbridge Abbey with Primm—if she'd allowed Piers to announce their betrothal

—Lady Delilah would not have been left alone. She would have been inundated with support.

The true reason Victoria had left was that...

He doesn't love me.

He'd told her he liked her. He'd all but worshipped her body, and God knew she'd worshipped his, but...

Piers Primm wasn't the sort to fall in love. And although her love for him would likely plague her for the rest of her life, there had been no way she'd allow herself to be the cause of great upheaval when the man involved did not love her in return.

Love wasn't something she'd been looking for—or hoping for, even. Victoria had been happy enough with her life at the school.

She lifted a hand to her chest. The pain of reaching for the richness of love, and then failing to lay claim to it—it hurt.

She'd never comprehended how someone's heart could be broken until this past week. Because whenever her thoughts drifted to Piers, she felt an actual stabbing in her chest. And when she allowed herself to recall something he'd said, or a certain way he'd touched her, it bled.

This too shall pass. It was a quote her aunt had told her numerous times. But would it?

Perhaps the sharp waves of despair would lessen and become less frequent, but how did one go through life when the one person they wanted to share it with didn't love them back?

He'd said he would marry her. Of course, he would have. She could have at least had that.

Had she made a mistake in leaving? Should she have stayed and fought for him?

Victoria swiped at her eyes, annoyed with herself for following this dark tunnel of what-ifs and should-haves.

She needed something to do.

The door to the library caught her eye. The room had gone mostly unused by her aunt, who'd claimed it reminded her too much of her father, long deceased.

Victoria stepped inside, inhaled, and nearly choked on the dust. But once she was over that, with tears streaming down her face, she crossed to a large window, and then over to the empty hearth.

She did not have sad memories of anyone in this once-stately room. It was a library! With a surge of energy she'd not known for days, she made the decision to turn this room into something special. It would be uniquely hers.

Whipping the tarps from the furnishings, Victoria first took stock of what could stay and what must be replaced. And then, unwilling to wait until the new servants were settled in, she located a broom and linens and went to work cleaning, sweeping, and dusting everything she could reach.

It was hard work, but also rewarding. She found a first edition of *Gulliver's Travels* by Jonathan Swift, and a leather-bound edition of *A Vindication of the Rights of Woman* by Mary Wollstonecraft, and hundreds of others, some she'd heard of and some not. But there was a stack of maps, a gorgeous chess set, and even a collection of letters. She'd just opened one and lowered herself to the floor upon realizing it had been written by her great-great-grandfather when a knock sounded at the door.

"Martin?" When he didn't answer, Victoria remembered he'd gone along with Mr. Hill, and they must not have returned. Whoever was outside was, no doubt, a straggling applicant. It couldn't be anyone she knew because no one even knew she was here.

Reluctant to abandon her project, Victoria pushed herself to her feet and groaned when her back protested, along with her shoulders and knees. This sort of pain was the good kind, however. It meant she had purpose. It meant she was moving on.

She swiped at the apron covering her gown and laughed that her hands only made it worse. The caller would easily believe she was a housemaid—and an untidy one at that.

With one last glance at the progress she'd made, she left the room feeling satisfied.

This was helping.

A little.

Over the past few hours, she only thought of Piers when she found something she wanted to show him. A book about traveling. A journal of one of her great-uncles' adventures in India.

But she also found books that caused her to miss the school, and Primm and Priscilla. Likely, she would have even been happy for Allison Meadowbrook's company.

She grimaced and almost laughed to herself.

She wasn't that lonely yet.

The laughter caught in her throat, however, the moment she threw the door open.

She knew she wasn't dreaming, and yet, her eyes couldn't quite reconcile what she saw with her brain.

Standing on the stoop was the one person she'd been trying not to think of all day.

"Have I come to the right address?" Piers looked her up and down, that familiar teasing glint lighting his hazel eyes. "London fashions have changed since I've been gone, but you still look better than anything I've seen in days." His voice caught on his last few words.

It was as though all her thoughts had magically conjured his appearance.

But he looked almost as haggard as he had the night he'd fallen into the residence half-frozen.

Whiskers covered the lower half of his face, and shadows rimmed his beautiful eyes. And even though he smiled, tension tugged at his mouth.

He was real. He was not a figment of her hungry imagination. Instinctively, she smoothed her hands over her apron.

But there was no repairing the mess she'd made, so she simply stared at him.

"I thought you were one of the applicants sent over by the agency… What are you doing here?" she asked.

"You have need of a weary gentleman, then?"

"No. I-I thought you were someone responding to Coachman John's advertisement." She shook her head, feeling dazed. "But all the positions are filled."

He removed his hat and then tilted his head. "Are you going to invite me in? Or must I break one of the windows?"

He'd broken a window that first night, when they'd been alone. It felt like ages ago.

A time set away from the real world, from the world's expectations and rules.

His smile was sad. Tired.

Realizing he was standing in the cold, she took an abrupt step back. "Of course. I mean, no, you needn't break anything this time."

When they'd been together in Primm's residence, he'd

witnessed her in all manner of dishabille. And then, driving, he'd witnessed her casting up her accounts, for heaven's sake.

She half-wished she could have been at her best for this conversation. But, why was he here? Why had he come?

"May I take your coat? Mr. Hill, the new butler I've just hired, is running some errands, along with my only footman." Her hands settled on his shoulders but rather than straightaway drawing his coat off, she savored the strength and warmth beneath her palms.

She savored *touching* him.

It was a little thing. And yet, she'd expected to never be able to do so again.

"The house was a disaster when I arrived," she rambled, tugging at the heavy coat, and saying anything to keep from embarrassing herself. "I found my aunt's former housekeeper sloshed in my aunt's former suite, so I had to let her go. That left me..."

Piers slid his arms out of the greatcoat and turned around, pinning his gaze on her, and her mind went blank.

The bleakness of his expression tore at her heart.

"You left me," he said.

"I..." Yes, she'd left him. Why *had* she left him? She struggled to find words when he looked at her like that. "I left you," she finally agreed.

"Primm said you'd rather teach than marry me." The look in his eyes wasn't at all teasing. In fact, it was almost vulnerable. "But you didn't return to the school."

Her reasons had been so much more complicated than that. Surely he must understand!

"What else did she say?"

"Nonsense about wrecking my family." He scrubbed one

hand down his face. "I was sick with worry when I got to the school and found that you'd never arrived. But then I remembered you mentioning your aunt's townhouse and took a chance that you'd be here."

Which meant he'd barely stopped to rest at all since she'd left.

She swallowed the thick emotion that threatened her equilibrium.

"Come into the parlor where we can talk. I'll light the fire." She turned, relieved that he was following. "Would you care for some tea? Better yet, perhaps Cook can scrounge something together for dinner."

He didn't answer but instead caught her hand.

"Victoria." And then both his arms slid around her from behind, pulling her into him.

She should resist.

Was he engaged to Lady Delilah now? Had he defied his father and abandoned his family once again?

And yet, despite not having any of these questions answered, she relaxed in his embrace. And once there, she absorbed the security of his chest.

Her skin came alive, and her heart felt whole.

Dash it all. Was she going to have to start all over again after he left?

She dropped her head back, resting it beneath his chin. "Why are you here?"

"Isn't it obvious?"

"No," she whispered. Nothing was obvious where he was concerned.

He loosened his grip enough to turn her around, and she could either stare at the knot in his cravat, his mouth, or into his eyes.

"Why did you leave?" His eyes demanded her attention.

"Wasn't it obvious?" She echoed his ambiguous answer.

"No, Victoria." He frowned. "But perhaps I'm simply too thick-headed to believe you don't care for me—"

"Of course I care for you. But... Your family loves you. And they need you. And I refuse to be the person who keeps you from them." She stiffened and made a feeble attempt to step out of his arms.

Her effort was a feeble one because once she left his arms, she might never feel them around her again.

"What about Lady Delilah? You need to marry her."

"Marry Delilah?" Piers shook his head. "That was never going to happen, and my father knows that now. She and Liam are in love, and they were already setting the date for their own nuptials before I left."

"But Primm said—"

"I'll be the first to admit that my sister usually knows what she's talking about, but trust me, she was all wrong about this. Since you ran away—"

"But I didn't run—"

He touched two fingers to her lips. "Since you *secretly departed* without coming to me first, my siblings and I have cleared up a few issues. More than a few, in fact." Piers moved his hand to cradle her cheek. "Contrary to my behavior, and a good deal of my rhetoric, I do value my family. I need them. I even love them."

"Good," she whispered. She was so happy that he would have them!

"But I don't need them nearly as much... I don't *love* them nearly as much as I love you." His eyes blazed.

"As you...?"

"As I love you," he said. "But you left."

At that moment, Victoria truly comprehended what it meant to be speechless.

She was saved, however, from having to come up with a coherent response when Mrs. Teller peered inside the parlor. "My apologies for interrupting, Miss Shipley. I thought I heard a guest. Can I bring you anything?"

Without looking away from the man before her, she answered. "Tea, please, Mrs. Teller. And a meal for Lord Rosewood."

Piers's gaze might as well have caught her in a web.

"Right away." As quickly as she'd come, the housekeeper closed the door behind her.

"What I need to know," Piers said, as though they'd not been interrupted. "Is whether you left because you didn't want to give up teaching or because you—" His throat moved. "Because you didn't want to marry me?"

There were so many reasons why she'd left: his mother's health, Lady Delilah's feelings, his relationships with all those brothers, not to mention the reason he'd proposed in the first place, and the reason she had accepted.

But rather than attempt to go into all of that, she opened her mouth and...

"I want to marry you," she said. "Do you really love me? As in, love *me* romantically? Or do you love me more in the general sense? Because—"

"God." His mouth landed on hers.

His taste. It was home. It was better than eating her favorite meal, sipping her favorite wine, and a good night's sleep all rolled into one.

He released her mouth as abruptly as he'd taken it. "I'm *in love with you*, damnit," He shook his head. "*And* I love you. Is there a difference?"

There was. Kingsley had told her he'd loved her. But he'd been *in love* with Olivia Redfield.

And yet Piers was telling her that *he loved her* but also that he was *in love with her—Victoria Shipley.*

"Good." She absorbed what this meant even as she tried to breathe normally. "Because I'm in love with you, too. And I was afraid I was going to have to spend the rest of my life recovering from that." She touched his face.

"Why on earth would you leave, then?" He looked mostly relieved but also confused.

"Because, *Amor vincit omnia, et nos cedamus amori.*" She quoted the Roman poet, Virgil.

"Love conquers all?"

She was pleased to see understanding dawn in his gaze.

"Yes." It was part of it. "I didn't think you loved me. If I had stayed, I would have forced myself on you. And your family. And Primm's school. I didn't want to be the outsider... I didn't want—"

"Never."

Victoria shivered at the conviction in his voice, but continued her explanation. "I let you go." She shrugged. "And like a miracle..."

"Love won."

"It did." She hated that she felt like crying.

He touched a fingertip to her lashes, and she laughed.

"I'm happy. I am." And then she smiled.

THAT SMILE.

She was happy.

Piers's heart overflowed and took flight at the same time. Rather ecstatic himself, Piers swooped her into his arms and carried her to the settee—a rather tired-looking piece of furniture that he lowered both of them onto anyway.

She loved him. She was *in love* with him.

And he wanted nothing more than to make love to her right there. But the two of them had already put the cart before the horse more than once, and he refused to allow any more of these issues between them to go unresolved.

So he squashed the urges that weren't nearly as rational and settled her primly across his lap.

When she turned to put her arm around him, she wiggled her bum on his erection.

"Oh, hell, Victoria." Piers took a deep breath, reconsidering the timing for this discussion.

But the last time he'd made love to her without clearing the air between them, she'd disappeared the following day.

The discussion won out—for the moment.

"We need to talk first."

She stilled and made an attempt to look somber. "I suppose you are right." Her disappointment would have been laughable if he wasn't experiencing the same frustrations himself.

Focus, Piers.

She touched his face. "I should have taken the time to talk with you before I left. I always want to be able to talk with you." Her words were so simple but rang of great wisdom.

"From here on, we won't keep concerns from one another."

"Agreed." And then she tilted her head. "In that spirit, you were going to say…?"

Ah, yes.

"My father may never take to you." He wouldn't dissemble with her on this. This woman, the woman who would be his wife, had fierce opinions regarding family.

Which meant they must face a few obstacles where his was concerned.

But love was already living up to Virgil's line, so he wasn't going to avoid the most prickly issues.

"Never?" Her eyes looked sad.

"He wasn't at all happy when I left." Piers described the terms he and his brothers had insisted upon. In the end, Piers had almost felt sorry for his father, who'd finally conceded and then ordered them out of his study. "If it makes you feel any better, I doubt he'll ever take to me."

"It doesn't, but... thank you for being honest about that."

His sweet Miss Shipley managed to look prim and proper in his arms as she contemplated everything he'd told her.

"But one never knows." He tipped his head forward to meet her gaze. "And after we marry—you are going to marry me, aren't you?"

"That's what you want?" she asked. "To marry me?" Her warm gaze searched his.

"Is it what you want?"

"Neither of us must feel compelled, you know."

Piers squeezed her hand. "Seeing as I love you and I am also *madly in love* with you. I'm compelled by myself. Yes. Victoria. I want to marry you. I want to marry you more than anything."

"I feel the same." She exhaled. This discussion likely wouldn't sound all that romantic to anyone who didn't know them, and yet, Piers was incredibly moved by her acceptance of this proposal.

"Good to have that settled," he teased before observing the moment with a kiss that might have gotten out of hand had the housekeeper not chosen that moment to return.

Beautifully flustered, Victoria burst to her feet to relieve the housekeeper of the tray of food she carried. "Thank you, Mrs. Teller."

It was loaded up with tea, fresh bread, and two bowls of hot beef stew.

"I didn't even realize I was hungry until now," he admitted.

Which earned him another brilliant smile from his... *fiancée*.

He could never tell her how powerful that was. If she decided to take advantage of such a weapon, he'd be incapable of denying her anything.

Although, he knew he'd give her the world if she asked.

Seated straight-backed beside him now, Victoria proceeded to pour two steaming cups of tea. "So," she said as she handed him the saucer. "We are engaged once again."

"Yes," Piers agreed.

"And not because we have to be."

"Not even close."

He draped a napkin over one knee. "Which leads us to my next item to discuss." Catching her glance, he winked.

Another smile.

He'd bring her the king's head if she wanted it. Piers simply stared at her, overwhelmed with gratitude that he was being given the gift of sharing his life with this woman.

Victoria—his angel.

"Yes?" she prompted.

Momentarily entranced by her mouth, he blinked away thoughts that would prematurely end this very important discussion. "You asked me before if I wished to continue traveling. The only journeys I want to make are journeys with you. So, if we're to settle down, we need to agree on where we will make our home."

"You truly have no wish to live at Starbridge Abbey?"

"God, no." Liam was more than passionate about running the estate. Why should Piers step in and take that over for him? "The Abbey is, and always will be, my heritage. But... Liam seems to need it. All I need is to be with you." He studied her expression. "There is an old estate just north of Warstone Crossing and while I was there, Mr. Driver mentioned that it is unentailed and the owner has plans to sell. It's sat empty for nearly a decade and I have no idea what it's going to take to return it to its former glory. But seeing as it's near the school, and if you truly are passionate about teaching—"

"Yes!" Before he could finish, she had twisted around and was nearly strangling him in her exuberance. "You mean Longbow Castle? But are you sure? It's a shambles. Do you really want to take something like that on?" She laughed. "It could be beautiful, but I'll live wherever you want—"

"I'm quite sure. And I'm rather intrigued by the challenge of making such an ancient landmark functional again." He glanced around the parlor which, although shabby, had potential itself. "If you're agreeable, I'd like to make Starbridge House here in Mayfair available to my brothers. When I have to come to town, we could stay here."

Again, she was nodding eagerly. "That way I won't have to let go of the staff I've just hired."

So very practical.

"Good point," he said. "But you will teach," he said.

"Agreed." She held his face in both her hands and pressed her mouth to his.

"All of our traveling will be done together."

"Agreed." She kissed him again.

"Do you have any other items we ought to address?" Piers wondered how he'd never experienced this... completion before. The weight of her curves in his arms, the taste of her kiss on his lap, the... pure happiness.

More happiness than he deserved.

"Actually, yes." She frowned. "There is one more thing."

What had he forgotten? "Out with it, Miss Shipley."

"I don't want a long engagement. In fact, I'd like to have the ceremony as quickly as possible."

"Are you...? But we...? Of course—"

Her eyes widened. "No." Then she laughed. "Not that I am aware of, anyway." She grew somber again. "I told you about the length of my betrothal with Kingsley and as long as you have no objections, I'd prefer to get ours over with as soon as possible."

"The ceremony?" He would have thought she would prefer all the pomp and circumstance of a grand *ton* affair.

"Gretna Green is nearly a week's journey this time of year. And as we've both recently endured more travel than either of us planned, would it be possibly, do you think—?"

"You want me to secure a special license?" So they could *get theirs over with as soon as possible.* Piers couldn't have agreed with her more.

She exhaled. "Would you mind?"

This woman could not have been any more perfect for him.

"Not at all. We'll do it tomorrow if you wish. St. George's?"

"If that's possible."

"St. George's it is." He grinned. "Anything else?"

Victoria turned to straddle him. "I believe that's everything." She moved her hips in a most unladylike manner, making it impossible for him to keep his cock in check a second longer.

"You're sure?" Piers thrust up, teasing her—teasing them both. "You don't wish to discuss who to invite... finances, perhaps?"

"Not right now. You see, I have this other problem." Her hands reached for the fastening on his falls. "And I believe it requires your immediate attention."

Piers slid his palms under her skirt. "In that case, this meeting is adjourned."

*L*ogistically speaking, as it turned out, Piers and Victoria were not able to schedule a ceremony the next day. Which in the end, they both agreed, was rather serendipitous.

And since Piers had made arrangements for them to meet with the owner of Longbow Castle just after the new year, it meant they would be traveling back to the school immediately following their wedding. Victoria took advantage of the additional time in London to do some shopping.

She could not have been more startled when, while exiting a teahouse late in the afternoon, she and Piers ran into Lord and Lady Kingsley. The storm that had stranded Victoria with Piers at the school had caused them to postpone the more distant travels they'd had planned for the holidays.

Victoria would have imagined such a meeting would be awkward, but with Kingsley's easy charm and his countess Olivia's welcoming warmth, it was anything but.

Olivia, who was uniquely beautiful with blond hair and

violet eyes, had enchanted Victoria the same as she had on other occasions. And after sending Piers a questioning glance, Victoria had surprised all of them by asking the couple if they would be willing to act as witnesses at their ceremony.

As luck would have it, Piers and Kingsley, having attended school around the same time, had already realized they had several friends in common.

"That is, if you aren't leaving London before Saturday," Victoria had added. Because although she felt perfectly comfortable with the arrangement, it was possible that one of them might not.

"We would be honored," Olivia answered for both of them with a good deal of sincerity. Olivia's gaze, of which one of her eyes tended to move independently of the other, had initially been disconcerting. But since coming to know her, Victoria hardly noticed it anymore.

"I second that wholeheartedly," Lord Kingsley had agreed.

That had been three days before, and Piers's and Victoria's wedding ceremony had taken place at St. George's that very morning. With only the four of them in attendance and the bishop, the vows she and Piers recited to one another echoed even more meaningfully in the sacred building.

After their small party emerged from the church, Victoria and Olivia shared an unforeseen emotional farewell while Kingsley congratulated Piers. All in all, Victoria decided her wedding could not have been more perfect.

Seated in the coach that would carry them north, she marveled that she was no longer an engaged woman, nor a bride—but a wife.

The coach, which was the most luxurious she'd ever ridden in, had been a wedding present from her husband.

When they'd initially climbed in and Victoria had taken a seat on the front-facing bench, scooting over so he could sit beside her, she'd been taken aback when he'd chosen to sit opposite her.

Piers, however, had casually raised both his feet to rest them on the bench, bracketing her between his long legs.

"I must admit, I didn't expect to like Kingsley," he admitted, snugging his feet up beside her.

"I never would have expected to grow so fond of Olivia," she said.

"She seems the perfect match for him. She isn't self-conscious at all."

"Because of her eye?" When he nodded, Victoria continued. "For most of her life, she considered it a curse. Her family experienced a few tragedies, and from my understanding, her father blamed them on her. Kingsley has done well to dispute such ridiculousness. I am happy they found one another."

Piers was staring at her with an expression she hadn't gotten wholly used to yet. It was possessive and fiery and tended to result in activities that left both of them breathless, and if not in an all-out state of dishabille, at least a little undone.

"I am forever indebted to Lady Kingsley." His voice lowered. "Because although Kingsley was a fool to let you slip away, if he hadn't, I wouldn't have found you."

His words sent the most wonderful river of joy flowing through Victoria.

"I suppose I owe her as well." She flicked a meaningful

gaze to the space beside her and cocked a brow. "Now, why are you sitting way over there?"

Piers flicked a glance out the window. Although they'd made it to the outskirts, they hadn't quite left the city entirely.

"Because, my dear Miss Shipley," His eyes danced. "Wife."

"Yes? My dear Lord Rosewood?"

"I don't trust myself not to do something that might be embarrassing for anyone who happens to get a glimpse inside. Or, my very proper wife." He winked. Because, of course, they both knew she wasn't always concerned with propriety.

"Although," he added. "I also want to make a few notes about your preferences regarding our future home. I'll be meeting with Longbow's owner shortly after we arrive, and I've also made arrangements to meet with a contractor—the Duke of Bedwell's brother, coincidentally. He says Bedwell married one of your former teachers."

"Miss Jones. She was the teacher your sister and I had to fire a while back." Victoria frowned because that reminded her that she was going to have to face Primm again. And also, perhaps, a messy scandal.

"Don't think about it." Piers had come to read her mind with uncanny accuracy.

Most of the time.

"Easier said than done."

"Even if Auggie can't hire you back right away, once you've become established in the area as the Countess of Rosewood, any annoying gossip will quickly be forgotten. Trust me?"

"I do." But she hoped it wouldn't have to come to that.

"Meanwhile." Piers removed a small book and pencil from his pocket. He'd told her that she had inspired him with her organizational skills. And since setting up this new estate while keeping in contact with Liam, figuring estimates and bids, and noting ideas, he'd purchased one for himself. "I have a few questions for you."

Victoria relaxed into the cushioned seat. "Ask away, my love."

My love.

Because he was just that. Less than an hour as a married lady, and she was already enjoying it.

"The castle is going to require a large music room. You'll want a pianoforte, of course, and a harp. Did you have any particular specifics I need to know before ordering them?"

He was planning their home. No, *they* were planning their future home—*together*. She supplied him with a few of her preferences, and then he moved on.

"Mr. Steward says he can provide some plumbing—but he'll have to look it over before knowing to what extent. I told him wherever possible, we want modern facilities."

"Agreed," Victoria nodded. "It will make the work easier on the servants."

"Precisely." The next look he sent her was a mischievous one. "And if I'm to provide you with additional cooking lessons, I want the kitchen to be bright and well ventilated. Because I rather like rolling dough with you."

Three days before, at Beasley House, while the cook had gone shopping for fresh produce, she and Piers had cooked some fruit pies. Victoria was still thoroughly impressed with the manner in which he'd utilized the left-over fruit mixture—which had been warm and gooey and... She squeezed her thighs together at the memory.

"Yes," she agreed. "We want a spectacular kitchen. We can have it on the main floor, near the dining room for convenience."

"And a nursery?" His mouth twitched.

"Near the master suite."

But the reminder of the fruit mixture, along with a mention of a nursery and master suite, had caused Victoria's mind to travel in a less practical direction.

She reached across the interior to slide closed the drapes on the far side of the coach and then closed those right beside her. Having assured them of privacy, she then met her groom's gaze and deliberately sent him a most meaningful...

Smile.

Piers licked his lips and tucked the notebook back into his jacket, and then, dropping his feet, leaned forward.

She gasped when he reached out and edged her thighs wide. "You are in big trouble, Miss Shipley." He lowered himself onto the floor to settle himself between her legs.

"Wife," she corrected him, her voice raspy in anticipation.

Her gaze locked with his; Victoria removed both her gloves and then cradled his face between her hands.

The wave of tenderness she felt in that moment nearly overwhelmed her.

"I'm so glad I waited for you," she whispered.

She would never grow weary of seeing the expression he wore for only her. There was a hungry look of warmth in his eyes, he parted his lips softly, and two delicate spots of red blossomed in his cheeks. Moments like this—when they shared a silent language—she could not believe this was her life.

Piers edged her skirts up until his gloved hands settled at the tops of her stockings. "Do you know how beautiful you are? I'm the luckiest man in all the kingdom."

And staring down at him, so happy she could hardly contain it, Victoria realized that her heart was not only *healed,* but it was *whole.*

Because after taking a most unexpected journey to get to this point, she not only believed in hope again, but she also believed that dreams could come true.

She, Victoria *Primm* now, was no doubt the luckiest *lady* in all of the kingdom.

And that, she thought as she slid lower on the seat to enjoy the attentions of her most talented husband, was something worth celebrating.

Determined to seize every moment, Victoria closed her eyes and… celebrated.

BONUS EPILOGUE

JAN. 7, 1831

*A*s it was, the newly married couple did not go directly to the school. But when another storm had whipped up to slow their travels, Piers checked them into a charming inn where the two of them spent what they'd later refer to as their honeymoon. The stay ended up lasting an entire week, most of which—excepting a few necessary outings—was spent sleeping and eating and making love in their small but comfortable chamber.

By the time they finally arrived in Warstone Village, the gentleman who was selling Longbow Castle, as well as their contractor, had already arrived and were anxious to meet with Piers at the property.

Since Victoria was apprehensive about facing Primm, she had Piers deliver her to the school rather than attend the meeting with him.

Best to get this over with so she could continue her happily married state without it hanging over her head any longer.

"Miss Shipley!" Primm greeted her but then corrected herself. "Or must I call you Lady Rosewood now?"

"Victoria is fine." Except around students. Victoria and Piers had agreed that she would remain Miss Shipley if she were allowed to continue teaching. The school couldn't very well have two teachers who went by the name of Primm. That would be too confusing by far.

She'd barely removed her coat before both Primm and Priscilla peppered her with questions about the ceremony and also how that ceremony had come about.

Apparently satisfied with Victoria's answers, Primm then led them into the parlor to sit down for tea.

"So, you and my brother are married, and he is this very moment making arrangements to purchase Longbow Castle, and, although you are a countess now, you still wish to teach?" Primm was all business now as she stared across at her from behind her spectacles.

"I do. Was Mr. Driver able to right the damages inside the school?" The students would begin returning any day now.

"Most of them. But he's also, most unfortunately, found a few issues concerning the foundation now." Primm frowned.

"Perhaps Mr. Steward, the contractor Piers is looking to hire to help put Longbow to rights, will have time to assess what needs doing. But I realize," Victoria inhaled a fortifying breath. "That there are other issues we must address first."

Primm's chest rose. "Yes." Her eyes narrowed on Victoria.

This formidable woman, Victoria's former employer, who was also now her sister-in-law, did not need to speak a single word to convey that she was fully aware of what had occurred that Christmas morning when Priscilla and Miss Meadowbrook arrived.

In Primm's bedchamber.

"I am so very, very sorry." Victoria stared down at her hands. And then she considered all that had happened over the last few weeks and lifted her chin. Meeting Primm's stern gaze, she added. "But I am not sorry. I mean. I'm sorry if we've done anything that could potentially harm the school, but I am so very in love with him, Primm. And we are so very, very happy." And at that moment, Victoria allowed all the joy inside of her to show.

"It was… fate." She added with a smile.

Primm blinked, and Priscilla made a small cry beside her.

"I'm so glad," Priscilla said. "I knew it. I wasn't happy with how it came about, but I could see it on both of you. And I could not be more pleased that the two of you went ahead and got married."

"Yes," Primm's mouth, although pinched, edged up in what one might almost consider a smile as well. "I am happy to have you as a sister."

If Victoria didn't have the scandal part of this discussion looming over her head, she might well have burst into tears. *Primm considered her a sister.*

"I am happy to have you as a sister as well." Her voice wobbled and her eyes stung.

Primm cleared her throat and then went back to their original subject. "As for coming on to teach again—"

"I understand that may not be possible right now," Victoria interrupted, prepared to be disappointed. "But I hope you will keep me in mind for some time in the future."

And then she asked the question she'd been wondering for weeks now. "What are they saying about me in the village?" Because no matter how much one tried to convince themselves that they didn't care, these things mattered.

Before answering, Primm turned to meet Priscilla's stare and then back to Victoria.

"Mr. Driver, it seems, is more shrewd than I realized. As luck would have it, he did not, after all, tell Mrs. Driver that my brother had been staying at the school—that he shared the residence with you for all of four days—alone."

Victoria touched her fingertips to her chest. "So no one knows?"

"Only Miss Meadowbrook."

Drat. Victoria had been excited for a few seconds. "Has she told anyone?"

"She has not," Priscilla answered. "Yet."

Victoria knew that such a difficult girl wouldn't make matters easy. "Has she indicated that she is going to, then?"

At this question, Prissy winced. "She… is trying to strike a bargain with me." She slid a knowing glance toward Primm. "Miss Primm and I have been discussing the ramifications." She bit her lip.

Although her answer seemed to offer some hope, whatever they had yet to reveal about Miss Meadowbrook's bargain seemed troubling indeed.

"As you remember, Allison and I returned early because Miss Meadowbrook's father wants her to marry the Earl of Hardwood. And Lord Hardwood is insisting her father honor the contract. Apparently he is desperately in need of funds."

"Yes," Victoria answered. "But what does that have to do with the scandal?"

"The Earl is coming to the school and is expected to make a formal offer. His father impoverished their estates while he was alive, and so the new earl insists he has no choice but to marry her."

Victoria nodded. Such a match was not unheard of—an impoverished lord to the daughter of a wealthy but socially inferior gentleman.

"And?" Victoria prompted.

"Allison says that if I can convince him to break the contract with her father, then she will never mention a word to anyone of what she saw on Christmas morning."

"Can you? Convince him?"

Priscilla shook her head. "As her teacher, I doubt it. What Allison wants me to do is…" She inhaled. "She wants me to meet him when he arrives—as her. She wants me to convince him not to marry her while pretending to *be her*."

"But the two of you don't even resemble one another!" Prissy could most likely pass herself off as a student, but whereas Allison was of average height and figure and *blonde*, Priscilla was slim, petite, and *brunette*.

And Priscilla possessed that unique quality inherent in most teachers—the one that projected a most adamant disinclination for marriage.

"The two of them have never met. We left before the earl arrived, if you remember."

"If Miss Fellowes refuses," Primm said, "Allison has promised to spread word of my former assistant director's indiscretions in great detail to anyone who will listen."

This.

Was not good.

"I can't let you do that! I'm the one who should pay." But

305

unfortunately, there was no way that Victoria could pass herself off as a girl of ten and seven.

"But the school would pay," Priscilla pointed out.

"I am so sorry." Victoria felt terrible that she'd confessed two minutes earlier that she was not. Because where it came to the school's continued success, anyway, she was dreadfully, horrifically, sorry.

"All I need to do is be so forceful—so adamantly against the marriage that he cannot help but reconsider," Priscilla said. "And hopefully he will give up on the betrothal with no one being the wiser."

"Are you going to do it?"

Again, that glance between Primm and Priscilla. Only this time, it was resigned.

"We haven't a choice, really," Priscilla said.

"And you trust Allison? That she'll keep her word?"

"We do." Priscilla nodded. "Because if her father ever gets wind of any of this, he may very well send her off to join a convent."

Even that, Victoria realized, could put the school at risk. It most certainly put Priscilla at risk. "Then you must have all of our support," she said. "It has to work."

All three of them sat silently until Priscilla rose. "I'll go tell her now. I need to go over every possible detail that might arise. I'll be mortified if he finds me out."

"We'll go over the best reasons to give for refusing him. Then, after that, we'll help you rehearse. And Piers will be returning from his meeting soon. He ought to have some insight as well."

"True," Primm agreed. "But first, perhaps he'll take a moment to actually say hello to his only sister."

"Of course he will," Victoria soothed.

"Very well, then." Priscilla straightened her shoulders and went to move toward the door.

"Miss Fellowes." Primm stopped her. "After you've informed Miss Meadowbrook of your decision, tell her that I wish to speak with her as well—to ensure that she fully comprehends every last detail of this little arrangement."

"Good idea," Priscilla winced.

"Good luck," Victoria added.

Once she'd left, Primm seemed to relax. Relax in that she was no longer on the edge of her seat looking as though she was strapped to a posture device.

"Now, tell me about these curriculum changes Miss Fellowes mentioned."

Victoria withdrew her notebook from the reticule she'd brought along and time flew by as Victoria explained her ideas. When Victoria heard the coach draw up outside, Primm seemed entirely on board. She had even added more details that would be helpful to better prepare their girls to graduate, not only as ladies but as independent and capable women who could fend for themselves if necessary.

The two of them went to answer the door together and were surprised when they found not one man waiting to enter but three.

Piers first introduced Mr. Rowan Stewart, the contractor considering taking on their project. He was a tall and powerful-looking gentleman with dark skin and flashing, intelligent eyes. He appeared to be in his late thirties, and when he removed his hat to bow over Victoria's hand, revealed black hair that was so short she was certain he regularly shaved it.

"It is my pleasure to meet you," Victoria said.

"Likewise," he answered before turning to Primm. "And this lovely lady is…?"

"My sister, Lady Augusta, who also happens to be the most famous Miss Primm." Piers gestured toward the school. At that moment, Primm blushed like a schoolgirl.

She recovered quickly, however, and scowling, sent her brother a reprimanding glance.

"My Lady." Mr. Stewart stepped forward to bend over Primm's hand. Who, of course, clasped his instead and shook it firmly. This was not the first time Victoria had witnessed Primm greeting a gentleman like this.

Piers was relatively unfazed by his sister and took hold of Victoria's elbow to introduce her to his other companion. "This gentleman, my dear, has agreed to sell us the estate that will one day be our home."

He wasn't as tall as either their contractor or Piers, nor was he as well dressed. But as Victoria noticed the manner in which he held his hat, and his solemn light green eyes, she found him to be slightly familiar.

"Have we met?" she asked.

"I believe we were introduced a few years ago." Then the wind lifted his dark brown hair off his face, and that was the moment she realized who he was.

"Victoria, I'd like to present the Earl of Hardwood, who, coincidentally, has informed me that his primary reason for traveling here was to meet with one of your students."

The earl lifted his chin. He wasn't as tall as Piers, but Victoria judged him nearly as handsome.

"Is Miss Meadowbrook in residence?" he asked. "I'd very much like to meet with her if I may."

THE NEXT BOOK in Miss Primm's Secret School for Budding Bluestockings Series, **PRETENDING TO BE A DEBU-TANTE**, releases Feb 1, 2022.

Preorder today! Lady Priscilla, declared ruined the year of her come-out, loves teaching domestic sciences and history at Miss Primm's Private Seminary for the Education of Ladies. She adores most of her students and will do almost anything for them. In fact, under the direst of circumstances, she's even willing to pretend to impersonate one of them...Everything goes swimmingly until she finds herself falling in love with Emerson Huntington, the Earl of Hardwood--aka—her student's betrothed...

Meanwhile, you can read **THE PERFECT SPINSTER,** Lord Kingsley Olivia's story. Download it now!

MISS PRIMM'S SECRET SCHOOL FOR
BUDDING BLUESTOCKINGS

A NEW ANNABELLE ANDERS SERIES

TRAPPED WITH THE DUKE

Miss Colette Jones

EDUCATED BY THE EARL

Miss Victoria Shipley

PRETENDING TO BE A DEBUTANTE

Lady Priscilla

RESCUED BY THE RAKE

Miss Chloe Fortune

ADVISING THE VISCOUNT

Miss Addy

SCHOOLED BY THE BASTARD

Miss Primm

REGENCY COCKY GENTS

Cocky Earl

Jules and Charley

Cocky Baron

Chase and Bethany

Cocky Mister

Stone and Tabetha

Cocky Brother

Peter Spencer's Story

(Formerly Mayfair Maiden)

Cocky Viscount

Mantis and Felicity

Cocky Marquess

Greystone's Story

Cocky Butler

Blackheart's Story

THE DEFIANT DAMSELS SERIES

Lady at Last

Penelope's Story (Viscount Danbury)

Lady Be Good

Rose's Story (Viscount Darlington)

Lady and the Rake

Margaret's Story (The Marquess of Rockingham)

ABOUT THE AUTHOR

Married to the same man for over 25 years, I am a mother to three children and two Miniature Wiener dogs.

After owning a business and experiencing considerable success, my husband and I got caught in the financial crisis and lost everything in 2008; our business, our home, even our car.

At this point, I put my B.A. in Poly Sci to use and took work as a waitress and bartender (Insert irony). Unwilling to give up on a professional life, I simultaneously went back to college and obtained a degree in EnergyManagement.

And then the energy market dropped off.

And then my dog died.

I can only be grateful for this series of unfortunate events, for, with nothing to lose and completely demoralized, I sat down and began to write the romance novels which had until then, existed only my imagination. After publishing over twenty novels now, with one having been nominated for RWA's Distinguished ™RITA Award in 2019, I am happy to tell you that I have finally found my place in life.

Thank you so much for being a part of my journey!

To find out more about my books, and also to download a free novella, get all the info at my website!

www.annabelleanders.com

Printed in Great Britain
by Amazon